Where You Belong

Nicole Baker

Contents

Little Italy

This book takes place in a little neighborhood in Cleveland, Ohio called **Little Italy.**

<u>All of the restaurants and stores are real.</u>

If you ever find yourself in Ohio, or passing through, please stop in and enjoy! It will be worth your time!

Corbo's Bakery

Ever had the famous Italian pastry known as a cannoli? You will find the *best* cannoli's here, ALWAYS freshly filled!

If you are familiar with the movie *The Godfather* or *You've Got Mail*... you will recognize the sign displayed above the cannoli fridge. *Leave the gun, take the cannoli.*

Tavern of Little Italy (TOLI)

If the weather is nice, stop in at TOLI for a *great* outdoor atmosphere and quality Italian inspired pub food!

Michaelangelo's

Looking for exquisite Italian cuisine found a little off the path in Little Italy? Michaelangelo's is your place. Award winning Executive Chef Michael has created a perfect menu to bring Italy to Ohio.

Marble Room

If you want some of the BEST food that will ever touch your tongue, and you're willing to spend the money, Marble Room will NOT disappoint. A restaurant in the setting of an old bank, with grand architecture featuring marble walls and Corinthian columns.

The restaurant has been awarded the Silver Spoon Award four years in a row, and received the Best of Award of Excellence by Wine Spectator in 2022.

The Executive Chef has made a menu that will make you want to keep coming back so you can try everything on it!

Chapter One

Gabriel

"You can't seriously think this tastes good," Marcus mutters behind his wine glass.

I glance down at my drink, swirling the contents of the glass as Dean Martin plays in the background, setting the mood.

Marcus has always been impulsive. From the second he rushed through assessing the aroma, I knew he wouldn't understand the beauty lying in the glass in front of him.

Women are like a glass of wine. To truly appreciate them, you have to take your time, draw out the taste...the pleasure.

Not like I do much of that these days. No, lately, I'm hollow inside. Bitter with resentment from my own mistakes that led to the biggest regret of my life.

I bring the glass to my nose and take quick sniffs. If you don't sniff the wine first, your senses aren't fully opened to take in the tastes.

This particular wine gives off a berry aroma with notes of chocolate. Most Italian wines, like Chianti, are only made from eighty-percent Sangiovese grapes, but this one is fuller-bodied, made entirely from Montalcino, Italy's famous grapes. Is there anything sexier than a full-bodied wine that can take on your pallet with only one grape as the star of the show?

"How much beauty do you let pass you by on a daily basis? This wine is sexy, elegant, and bold," I tell him. "I feel sorry for the ladies in your life. Do you even get them off? You know you have to take your time with them. Women are complex, and just like these wines, you have to get to know them first."

Marcus rolls his eyes while my other brother, Lucas, snickers at my remark. Little do they know, I'm the guiltiest culprit in the room. I let beauty pass me by every single day, too wrapped up in my misery to bother noticing it. Being with a woman nowadays is simply for a quick release, just to scratch an itch.

"I think Gabe just accused you of not being able to please your women." Lucas smiles at Marcus in delight. "What do ya have to say to that?"

Marcus huffs, like the mere idea is ludicrous. "I know damn well what to do with my women. What would you know about women anyway? You refuse to get back out there and actually settle down with someone."

My hand tightens around my glass at his comment. Lucas shakes his head, knowing that Marcus never knows when to keep his mouth shut.

"I may not know a damn thing about how to keep a woman, but I definitely know how to make her scream in the bedroom," I spit out, the words tasting sour on my tongue.

Does anybody *really* know how to make a woman happy enough to stick around in a marriage? I sure as hell didn't. Angie left both me and our daughter high and dry two years ago for a fresh start in California.

"Let's not get into it tonight," Lucas jumps in. "We're here to sample these wine and food pairings. I also don't think I have the energy to deal with you two tonight."

I shift around in my seat, not wanting to admit he's right.

It's been a long two weeks since Ma took a spill down the stairs and scared the crap out of us.

The fall resulted in a herniated disc that began pressing on a nerve causing some excruciating pain. Surgery was the quickest option for relief and since she went in for it last week, we've all been checking in on her non-stop. Pa isn't great with blood or incisions, and the last thing we need is him hitting the ground, too.

My parents still live in the same house we grew up in in Cleveland, in a neighborhood called Little Italy. I'm the oldest of four kids. Me, Lucas, Marcus, and then our baby sister Mia.

Four years ago, my siblings and I started our own wine brokerage company called Giannelli Family Selections. We travel the world to taste the finest wines, and then we recommend them to restaurants all over the United States. Tonight we are eating at one of our client's restaurants, Michaelangelo's, which is owned by award-winning Chef Michael.

Mia had to stay home in Shaker Heights with my four-year-old daughter Sienna because I'm out a babysitter. We've been scraping by since Ma, my usual babysitter, got hurt. The four of us taking turns watching Sienna, depending on our work schedules.

There's no way we can keep up like this for much longer, and I know I need to hire a nanny. The problem is that ever since Angie left us, I've had trouble trusting people.

Sienna was too young to understand or even remember her mother, but I remember the day my little girl lost the most important relationship in her life. All for what? For more sun and a higher cost of living? Giannelli Family Selections was still experiencing growing pains at the time, and life was tough financially. Sometimes I wonder if Angie would have stuck around if I had taken a normal corporate job and could have adequately provided from the beginning.

Last year was a huge turning point for our business. We scored some major clients around the country and have been growing exponentially ever since. Six months ago, I was able to move into a beautiful home with Sienna, and it feels so good that the blood, sweat, and tears we put into the business have finally paid off.

"Well, I, for one, like this Brunello di Montalcino paired with the sacchetti al tartufo. The Chianti pairs well with the taglioni pasta," I say firmly.

"I agree. The Brunello is a great wine. I think customers will enjoy the addition," Lucas comments before taking a bite of his veal, moaning as he chews. "Shit, this is so damn good. Is this really what we get to call work? It doesn't feel like it."

Marcus laughs, and I even break a smile. He's right. While we're in California, Italy, or France, I often want to pinch myself when we taste these unbelievable wines and foods made by incredible people.

"Too bad Mia is missing out on this," Marcus adds. "Any luck on finding a nanny yet?"

My body stills at the mention of a nanny.

"Not yet. I interviewed a couple of women yesterday," I tell them, thinking back to the interviews.

I wouldn't say they went terribly, and some of the candidates were more than qualified to watch Sienna. I don't even know what I'm looking for. I just know I didn't *feel* it.

"Annnnd. How did they go?" Lucas eyes me skeptically.

I shrug my shoulders. "They were alright. None of them were a good fit."

They both make an audible sigh.

"Look, you know how much we love Sienna. I have a blast watching her. I'm also pretty sure I'm her favorite uncle." Marcus smiles over at Lucas, who just rolls his eyes. "But we can't manage this rotation anymore. I have to fly to New York tomorrow, and Lucas goes to Cali on Thursday. Mia can't be a full-time nanny while also managing all her responsibilities for the company. You have to find someone to start by Monday."

Today is Tuesday. They want me to find someone who can start in six days? Fuck, I know I've been leaning on them a lot, but I didn't realize it was that bad.

I run my hand through my hair. "I'm sorry. I just...it's hard to find someone I trust. What if Sienna gets attached, and they just...leave?"

I watch as a solemn look takes over each of their faces.

"I know it's been tough, man. You're doing a great job, especially given the circumstances." Lucas pats my shoulder. "No matter what happens with this nanny, Sienna will be fine. Besides, this is just for the summer. Until Ma gets better."

"About that...I've been thinking. Ma's fall makes me worry about her running around with Sienna all day. I haven't decided yet, but if the summer goes well, I may consider getting a full-time nanny."

Marcus's head falls back, and he lets out a ripple of laughter. "Good luck telling Ma that. She will never go for it."

Lucas chuckles. "Yeah, sorry, man. I'm with Marcus. Ma would never agree to that."

"I'm not saying she can never have Sienna. She can take her for a couple hours every couple days, but it's too much for her to watch her all day, five days a week. She needs time to relax and enjoy her retirement."

They both shake their heads at me.

"Well, you have the summer to decide. Right now, you need to work on finding someone...anyone to take over. Even if they are only temporary until you find someone more permanent," Lucas says.

"Didn't Allen's daughter say she had a friend from college looking for some summer work?" Marcus suggests.

I've been reluctant to take Allen up on the offer. I don't know his daughter, much less her choice of friends. What if she is a big partier and my nanny is constantly showing up hungover? I don't even know how old she is. Is she eighteen, nineteen? How mature can she be?

"I see the wheels spinning in your head." Lucas points at me. "No excuses. Allen's been a client of ours for years now, so you know he's a good guy. You no longer have the time to be picky, and he wouldn't recommend somebody he doesn't trust. Call him on the way home tonight."

My body deflates. I know he's right. Part of me does feel better about hiring through somebody that I know. These other possible nannies I found on a website. They could be crazy, for all I know. Screw background checks. Just because you've never been caught doing shady shit doesn't mean I trust you.

After we settle our tab with the waitress and say goodbye to Terry, we walk outside. It's mid-June, and the nighttime temperature is starting to feel muggy. I roll up the sleeves of my dress shirt in an effort to combat the heat.

"Make sure you call Allen on your ride home." Lucas slaps my back. "I'll see ya tomorrow, brotha."

I turn around and walk up the street toward my car. Murray Hill is still an all-cobblestone street that has been around since the mid-eighteen hundreds when the Italian immigrants settled here. It's remained strong in its Italian heritage with restaurants, cafes, shops, and art galleries. It was an amazing place to grow up as a kid.

I hop in my black Range Rover, easing my way down the cobblestone street as the imperfections of the road knock me up and down. When I finally turn onto the paved road, I scroll through my phone until I find Allen's number. As soon as the ring echoes through my car speakers, I clench my steering wheel as I brace for the conversation.

"Gabriel. To what do I owe the pleasure?" Allen answers.

"Hi, Allen. I hope it's not a bad time." I take a sharp right as I get closer to home.

"Not at all. Just not used to hearing from you this late."

"I'm sorry about that. I was just calling about your daughter's roommate. You said she was looking for some summer work, and I could really use the help."

I hear him chuckle in the background. "Marcus told me you were gonna get to the end of your rope and need some last-minute reinforcements. I take it this call at this hour means you're desperate."

I take an annoyed breath. I'm gonna beat Marcus tomorrow morning.

"Yeah, I suppose you could say I've let it get down to the wire. I don't suppose she's still looking?"

"Well, as a matter of fact, she is still looking for something. She's spending some time with Alicia this week. I'll text you her number so you can set up a meeting."

"Thanks, Allen. I really appreciate it."

"Not a problem. You take care of yourself. We'll talk soon, I'm sure," he says.

"Will do. Talk to you soon."

When I click off the call, I'm turning into my driveway. I open my front door to Mia lounging on my couch as she stares at her phone. She hears me enter and looks over, smiling.

"How was it?" she asks, making no attempt to move as I join her.

I take a seat on the opposite side of the couch as I unbutton the top buttons of my shirt.

"It was good. Food was delicious, as always. Lucas and I agreed on the Brunello as the winner to present to the restaurant. Like usual, Marcus tried to argue with us about it. How was Sienna?"

"Perfect, as always," she says, a hint of adoration in her voice as she talks about my daughter. "Did they talk to you about finding a nanny?"

Well, that didn't take long. I guess I've been stressing all of them out the last two weeks. I try to rub the tension away from my neck with my hand. It feels like the stress is constantly there these days.

"Yeah, they did. I'm sorry if I've taken advantage of you guys lately."

She rolls her eyes. "You know that isn't true, but we do all need to get back to work with our regular hours. It will start to affect our business if we let it go on too long."

"I know. I called Allen on the way home, and he texted me his daughter's friend's contact information. She's looking for summer work. I'm gonna call her as soon as you leave."

"Oh, well, don't let me hold you up." Mia stands and begins to gather her things. "I'll see you in the office tomorrow?"

I nod my head. "Only for a couple hours. I'll be bringing Sienna with me, so I can't stay too long."

"Open yourself up a bit. Whoever you choose will be great with her. I trust your instincts," she assures me before kissing my cheek on her way out.

When I close the door, I reflect on her words. She trusts my instincts...the same ones that told me Angie was someone I should settle down with. Sure, we weren't perfect together, but it was good enough. I was so focused on getting the business off the ground, I didn't put much thought into the marriage. It just seemed like the obvious next move. Never would I have imagined she would be the type to up and leave a two-year-old daughter behind.

I pull out my phone and open the text from Allen, hovering over the number as I debate if it's too late to call. It's not even ten, and given she's fresh out of college, I'm sure she's awake. I click on the number as I wait until a happy voice answers the phone.

Chapter Two

Alexis

During my last year of school, the college scene held little to no appeal to me anymore. Instead of time spent in the bars or at frat houses, I chose to focus on my classes, my weekends consisting of lounging in my pajamas with a pint of ice cream and *New Girl* reruns.

As I glance down at my black slacks and white button-down shirt, the couple pounds I gained as a result of my ice cream habits are now obvious by my breasts stretching the material, begging to break free.

Now here I am, a twenty-one-year-old graduate from *The Ohio State University* and going on an interview for a summer nanny gig. Call it a quarter-life crisis, but it wasn't until after receiving my degree in finance that I chose it on a whim, believing it would give me the most opportunities. In reality, I have no idea what I really want to do with my life.

I've never understood how anyone can possibly know what they want for the rest of their lives when applying for college at the age of seventeen. Maybe it's because I've spent most of my life without anyone considering my feelings, so when it came time to pick something all for myself, I didn't even know where to start.

I'm not saying I didn't enjoy the major. I'm just not entirely sure finance is where my heart is.

Alicia has been such a lifesaver. She has a cute little apartment near the city and lets me crash on her couch whenever I want to visit from Columbus—which is often.

Living in my mother and stepfather's house isn't going to work for me long-term.

I've had my degree for a total of two weeks... am I supposed to have it all figured out right away? I didn't think so, but they keep incessantly breathing down my throat about when I am going to settle down and find work.

I think they just want me out of the house. They think I'm a distraction for my half-sister Emelia and half-brother Carter. My dad and stepmom live ten minutes away, but they aren't much more welcoming.

When Alicia told me to stay with her tonight, I was in my car driving up Highway 71 faster than a puppy chews up a new toy.

"Why are you so dressed up?" Alicia asks from her bed as I straighten my shirt in front of her mirror. "It's just a nanny position."

I laugh. "I nannied all of my summers home from school. People with money, who are hiring you to protect their children, want to feel like someone with equal wealth and power will be the ones they are leaving their children with."

"That's kind of ridiculous." She kicks off the bed and stands behind me, looking at me through the mirror.

"Yeah," I agree as I put on a subtle pink lipstick. "Rich people are insane."

"Well, my dad said Gabe is a great guy. He's apparently kind of young for all the money he has come into recently. Maybe he won't be a total dick."

I shrug my shoulders. "Doesn't matter to me if he is or not. I'm just there to watch his daughter and make some money."

"If he's the man I'm thinking of, he's also fine as hell."

Alicia raises her eyebrows suggestively.

Even if he is hot, I'm not sure what she thinks I'm going to do. I've been around attractive men before, I'm sure I can manage to watch a good-looking guy's child without catching a crush. Besides, it's not like I've ever felt tempted since my first and only boyfriend. It's something I've never really told anybody, too embarrassed to even talk about.

"I'm not bothered by that. There are good-looking people everywhere. I still manage to go about my life," I counter.

With one last glance in the mirror, I scrunch my fingers into the roots of my hair in an attempt for some last-minute body. I have long, thick brown hair. It's both a gift and a curse. If I put forth the effort, I can make it look pretty good with long waves cascading down, but it's so heavy that getting body up top is challenging.

"We'll see about that," she mutters under her breath, laughing at me. "So, he wants to meet you at his office? That's kind of odd."

"Yeah. He said he needs to get some things done at the office and wants to spend some time with his daughter tonight. I guess if things work out, I'll be starting on Monday. That will give me the weekend to drive home and pack up my clothes."

"How amazing would it be if we still get to live in the same city this summer?" She claps her hands in excitement as she follows me to the front door.

The idea of still getting to spend one more summer with her would be amazing. Over the last four years, she's become my family. Even her parents have taken me in as one of their own, letting me spend Easters and Thanksgivings with them when my own parents decided to take vacations with their *new* families.

"I can't even think about it right now. I may cry if I have to go back home this weekend and live with my mom."

I grab my purse and slide into my black pumps.

"How do I look?" I open my arms to Alicia.

"Hot, yet...professional," she says, looking me up and down. "Very nice."

I smile and shake my head at her. I wasn't going for hot, but I'll take it.

When Gabriel called me last night, I was a bit taken aback. I knew Mr. Albertini was going to give him my number, but that was two weeks ago. When I never heard from him, I assumed he had already found someone. He is clearly desperate now, though. A phone call at ten p.m. asking me if I would be available for an interview the next morning doesn't exactly sound like someone who wants to take their time.

"Okay, I have to go. Wish me luck," I say as I blow a kiss.

"Good luck, girl. You got this," she shouts as the front door closes.

I take the elevator down the three flights, not wanting to work up a sweat or trip in my heels.

I put his address into my phone and let navigation lead me to his office in Shaker Square. As I drive through neighborhoods of beautiful homes that look old and yet well-maintained, I'm surrounded by large trees that look like they are going to engulf you if you continue down the street.

When I get to the square, I notice a sign that reads *Giannelli Family Selections.* As I park my car, I look around at the beautiful architecture, and a flutter of nerves begins to dance around my stomach.

Upon entering the building, I am in awe of the crown molding and what appears to be the original hardwood floors that are still in amazing condition. The large staircase on the left leads up to French doors, and I slowly take the steps one at a time as I look around at the mosaic ceiling. I could get lost in the beauty of this building.

I open the door and am greeted with a beautiful display of wines and barrels surrounding another sign of the company name. As I approach the display, I'm struck by the labels that seem to be from countries all over the world.

"You can take one, I won't tell anyone," someone says, startling me. "Sorry, I didn't mean to scare you."

The man approaches me as he extends his hand. I shake it, trying to take in all his handsome features. He is tall and lean, with dark hair. He has a distinct jawline, made even more obvious by his perfectly shaved skin. The most shocking feature is his blue eyes against tanned skin.

"Hi, I'm Alexis. Are you Gabriel?"

He laughs affectionately. "I'm his brother, Marcus. I'm the friendly one. You must be the new nanny."

I adjust my blouse. "Oh, no. I mean, I'm here for an interview. We'll see if I get the job."

He looks me up and down, not subtle in his appreciation. "Gabe will hire you. He'd be crazy not to."

A deep voice clears his throat from behind Marcus. I step back from Marcus as another man walks forward, stopping in front of me as my body instantly covers in goosebumps. This man looks very similar to Marcus, with the same dark hair, darker complexion, and tall build. The differences are that he has muscles that show through his suit, a light stubble covering his jaw, and dark eyes. They hold mine as I feel them assess me. I shiver at having this man's full attention. There is something eerie in his stare...like I can feel his anger as he takes me in.

I'm not sure if I'm intimidated or turned on.

"Marcus," the man says with authority. "Mind your business."

Marcus gives him a serious look. "Just getting to know your new nanny."

This is Gabriel? I'm not sure what I was expecting. Maybe someone like Marcus, a bit more friendly and laid back. Certainly not the man standing in front of me.

"You can follow me, Miss Moretti," Gabriel instructs.

"Oh, you're Italian! Ma will love that." Marcus smiles at me mischievously.

Gabriel doesn't acknowledge his comment as he begins to walk back down the hall he came out of. I don't miss the glare that takes over Gabriel's, or Mr. Giannelli's, face. I'm not sure what he wants me to call him after his formal use of my name.

This man is seriously uptight. I want to whisper for Marcus to *help me*, but I'm not sure he would do anything to save me. Instead, I follow Gabriel until we are walking into a room with Gabriel Giannelli on the door.

He gestures for me to go in first. "You can take a seat in front of my desk."

I walk into a large office with wooden floors, walnut crown molding, and antique-looking furniture. It screams power and wealth, but also someone who has appreciation for history.

When I take a seat in one of the leather chairs, Gabriel sits in his chair across from me. The desk divides us, reminding me that he is going to be my boss if I get the job. The other people I nannied for were a bit more laid back. We discussed my qualifications at their house, sitting on the couch or at the kitchen table with children running around.

I feel like I'm interviewing for a position at this company, not to be the nanny.

"I see you already met my brother, Marcus," he says as he straightens his tie. "I assure you the rest of the family is normal."

I smile. "He seems very kind. I didn't realize he was your brother."

Gabriel nods his head at me. "This is a family-run business. I started it with my siblings four years ago."

"It's a beautiful building you have here. I love the history it portrays."

He nods his head but doesn't offer any further comments. "Thank you for meeting with me on such short notice."

"It's no problem. It worked out that I was in town already."

I squirm in my seat, still not sure how to act around him.

"I'll get right to the point. I need someone to be a live-in nanny for the summer to help take care of my four-year-old daughter, Sienna. My mother took a fall a couple weeks ago and needed surgery, so I need help while she recovers."

"I'm so sorry to hear about your mother," I sympathize with him. "But I would be happy to help you out this summer. I have a lot of experience with kids as I used to nanny during my summer breaks."

His eyes are looking at me all dark and broody again as he assesses me. "How old are you, Miss Moretti?"

"I'm twenty-one," I say with a smile. "And you can call me Alexis."

I think I hear a grumble come from his throat. "Okay, Alexis. I'm gonna be honest, I'm not the most trusting person. I'm only coming to you because I'm desperate. The idea of leaving my Sienna with someone I don't know makes me nervous, but I can't be picky at this point, and Allen speaks highly of you. If I hire you, I would need your full cooperation. This is not one of those summer gigs where you can show up hungover to take care of my daughter or bring around other party-going college kids."

I sit up straight in my seat. I don't care how intimidating he is, I won't let anyone talk to me like that. I'm not sure who he thinks he is.

"With all due respect, Gabriel. I am not some teenage babysitter. I would never behave that way. Mr. Albertini would never vouch for me if he didn't think I was a responsible *adult*."

I put emphasis on the last word because I'm not sure he understands that I'm not a sixteen-year-old who is going to invite her boyfriend over and sneak in beers.

"Very well," he says, offering no apology. "What was your major at Ohio State?"

"Finance."

"And you didn't want to find a job in finance instead?" he asks condescendingly.

"I just didn't want to make a rash decision without weighing all of my options first."

It's getting exhausting explaining myself to people. Why are we expected to have our job lined up the day after we graduate? I'm not interested in taking the first job that comes my way just to quit within the first year.

Before Gabriel can speak, his door swings open, and a little girl with beautiful dark brown hair comes running in, chuckling.

"Daddy." The girl smiles as she throws herself into the stone-cold man in front of me.

His eyes sparkle for her as a small smile spreads across his face.

"Sienna, I told you that you can't come in here right now. Daddy's busy," shouts a man I haven't seen yet as he barrels into the room.

This must be another brother. The genes of this family have blessed these men with incredible features. It's really quite difficult to see this many attractive men in the span of fifteen minutes.

"Who are you?" the little girl asks me while sitting on her father's lap.

I smile at her, taking in her adorable outfit. "My name is Alexis. What's your name?"

"I'm Sienna. Alexis is a pretty name."

"Thank you. I think your dress is very beautiful, Sienna. Did you pick it out yourself this morning?"

Gabriel is silent as he watches me interact with his child.

"I did. Daddy picked out boring clothes. I told him I wanted to dress up for work. I'm helping them today!"

I chuckle at her answer. She is completely serious, and it's adorable.

I can understand why Gabriel is so set on finding someone he trusts, but he has been trying to dissect our conversation, looking for something to criticize me about. The dude needs to chill out.

Chapter Three

Gabriel

Dammit, I didn't want to like her. When I walked out of my office to see this beautiful woman standing in front of me, I knew I was in trouble. I was picturing some tiny nineteen-year-old. Instead, I was met with a gorgeous brunette whose curves made my hands actually flex as they ached to touch them.

I'm not shy about taking a woman home when I have the chance to curb my craving for intimacy, but I've never had such an immediate reaction to a woman.

Now I'm sitting here with my daughter on my lap as the two girls chat like I'm not even in the room.

"And my favorite ice cream flavor is chocolate with a whole bunch of rainbow sprinkles on it. What is yours?" Sienna manages to stop long enough to let Alexis answer.

Alexis smiles widely at my daughter. "Ooh, that's a tough one. I would have to say mint chocolate chip *or* cookies and cream."

Sienna nods her head approvingly. "Those are good flavors too. I would eat them. I also like to bake cookies, but Daddy never does that with me. Grandma lets me bake with her all the time. What about you? Do you like to bake?"

"I *love* to bake!" Alexis answers enthusiastically.

"Okay, honey. I need you to go with Uncle Lucas. Daddy and Miss Alexis need to finish their conversation. When we're done, you and I get to go home and have a nice lunch together," I tell her.

Sienna jumps off my lap. "Oookay, Daddy. Bye, Alexis." She waves as Lucas grabs her hand and leads her out of the office.

"Bye, sweetie!" Alexis responds with a wave.

When they're gone, I attempt to bring the meeting back to where we left it.

"I'm sorry about that," I start. "As you can see, we're struggling to keep up with her at the moment."

Alexis doesn't seem bothered at all by the interruption.

"No worries. I'm glad I got to meet her. She's adorable and very talkative."

Sienna never fails to charm the socks off anyone she meets. She trusts and loves like she has never known heartache. I'm thankful her mother leaving hasn't seemed to affect her yet. Not like it has me. I'm the one who can't quite get over the depression or guilt...or whatever the hell it is that I'm feeling these days.

"She took a liking to you. So, where were we?" My frazzled brain tries to remember what we were talking about before Lucas lost control of his niece.

Alexis's eyebrows raise with a challenge. "I believe you were trying to figure out why a recent college graduate with a degree in finance would be looking for a nanny position. And just so you know...the reason this position is perfect for me is because it's temporary. I'm not looking to settle into something completely outside my career interests. I just want to take the summer to really think about where I want to settle down."

I try not to get distracted by her delicately carved face or her full mouth. She does this thing where she purses her lips when she's thinking, and it's incredibly distracting.

"I can understand that. I suppose not jumping into something you aren't committed to is admirable."

"Thanks," she says earnestly as she struggles to meet my eyes.

It feels like there's something deeper in her reasoning for not settling down somewhere yet. Something that few people understand.

I lean back in my chair. "I'm not known for giving compliments out easily."

"I'm not known for receiving them easily. I think we would work well together," she says softly.

This feels dangerous. I know what I'm about to do could really come back and bite me in the ass. How am I going to live with this woman all summer? I can barely look at her now without having a strong reaction. My dick twitches in my pants at the thought of her showering naked in my house.

Fuck, I need to get a hold of myself. I'm fourteen years older than her.

"Look, I'm not going to beat around the bush. I need you, so the job is yours if you're interested. I have a guest bedroom with a private bath that you would move into. I would need you to move in by Sunday so you could be ready to start on Monday morning. It would be nice if we could eat dinner together Sunday with Sienna, so you two can get better acquainted."

She does that damn thing with her lips again as she considers my words.

Fuck my life! Why couldn't I just have hired the old lady I interviewed a couple days ago?

"I accept. I can drive home tomorrow and pack my things."

The breath that I didn't know I was holding releases.

"I'll email you all the information, including a formal offer with pay before you officially accept, but I do appreciate you coming in and willing to be so flexible." I stand up and shake her hand, surprised by how nice the soft, warmth feels against my skin. "I'll be in touch."

She follows me to the door.

"Thank you again for considering me," she says.

We walk out to the main area of the office, and I lead her to the exit, holding the door open for her.

"You'll see an email from me within the hour. Nice to meet you, Miss Moretti."

"Please, call me Alexis," she offers.

I nod my head. "Very well. You can call me Gabe."

"I'll see you around, Gabriel," her silky voice drawls out.

Ugh, the sound of my full name coming out of those lips is dangerous. No one but my parents call me Gabriel, and they only do that when I'm in trouble. But that seems fitting for Alexis because everything inside me is screaming that she's risky.

When I walk back inside, Lucas and Marcus are standing there with shit-eating grins on their faces. I choose to ignore them as I take long strides back into my office, knowing they will be following me.

When I walk in, Sienna is sitting on the couch.

"Where'd the pretty lady go?" she asks.

Before I can answer, Marcus walks in and beats me to it.

"She was quite pretty, wasn't she?" He takes a seat in my chair. "I think I might be asking her out on a date this summer."

My hands tighten in fists by my sides at the idea of Marcus going on a date with her.

"You. Stay. Away," I say through clenched teeth.

Lucas shakes his head and laughs while Marcus looks mischievously at me.

"What? Would that make you jealous?" Marcus presses me.

"Not at all. I just don't want you scaring her away. We all need this relationship to remain professional for the sake of Sienna."

Why does the reality of that make me feel so disappointed? I don't plan on crossing the line, but the idea that I can't makes my body deflate.

"Is that pretty lady going to watch me?" Sienna smiles excitedly.

I can't help but match her smile.

"Yes, sweetheart. Alexis is going to live with us and help take care of you this summer while Grandma rests."

Lucas and Marcus chuckle as they stand up and begin to leave the room.

"One happy little family," Lucas teases as he walks past me.

I choose to ignore my brothers. Right now, I just want to focus on the fact that I finally have someone lined up for the summer. It's a huge weight off my shoulders. I was beginning to think I was going to have to take some time away from work.

"Come on, sweetheart. Let's go home and get some lunch."

I extend my hand to her, reveling in the feeling when she rests her small hand in mine. It's such a precious moment where her innocence and age emanate.

I'm lost in thought during the drive home, thinking about the company, my daughter, and especially our new nanny.

"Can we get a doggie, Daddy?" Sienna's angelic voice breaks my concentration.

I look in the rearview mirror to find her looking outside longingly as a woman walks her dog.

"I've told you before, we don't have time for a dog. Daddy wouldn't have the time to train the dog properly."

She sighs as she continues watching on outside.

"I know. I just want one so bad. They're so cute. It could sleep with me every night, so I wouldn't be scared of the dark."

"Maybe when you're older and can help out more," I suggest, not wanting to break her heart completely.

She nods her head in agreement.

When we get home, I make us some lunch which we eat together at the kitchen table while she tells me all about the "work" she did for Uncle Lucas. I love that she wants to help out. She enjoys spending time with her family and will do so in any capacity that she can.

We spend the rest of the day hanging out with each other as I build a new wooden playhouse that I got for her. I say one too many cuss words under my breath, as it's a bitch to put together. When I finally finish, Sienna plays in it all evening while I get some work done.

Now that she's asleep in her room, I pour myself a glass of Vino Nobile di Montepulciano. It's a dry wine with soft tannins that stick to my tongue in the best way. One thing I've learned from tasting hundreds of wines, is that one of the most important attributes is distinctiveness. When you taste your wine, you want the flavors to jump out at you and show you who they are. This particular producer knows exactly how to make sure I know I'm drinking a Montepulciano wine.

It's bold, crispy, and has a powerful aroma of earthy tones mixed with berries. When I close my eyes, I can imagine the grapes growing in clay-rich soil as the fullness of the wine comes through.

When I think of fullness, Alexis's lips come to mind. I bet they taste just as bold and powerful as this wine. Just the thought alone makes my dick react. I groan at the power that woman's mouth has over me after just one interaction.

After my glass of wine, I stand up and walk into my bathroom, stripping out of my clothes and getting into the shower, intending to do something about the situation going on in my jeans. Before I can do something stupid like indulge in the fantasies taking residence in my brain, I turn the temperature of the water to ice cold and stand underneath the stream as I let the water chill both my body and my thoughts.

Chapter Four

Alexis

I pull into a long driveway shadowed by towering trees. Lining the driveway on my right are perfectly trimmed hedges, while along my left is a stone wall, offering privacy to the house. I continue driving for what feels like minutes but is probably only seconds until I finally pull up to an insanely large cream house. It has three massive arches and a statement fountain displayed in front.

I'm not sure what I was expecting, but this definitely wasn't it. The house is clearly older, but given its amazing condition, it's obviously well-maintained. As I glance around the front yard, I find that I could get lost in the landscape alone. It feels like I just turned into an old Tuscan mansion.

I park my car and walk past the large fountain surrounded by greenery and vines climbing large trellises. I walk under one of the stone arches, which leads me up to a wooden double door. Knocking on the door gives off a loud echo, vibrating through my arm.

The door swings open, and my eyes land on Gabriel in a black button-down shirt paired with dark-wash jeans. He is wearing his signature scowl as he looks me up and down, eyes turning even darker than I remember.

"Where are your things?" he says without any other greeting.

I move my weight from one foot to the other, not used to anyone making me feel so nervous.

"I figured I would knock before I trekked all my things up to the door," I tell him.

"Come in." He stands to the side, motioning for me to walk past him.

"I love your home. It's beautiful," I offer as I slowly enter the house, slipping out of my shoes.

His eyes capture mine, and the familiar shiver from when we met runs through my body again.

"Thank you. We moved in not too long ago. We're still getting settled, but we like it so far."

I take a moment to orient myself, looking around the entryway. The foyer is huge, with two winding staircases and a large antique-looking chandelier hanging above us.

"I'll give you the tour, and then we can grab your things," he says with an edge to his voice.

I follow him upstairs, where he shows me there are four bedrooms. Mine is the last door on the right, with an amazing view of the backyard. The room is decorated in warm earth tones with a four-poster, king-sized bed, and a bathroom big enough for a freestanding bathtub.

"Sienna's room is directly across from yours," he says as he leads me across the hall into a light pink room filled with white furniture.

"Aw, I love her room," I tell him.

"Sienna demanded pink, but I told her it would have to be subtle. I didn't want to walk into a hot pink explosion every time I came in here."

I try to stifle my laugh. "I can see her enjoying a hot pink room. It would certainly match her big personality."

A glimmer of a smile crosses his face, one I'm sure doesn't appear very often, at least in front of adults. It appears his daughter is his only reason for smiling.

Once we're done with the tour, we walk out to my car to get my things. I open my trunk, revealing my two suitcases and a few tote bags.

"Doesn't look like you packed much," he says as he stares down at my luggage.

I shrug my shoulders, not sure how to respond.

"I wasn't sure what to bring. I didn't want to overpack, and I figured I could drive home on a weekend if I needed to get more things."

Once we lug the bags upstairs, he puts the suitcase next to the dresser and places my bags on the bed. I've never really been into older men, but I'd be lying if I said I didn't notice the muscles in his arms as he carries the weight of my things. To be fair, I also have never met anyone as attractive as him, even with the intense, mysterious thing he's got going on.

He's nothing like the college men I'd grown accustomed to over the last four years. With them, it was never too difficult to figure out what was on their mind's eighty percent of the time, and it left me feeling bored in their presence. Not to mention the dreaded insecurity I faced every time things were heading toward being intimate together that also had me running for the hills.

"I'll let you get settled," he says as he glances down at his watch.

Um, yeah, and his watch. There's something so sophisticated and sexy about a man in a watch, something college guys definitely don't wear.

"My sister Mia is going to drop by with Sienna in about fifteen minutes. I was going to whip up some chicken marsala in the meantime. Feel free to join me in the kitchen whenever you are ready."

"Sounds great. Thank you," I tell him.

He walks out of the room, and I immediately fall back on the large bed. There's a television hung in the corner of the room, and as I survey the ceiling, I notice the intricate woodwork splayed around the perimeter. I can't believe I get to spend the summer in a home this beautiful.

As I begin to unpack my clothes, placing them neatly into the drawers, I imagine what Sienna and I will do all summer.

Picturing tea parties in the backyard, cooking lessons in the kitchen, and fun arts and crafts. When I open the closet, there is a massive walk-in with custom drawers and shelving made of wood. Every inch of this house is updated, and it's obvious a lot of thought went into the design. This will be a nice space for me to still have some privacy, which will be important living where I work. Gabriel hasn't done much to make me feel like we are going to be hanging out to watch reruns of The Office together after Sienna is in bed.

This is my first time nannying for a single dad before, so naturally, the dad has to be insanely good-looking. Why couldn't he have a beer belly and a balding spot?

Hearing a commotion, I assume Gabriel's sister must be here. When I walk downstairs, I'm greeted by an enthusiastic smile from Sienna and a dark stare from Gabriel.

The sister, Mia, looks me up and down before a beautiful smile greets me.

"You must be Alexis. Sienna told me all about you this afternoon. I'm so happy Gabe finally agreed to find someone to help him out," Mia says warmly.

When I get to the bottom of the steps, I extend my hand to offer a hello.

"And you must be Mia. I'm looking forward to spending the summer with Sienna," I say as I look down at the little girl. "We are going to have so much fun together."

Sienna lifts her innocent little shoulders and giggles.

"Well, I will leave you guys to it." Mia claps her hands together. "It was nice meeting you, Alexis."

"So nice to meet you too, Mia," I tell her as she walks out the front door, leaving me standing here with a happy girl and her grumpy father.

"Want to come see my stuffed animal collection?" Sienna grabs my hand.

"Not right now, sweetie." Gabe stops her. "Dinner's ready."

"Awww," Sienna whines.

"I would love to come see your collection after dinner." I extend my hand for hers as we follow Gabriel to the kitchen table.

I take the seat next to Sienna, with gold silverware and a tall wine glass set in front of me. Gabriel walks over, casually holding two large white plates. He places one in front of me, which holds a healthy portion of delicious-looking chicken marsala. The chicken has the perfect brown color, and the marsala sauce wafts in my face. Growing up in an Italian household, I learned early on what fine cooking was.

"Looks yummy, daddy." She smiles up at him.

He offers her head a small pat, crinkles appear in the corner of his eyes when he smiles at her.

Shit, my entire body just broke out in a shiver at the exchange. These two obviously have a strong connection. And what type of four-year-old is excited about chicken marsala?

Gabriel walks over with his plate in hand to join us at the table. He takes a seat across from us before he grabs the bottle of wine sitting in the middle of the table.

"Would you like a glass?" he asks me.

Knowing this man's profession, I feel like he might kick me out if I say no.

"I'd love some. Thank you," I tell him.

He dips his head in approval and pours me a small glass before doing the same for himself. I pick it up and take a sip before placing it back down to grab my fork. I swirl the pasta, trying to get the perfect first bite. When I look up, Gabriel is still sitting there with his glass in his hand, staring at me with a curious look on his face.

I try to wipe around my mouth subtly, just in case I have something on my face.

"What?" I ask, feeling incredibly self-conscious.

"What do you think of the wine?" His eyebrows raise with the question.

"Oh." I look down at my glass before shrugging my shoulders. "It was good."

His head lowers, but his eyes keep boring a hole in me. I must have said something wrong; I don't know what that could be.

"Good? This is a Chateau La Conseillante. It's one of the finest French wines you can find."

He says this as if I have the slightest clue what the hell wine he just rattled off. I'm a poor college graduate who has survived off bottom-shelf wine for years. Now he expects me to offer some rave review of a wine I can't even pronounce? I'm the freakin' nanny, not some award-winning sommelier. Are there even awards for sommeliers? Probably not.

I guess I need to appease the man since he is going to be my boss for the summer.

"Oh. Um, it tastes lovely," I say, emphasizing the last word.

He shakes his head, a mocking chuckle escaping from his stupidly sexy mouth. Apparently, he is capable of laughing, but only when it's to make you feel like an incompetent idiot.

"It is *lovely*, Alexis." His voice drowns in sarcasm.

He begins to swirl the contents of wine in his glass before bringing it to his nose. His eyes close as he breathes in a couple long inhales. I'm not sure why, but watching it makes me feel something between my thighs. I squeeze them together as I watch him.

"You need to take a couple sniffs of the wine before you take your first sip. The tongue isn't going to take in the full flavor profile if you don't prepare it with your scent first. Try it. See what your nose can detect."

He watches me as I follow his instructions and bring the glass to my nose. I take a couple inhales as the smells invade my brain and begin to register. I keep my eyes closed as I answer, trying to focus on the task at hand, feeling a strange need not to disappoint him.

"Um, I think I smell some kind of peppery, spicy smell. And," I take another quick sniff, "like...a berry, maybe."

When I open my eyes, his are focused on mine in a way that makes me feel very aware of the attention.

"Good," he answers. "Now, you need to take a sip, but let the taste come to you. Let it tell you the story of how it was made. What kind of love and effort went into it, and how the flavors work together like a symphony. Wine is so much more than something to get you drunk or just a drink to go with a meal. It's an expression of the winemaker and what they are trying to say to you. Let them tell their love story."

The way this man talks about wine is doing more for me than porn ever could. My body has never felt more on edge and needy, wishing I could listen to him all day. How can he make the act of drinking wine so...erotic? And this is coming from the least sexual person in the world.

His eyes hold mine as I take another sip of the wine. This time, I pay attention to the flavors that dance around my tongue.

"In the beginning, I definitely tasted the berries," I tell him, "but it turned into a more woodsy, spicy taste."

He nods at me, which seems like a gesture he does a lot.

"Not bad for a beginner," he tells me.

"I've never put much thought into the wine I drink. I generally just buy my seven-dollar bottle of wine and pour it in a plastic wine glass."

Gabriel closes his eyes and groans at my admission. When he opens his eyes, he looks at me earnestly.

"Please...*never* bring one of your seven-dollar bottles of wine into this house," he begs. "Those bottles are made by people looking to make a large profit, not to inspire others with its beauty."

I can't help but snicker behind my glass of wine. I will admit, taking his suggestion does make me more aware of how good the wine tastes. I look at the bottle and make a mental note to google the name when I get to my room tonight. I'm kind of curious about what a bottle like this would set me back.

"This food is really good. You're clearly very good in the kitchen," I say to him after another large bite.

"Daddy makes the best food." Sienna smiles as she slurps in a long noodle.

I smile down at her. "I agree, his marsala is really good, but I bet my chicken piccata is better than this."

Gabriel takes the bait and sits up straighter, the challenge in his posture giving him away.

"I highly doubt that. No offense, but you're twenty-one. I've had a lot more time and practice in the kitchen."

Sienna chuckles next to me.

"Daddy is super competitive. He doesn't like to lose," she says, looking up at me.

"Oh, yeah?" I laugh. "Well, guess what? I'm really competitive, too, and I'll bet you like my chicken more."

Gabriel snorts at my words. Although I don't want to upset him, I do feel like this dinner has helped loosen me up a bit. He's still intimidating, but I don't want that to squash my carefree nature this entire summer.

Chapter Five

Gabriel

"How was the first evening with your new nanny?" Marcus asks with a smirk.

The four of us siblings are sitting in the office kitchen eating lunch. We haven't all been together since before Ma fell, but we can always count on Marcus to ruin a good thing.

I raise my eyebrows at him, letting him know I'm not impressed with his insinuation.

"What exactly are you trying to imply?"

Marcus shrugs his shoulders, acting innocent.

"Not implying anything. I'm just asking if your *hot-as-sin* nanny got settled alright in her new room at your house. Did you show her how to use the shower? Sometimes those knobs can be tricky. What would you do if she came out in only a towel and asked for some help?"

Lucas and Mia both cover their mouths to hide their smiles.

"I'm not living in a freakin' porno, you idiot," I say, smacking his arm.

"That's too bad. She's hot enough to star in a good porno," Lucas adds.

"How old are you two? What the hell has gotten into you guys?" I look at Mia to defend me.

She just smiles. "She is really beautiful."

I roll my eyes. Apparently, all my siblings are going to get on me about having a good-looking nanny.

I think back to dinner last night when I stupidly decided to teach her about wine. What was I thinking letting her onto such an important part of who I am? My dick nearly jumped out of my pants at the sight of her licking the wine off her lips as she released a soft moan. Sienna and wine have been the only two things to bring me out of my funk, and now Alexis drinking wine has been added to that list. I could watch her sip wines and explore the flavors all day.

Fuck, it was inappropriate of me to be so turned on by a twenty-one-year-old. While my daughter was sitting at the table, no less. I'm starting to regret hiring her, and it's only been one day.

I've tried to be good about not checking in, but it's beginning to get to me now. I reach into my pocket for my phone, deciding one text won't hurt anything.

Gabe: How are things going so far?

I try to get back to my food, but when I see the three dots pop up, I'm on the edge of my seat, waiting for her response. When the message finally comes in, I see a picture of the two girls smiling. Sienna is standing behind Alexis, who is sitting on the floor, hair in complete disarray with butterfly clips all over her head.

Alexis: Sienna's doing my hair. She's making me into a princess. Great day so far.

I do my best to control the smile that wants to break free at the picture. Something in my chest feels weird at seeing Sienna so happy with another woman besides her aunt or grandma.

Gabe: I think the princess will have trouble finding a prince looking like that.

That's not entirely true. Even with that hairdo, she's stunning.

Alexis: I think the princess doesn't care what the grumpy villain thinks.

Any other day, with any other person, I would wear the grumpy villain badge with pride. Hearing it from Alexis, though...it only makes me feel more out of control with desire.

I spend the rest of the day trying to fight off visions of all the ways I would like to show Alexis my grumpy side. I'm not sure what to do with this craving that only seems to be getting stronger. It's been a little while since I've gotten laid; maybe that's my problem. A man can only go so long without sex and *not* have a reaction to the beauty that's in front of him.

When I get home, I sit in the driveway, trying to mentally talk myself into going into the house and having no reaction to the woman I will be greeted by. As the door opens, I'm hit with Sienna's giggles, and my body instantly relaxes. It's the perfect reminder of why I hired Alexis. It doesn't matter what my body is telling me; all that matters is that Sienna seems to love her.

As I walk into the kitchen, I see Sienna carrying a basket of bread to the dinner table. She sees me and her face breaks out into an excited grin.

"Daddy!" she screams and runs into my arms.

I pick her up and breathe in her scent. When I put her down, I survey the room and see Alexis standing there with a small smile on her face.

"Hi," I say to her, not sure exactly how to greet her.

"Hi," she says back.

I see the table is set for two, with a flickering candle in between the plates.

"What's all of this?" I ask somewhat nervously.

"We made you dinner, Daddy!" Sienna exclaims.

"She wanted to make dinner for the two of you," Alexis clarifies. "We kind of decided to go all out and set the table as well."

I wonder if she saw the panic start to arise in me at the sight of two plates and a candle.

"That's so thoughtful of you." I look down at Sienna. "What are we having for dinner?"

Waiting for her to tell me she picked chicken nuggets and mashed potatoes; I'm not prepared for the answer that follows.

"Alex and I made chicken piccata with roasted vegetables. She promised me I would like the carrots and that I would like this chicken more than yours."

Alexis is biting her bottom lip as she smiles up at me.

"Oh, really?" I question Sienna while my eyes remain on Alexis.

"Come on, Daddy!" Sienna grabs my hand and leads me to the table while Alexis plates the food off the stove.

As she places the food between Sienna and me, I'm struck with a twinge of disappointment.

"You won't be joining us?" I ask her.

"Oh, um, I figured you wouldn't want to spend your dinners with your nanny. I'll just be in my room if anyone needs me. I had a lot of fun with you today, Sienna."

"Me too!" Sienna smiles.

With that, Alexis disappears out of the kitchen, and I remain lost in my own head.

"Don't you want to try the food, Daddy?" Sienna breaks my train of thought.

I shake my head, trying to rid myself of the funny feelings that have taken root in me. Why am I so disappointed she isn't joining us for dinner? That was never an expectation from the beginning, and it shouldn't be now.

"Of course, I do," I tell her as I give us each a big helping of food.

I cut up Sienna's chicken for her, followed by her carrots. Alexis already had a basket of warm bread on the table, which Sienna has buttered herself.

When I take the first bite of my chicken, my tastebuds weren't prepared for the flavors they were going to be treated to. The lemon, olive oil, cheese, capers...they all work together in the most delicious way. The texture of the chicken is perfect. It has an amazing crunch to the skin with a moist center.

I stand up immediately and walk to the large closet under the stairs that I had turned into a wine cellar. I know exactly what kind of wine I want to open with this meal. In the cooler part of the cellar, I reach for the Sauvignon Blanc that I picked up on a trip to France a couple years back. It will pair perfectly with the acidity of the lemons in the chicken.

Once I sit back down with Sienna, she looks at me quizzically.

"I guess you really like the chicken," she says matter-of-factly.

"Why do you say that?" I question her.

"Because you got a bottle of wine. You only do that when you really like the food," she says, sounding wise beyond her years.

I have to contemplate that for a second. I suppose it's true. I do only open wine at dinner when I feel like the food calls for it. As soon as I took one bite of Alexis's food, my body was in motion for something to accompany the food. It's a testament to how good it is.

"You're right, kiddo. The food is really good. You and Alexis did a great job," I offer, rubbing the soft skin on her cheek.

She leans into me with her hand over her mouth. "Alex did most of the work."

I laugh before taking a sip of the wine. "It's okay. I'm sure you were great company for her."

I enjoy the dinner with Sienna as we talk about her day with Alexis. She seems so smitten with her, and I realize she's not the only one. It's rare to find a woman who looks like Alexis and can cook like this.

After bath and story time, I tuck Sienna in. The speed at which her eyes flutter closed shows how busy she was today. When I walk back downstairs, I notice Alexis is in the kitchen making herself a sandwich. I'm momentarily distracted by the short pajama shorts and t-shirt she's wearing.

"What are you doing? Going for a second dinner?" I ask before I pour myself another glass of wine.

She shrugs. "Nah, making myself a first dinner."

I don't mean to slam the bottle down as hard as I do, but the reaction was immediate.

"What do you mean? You didn't eat some of your chicken before I got home?"

She looks a bit bewildered by my question. "Uh, no. I don't generally eat the food that my employers pay for. It's not part of the agreement."

It's then that I notice she is making a sandwich on cheap ass bread with meat that I would *never* have in my house.

"What the hell are you eating?" I spew out with anger.

When I notice she's not catching on, I grab her sandwich and throw it out. Opening the fridge, I grab the leftovers container and a plate to heat up the dinner she prepared. I'm so angry with her, I can't even think straight. How could she slave away over a meal for me and my daughter, and think a two-dollar sandwich is an adequate meal for herself?

"What are you doing? Why would you throw away my food?" she asks.

I manage to look over at her, seeing she's wearing a look of annoyance as her hand rests on her hip. Her posture makes her look more enticing, which only adds to my anger.

"I'm making sure you eat a decent meal. When you are under my roof, you do not put that crap in your body. Do you understand me?" I grab the microwaved plate and set it on the island.

I motion for her to sit, but she stands there defiantly.

"Did you not hear me, woman?" I enunciate my words.

"First off," She comes closer to me, finger pointing at me. "don't call me *woman*. Secondly, I will eat the meal when you ask me *nicely*."

Fuck, her opposition is hot as hell. There are so many things I would like to do to her right now. To do to that sweet ass of hers that shows just how much she enjoys her food. She has the perfect body. Curves in all the right places and a tiny waist I wish I could dig my fingers into.

I can tell she isn't going to back down from this, and I really don't want her going to bed hungry.

"Will you *please* sit down and eat this food?" I grit through my teeth.

She smiles up at me. "That was much better, thank you," she says.

I stand here and watch her eat for what feels like a weird amount of time. She confirms my thoughts when she turns her head and looks over her shoulder.

"Are you just going to stand there and stare at me like a psycho while I eat my food?"

"Just making sure you actually eat," I tell her, hoping she doesn't know I was lost watching her lips wrap around each bite.

"How was your first day with Sienna?" I ask as I wrap back around the island and put away the leftovers.

When I turn back around from the fridge, Alexis is smiling.

"It was great. She's so sweet and funny. She had me cracking up the entire day."

The sincerity in her words makes me crack a small smile.

"She seems smitten with you. I'm glad you both had a good first day."

She eats her food quickly and puts her plate in the dishwasher. I continue to stand in the kitchen, sipping my wine as I watch her.

"Well..." she starts awkwardly. "Thank you for dinner."

"You mean the dinner you cooked?" I point out.

She shrugs her shoulders as a laugh escapes. "Yeah, I guess so. I think I'm gonna go relax in my room, probably read a book. Try to conserve some energy to keep up with your little spitfire tomorrow."

I smile again. Something I'm not used to doing, but that she has gotten out of me twice in the last fifteen minutes.

"I'll see you in the morning, Alexis."

"Goodnight, Gabriel," her silky voice says before she walks away.

I put my wine down as I lean my hands against the island and hang my head. Fuck, I need to get a grip. That voice saying my full name...it's becoming a problem. How do I politely ask her not to use my whole name because it makes my dick twitch in excitement?

Chapter Six

Alexis

"So, what shall we do today?" I ask Sienna as I start to clean the dishes from our pancake escapade this morning. I may have fed off her energy and excitement a little too much and made three different kinds of pancakes.

In just two days, I've already learned that she's really good at claiming she's "done it a thousand times" while continuing to prove otherwise. Like cracking an egg or pouring milk.

"We can go to the park. Grandma used to take me to the park all the time. Oh, we could get gelato after!" she eagerly says.

"Did you just say gelato?" I question, looking down at her curiously.

Her eyes light up as she nods her head enthusiastically. What four-year-old asks for gelato over ice cream?

"Grandma gets a cannoli, Papa gets a coconut bar, and I get gelato," she says, counting as she holds a finger up for each order.

I chuckle at her knowledge of Italian desserts. "Where is it that you get all of this food?"

"Little Italy!" she exclaims. "It's where Grandma and Papa live."

Now I'm confused. Is there an actual place here called Little Italy, or just some imaginary name Sienna has given this bakery? If there is such a place, I need to go. How can I live two hours away from here and not know of such a place? Growing up with Italian grandparents, I've been introduced to all the food and the culture. It's a part of who I am. A part I love to explore. Going to Italy one day would be a dream come true.

I get my phone out and Google Little Italy. Much to my surprise, there is a neighborhood only ten minutes from us that, sure enough, is called Little Italy.

"If I drove us there, would you be able to show me where the playground is?" I ask her.

"Of course. I only go there *all* the time," she sasses.

I eye her, letting her know I'm not impressed, and she starts to giggle.

"Okay, little Miss. Smarty Pants. Let's hit the road. I could use a little gelato in my life."

Once I get her buckled in the car seat that Gabriel installed for me, I type in the name of a bakery in Little Italy, hoping that Sienna will pull through on her word to show me the playground.

I focus on following directions while Sienna looks out the window. We drive down a large hill until we arrive at Corbo's bakery on my left. I make a mental note to stop there after we play at the park.

"Okay, girl. Is the park near us?" I ask.

She points in front of us. "It's right there, silly. Right across from Grandma and Papa's church."

"Ah, there it is. Wow, you do know where it is. Well, this worked out. Now...where do we park?" I say to myself.

"My daddy turns down this road here. He parks on the street," Sienna chimes in.

I'm kind of amazed at this little one. She is so in tune with her surroundings and so articulate. I glance in the rearview mirror and see her looking curiously at the people outside. I guess that's what it's like to be an only child. You don't have someone to constantly bicker with and distract you. She reminds me of myself at her age. I had an inquisitive mind as well.

When I turn down the street, Murray Hill, I'm met with a cobblestone road, and it only adds to the charm of the neighborhood. I find parking pretty easily on the street, thankful college forced me to perfect my parallel parking skills. I'm in between two cars within seconds.

Sienna and I walk hand in hand down the sidewalk as I take in the businesses around me. I see a gift shop called La Bella Vita. A simple glance through the storefront windows and I know that I'm going in there another time for dinnerware from Italy.

There are restaurants on the street corner, and I spot an art gallery across the street.

"This way." Sienna grabs my hand as we cross the street and head toward the park.

Once we get there, I notice the ground is in the color of the Italian flag: green, white, and red.

"This place is super cute," I tell Sienna.

She smiles. "We could go visit my Grandma and Papa after this."

"I don't know where they live, and I don't know their phone numbers. Maybe some other time. I can talk to your dad about it." She seems content with my response as she shrugs and runs over to the swings.

"Come push me!" she screams as she gets herself situated on one.

When I'm standing behind her, I start to give her a good push as she tries to help by swinging her legs. She doesn't quite have the motion timed out right, but it's a nice effort.

"If you're four, does that mean you start kindergarten next year?" I ask her as I see a school bus drive by.

"Yes! I'm super-duper excited to start school. Daddy is sad, though. He says I'm not allowed to grow up, but I told him I have to so I can take care of him when he gets old."

Like I said, *wise beyond her years.*

"I don't think your daddy actually means he doesn't want you to grow up. It's just an expression. But that's sweet that you want to take care of him."

"Yeah. We take care of each other. Since I don't have a mommy, and he doesn't have a wife. My mom left when I was little."

My heart stills at the mention of her mother. I've been wondering, but obviously never wanted to ask Gabriel. He doesn't exactly give off the *go ahead ask me some personal questions* kinda vibe. But now that the topic has arisen, I'm kicking myself for not asking.

What am I supposed to say to that?

"Well, your mom missed out on a pretty amazing girl if you ask me," I finally say.

She looks over her shoulder with a smile. "Really?"

I poke her nose. "Really. I've only known you for two days, and you're already my favorite person."

I think I see a look of relief on her face like she was wondering if it was her fault, and my heart breaks. What kind of mother would leave a little sweetheart behind? How selfish of a person must she be?

Once Sienna gets bored of the swings and we are done talking about subjects out of my comfort zone, I chase her around the playground and then watch her go down the slides a dozen times.

It feels like we've both worked up quite a sweat by the end of it.

"Alright. I think I'm in desperate need of some sweets. What do ya say?" I extend my hand out.

She grabs it, and we both start to skip our way out of the park. As we make our way back to the bakery I saw on the way, I observe the green wood trim on the front and the red door. It looks super cute and feels very Italian.

Upon entering, my senses are hit with so many different flavors that saliva pools in my mouth. Yeah, there's no way I'm walking out of here with just gelato.

We walk to the back of the long bakery, lined with window cases full of pastries, until we get to the gelato.

"Do you know what you want?" I ask Sienna as my eyes roam the selection.

"I want chocolate." She claps her hands together. "In a waffle cone."

"Mmmm...that sounds yummy. I think I'm gonna get the mint chip."

I place the order and walk down the aisle with my tongue practically hanging out of my mouth. I tell the employee that I'll need a large box, and then I continue to rattle off different cookies, tiramisu, lobster tail, crème puffs, and this chocolate coconut bar that I've never seen before. I spot a fridge that holds cannoli filling with a sign that says, "Leave the gun, take the cannoli," and I burst into laughter at the Godfather quote.

The sign alone does me in, and you know you're in the right spot when they are freshly filled, never pre-filled. Of course, I ask them to add several cannolis to my box.

By the time we're done, I'm juggling my gelato and a heavy box filled with temptation. We finish our gelato as we walk back to the car, and it's a good thing I grabbed some napkins on the way out because Sienna has chocolate gelato all over her.

It's worth it, though, because we had such a great morning. Well, I did, at least. Sienna is such an easy kid to be around, with no commotion or stress involved.

The rest of the day flies by as we color, practice her letters, and top it off with a couple episodes of her favorite show. She surprises me by snuggling into my chest while we watch TV. It makes my heart ache at the thought of her not being able to do this with her own mother.

My thoughts go back to our conversation today. I wonder why she left. Is there something darker about Gabriel that I don't know about? No, that can't be it. I see the way he looks at his daughter, and there's no way he did something evil like lay his hands on his ex.

I rest my head on top of Sienna's as my eyes start to feel heavy.

"Alexis." I hear a faint voice calling my name.

When I open my eyes, Gabriel is standing in front of me with his hands in his pockets. I look around, feeling dazed until I realize Sienna and I both fell asleep on the couch together.

"I'm sorry." I feel embarrassed getting caught napping on the job. "We had a busy day today. I must have dozed off during the show."

I start to stand up, disrupting Sienna from her sleep. Her eyes flutter open, and unlike me, her energy is back in spades.

"Daddy!" She jumps off the couch and into his arms.

"Hi, sweetie!" He wraps his arms around her. "Did you have a fun day today?"

"It was awesome! We went to the park, and we got gelato. We colored, and Alex helped with my letters. She even snuggled with me!"

"Wow! That sounds like you had quite a day. How about you go get cleaned up for dinner?"

Sienna rushes to her bathroom so that she can get ready. I head into the kitchen to get something to drink, and as I pull out a bottle of water, I notice Gabriel has followed me.

"So, I take it Sienna convinced you to get her some gelato today?" he asks as he leans against the counter, arms crossed.

I hope I'm not in trouble. We never talked about the rules around sugar, and I know some parents are very strict about those things. But when I look over at him, I notice his shirt is unbuttoned at the top, revealing a scattering of chest hair.

Even his chest hair is beautiful. Nothing too much, just a subtle amount. The way he fills out his clothing is downright sexy. My brain short circuits until I remember he asked me a question.

"Um, yeah. I hope that's alright."

He shrugs. "I don't mind. I'm guessing that you went to Corbo's by the giant box of treats behind you."

"Oh," I chuckle. "I got a little carried away. That place is so cute, and all the restaurants there look amazing. I need to try some of them sometime."

I see a small smile break free on his face. "That's where I grew up. My parents still live over there; just a short walk down to the strip."

"Sienna mentioned something about that. It must have been so nice growing up next to all those restaurants and bakeries. I would have weighed a thousand pounds."

"I somehow doubt that," he says as he bites his lip.

His eyes roam over me in a way that makes every nerve in my body come alive. I can feel the appreciation in his gaze. What would it feel like to be on the receiving end of this man's touch? I know what would probably happen. I would start to freak out, mind racing as it recalled my first and only boyfriend. The words he'd said to me. The way he made me feel so damaged and unattractive.

Then, Gabe's eyes land directly on my chest, and my body over-rules the unpleasant memory while my body reacts again. My breaths begin to feel labored, and I can tell that he notices. His eyebrows turn up, though, like he's angry at what he sees.

Maybe he shouldn't eye fuck me if he doesn't want my body to respond like this.

I'm not in the mood to hear what condescending thing he will say to me, so I opt to change the subject.

"There's a lasagna in the fridge. I made it during breakfast this morning. It just needs to go in the oven to warm up."

He snaps out of his trance.

"Thanks. Are you actually going to eat it this time?" he asks indignantly.

Still groggy from my nap, I'm so not in the mood for his hot and cold game right now. I place my hands on my hips.

"Was that an invitation to dinner? If it was, it needs a little work."

I turn around and head for the kitchen, where I open the box of pastries. I need sugar to calm my anger and lots of it.

One of the cannolis is calling my name right now. I already let the poor things sit for too long in their shells. Not realizing Gabe is still standing behind me, I bring the cannoli to me as I eye fuck the shit out of it.

Who needs men when you can have a cannoli?

The long, slender pastry hits my mouth, and I can't help but moan at the rich flavors that dance on my tongue. It's exactly what I need to lift my spirits, to distract me from this madden-ing man who is making me feel things that I have no right feeling. I've never had a real man look at me the way he does—like all I need to do is breathe for him to be satisfied. It gives me a sliver of hope that I'm not a complete lost cause.

I hear movement behind me and see Gabe throw his head back in frustration.

"I'm so fucked," he mumbles before storming off.

Choosing not to worry about his mood at the moment, I finish my cannoli in peace before I dust off my hands. I'm definitely eating another one of those after dinner.

I realize Gabe walked away before putting the lasagna in the oven, so I turn it on and place the tray in. While I wait for it to warm, I walk upstairs to my bedroom to freshen up.

After brushing my teeth and washing my face, I throw on a little mascara, not willing to admit to myself who it's for. I sweat a bit too much at the park and feel kind of icky. I pull out a pair of jeans and an off-the-shoulder cream top. I throw them on the bed, pull my t-shirt off, and then pull my shorts down.

I'm standing in my room in my bra and underwear when I hear giggles pass by my room, followed by a deep voice. Thinking nothing of it, I grab my jeans and am about to step into them when my door swings open.

"Alex, let's go eat dinner!" Sienna screams, completely oblivious to the fact that I'm half-naked.

Gabriel runs in after her.

"Sienna, you can't just barge into..." he shouts as he comes to a screeching halt.

His jaw falls as he takes in my body, completely exposed to him. My lace bra and panties both show a good amount of skin underneath them.

"But it's time for dinner," she defends her actions. "I *needed* to tell Alex."

Gabe is now staring at the carpet like it's the most interesting thing in the world, his hand massaging the back of his neck.

"I know that, but you have to knock. Alexis needs her privacy. Now, say you're sorry, and let's give her some space."

"I'm sorry, Alex," she says with a sad little look.

"It's okay, sweetheart. I forgive you. I'll be downstairs in a minute. Just let me finish changing," I say as I throw my shirt over my head quickly.

"Okay!" she says enthusiastically as she grabs her father's hand and leads him out of the room.

Shit! How the hell am I going to face him ever again? I look down at my hardened nipples, knowing they're not hard because I'm cold. It's because of the hot-as-hell dad that just caught me half-naked.

Chapter Seven

Gabriel

"Daddy, is the food ready? I'm sooooo hungry!" Sienna pulls me from my thoughts.

I realize I'm standing in the middle of the kitchen doing nothing.

Well, nothing but thinking of what I just witnessed. If I thought Alexis moaning over a phallic-shaped cannoli was bad, seeing her in nothing but a sexy bra and panty set was ten times worse. How the hell am I supposed to sit across from her at dinner and *not* picture those perfect, taut nipples on display?

I need to get laid soon before I do something stupid, like act on these urges I have for Alexis. I think a night out with my brothers is something that has to happen this weekend.

Just as I'm taking the lasagna out of the oven, Alexis walks into the kitchen in skin-tight jeans and a damn shirt that falls off of one shoulder, exposing the black bra that I now have committed to memory. It makes my dick twitch. My inability to control my desire for her is beginning to piss me off, so much so that I literally growl as she walks past me.

"I can finish getting dinner ready," she says from behind me.

As I get a whiff of her perfume, my anger builds.

"I'm perfectly capable of taking a pan of lasagna out of an oven."

I don't mean for it to come out so rude, but damn if I know what the hell I'm doing right now. I've never felt this mixed up over a woman before. And this one is fresh out of college. She has her entire life ahead of her. She doesn't need me and my bitterness to drag her down.

"Oookay. Once again, your manners around all things dinner needs some serious work," she bites back.

I deserved that. And yet, I'm too much of a stubborn asshole to actually tell her that. I choose to let the current vibe of the night continue.

Once the lasagna is out and plated, I notice Alexis has put a salad on the table. She has her hands clasped in front of her like she's waiting for further instructions.

"I, um, didn't know if you wanted wine with the meal, but I'm not sure where the glasses or bottles are."

Shit, I know it seems like the safe thing to do to keep our relationship professional, but I kind of hate that I've made her this nervous around me. I guess the only way I know how to keep it appropriate with her is to be a dick.

"It's in the cellar. I'll go grab a bottle."

Before I turn around, I notice the curiosity on her face.

"You have a wine cellar in your house?"

"I do. Would you like to see it?"

She nods her head eagerly, so I motion for her to follow me out of the kitchen. When I open the door, I walk in first to turn on the light and feel her following closely behind me. It's not a huge space, so the proximity is far closer than I've allowed myself to get to her. A sudden image crosses my mind of her hands holding onto a shelve in just her bra and panties while I kiss my way up her long, toned legs, all the way up to her tight ass.

I clear my throat in an effort to regain my composure.

"Wow!" she exclaims. "This is incredible."

She walks all the way in, spinning in a circle to take in the three-sixty shelving that houses my collection. It's hard to ignore the feeling that having this beautiful woman appreciate my passion evokes.

"Where did you get all of this?" she asks.

"Everywhere. I've traveled all over the world tasting wine. It's more than just a business to me, it's my passion."

She continues to the wall opposite the door as she inspects the shelves. I try to dedicate areas of my space to different regions of the world. Right now, she's in my Italian section—my favorite.

I move closer to her, standing behind her as I watch her eyes scan the collection.

"This really is a passion of yours." She looks over her shoulder at me.

I chuckle to myself. "It is. It's like..." I begin but stop abruptly.

When she realizes I'm not going to finish my sentence, she looks over her shoulder. "It's like...." she drawls out, waiting for me to go on.

I struggle to swallow as I look down at her, our bodies close, her eyes focused on me.

"It's like women. It's tempting, it takes time to understand, and each bottle is unique. But most importantly, it's sexy. It always leaves you wanting more. One taste is never enough."

It's her turn to swallow down her arousal, because I know my words just turned her on. The sexual tension in this cellar is immeasurable.

"You think wine is sexy?" Her voice breaks.

"There you guys are!" Sienna shouts.

We both jump, completely unaware of the time or how long we've been standing here looking at each other.

"Sorry, we were just debating what bottle to choose," I lie.

"My tummy keeps talking to me."

Alexis laughs and picks Sienna up in her arms. "Well, let's get some food in that tummy of yours. I think it's telling you it's hungry."

When I'm alone, I take a couple of unsteady breaths before grabbing a bottle I've had many times before, so I know I love it. Sometimes you have to go with comfort instead of taking a chance and opening a bottle that you don't like.

Luckily, Sienna talks about her day throughout dinner, so I don't have to focus too much on the beauty sitting across from me. When we finish up, Alexis runs to get the remaining pastries, choosing another cannoli. I take that as my cue to get the hell away from her and do the dishes.

"Tell me, how's life with your crazy hot nanny?" Marcus smiles behind his beer.

I shake my head at him. Tonight is supposed to be an escape from any thoughts associated with Alexis. Thoughts that have been running rampant since the *incident* the other night. I'm not sure I can handle any more of this personal torture. Everything she does is so damn sexy to me, and that's how I knew I needed to get the hell out of that house tonight.

It's Friday, and Mia agreed to spend the evening with Sienna so I could go out with the guys. I need to get laid tonight. Surely that will be the ticket to moving past my inappropriate feelings.

"It's fine. Sienna loves her. Nothing to report," I take a huge swig of my beer.

"I don't know how you do it. I wouldn't be able to sleep knowing that girl was showering naked down the hall," he adds.

Lucas snorts. "That's because you have fewer brain cells."

"You ready for your trip next week?" I ask Lucas.

He's going to one of our favorite suppliers in Italy to try out a new product. These are normally trips I like to take, but I'm not ready to leave Sienna alone with Alexis for an entire week. They don't know each other well enough yet for me to expect Sienna to be fully comfortable with that.

"I'm always ready for Italy." He wiggles his eyebrows.

I roll my eyes. "Just make sure you don't play too hard and forget why you're there."

"I've literally never compromised our relationship with any client. No reason for you to think I will start now," he says bitterly.

I can't help it. I'm used to having control, and I don't like it when I have to give it up. As the oldest, I've always had to be the responsible one as I watch Lucas and Marcus behave like morons. Or the one that has to stay sober to make sure they stay out of trouble or don't get hurt.

Lucas and Marcus start bickering about something I'm not paying attention to when I see an attractive blonde smile at me from across the bar.

Nothing stirs in me at her attention, but I'm determined to rid myself of these feelings for Alexis.

"Excuse me, guys. I see a woman who looks like she could use my company," I say as I stand from the high-top table.

Neither of them seem fazed by my words. I'm waiting for them to try to stop me, but they just continue on in their conversation.

Do I want them to stop me? *No, of course not.*

As I approach, she bites her lip and looks up at me seductively. All signs point to her willingness to meet me in the alley or my car.

We strike up a conversation, and I can't help but notice that her lips aren't as full as Alexis's. Her hair is nothing in comparison to Alexis's long, dark locks. And the way she laughs, it makes her come off so desperate.

I'm just being foolish. This is why I needed to get out tonight; because I've been around Alexis for far too long already.

But as the conversation continues, I find myself bored. The usual appeal a strange woman in a bar would have on me is gone.

It's about the time she takes a sip of her wine, and I compare it to how Alexis drinks hers, that I know I need to get out of this conversation.

I don't even know what excuse comes out of my mouth. All I know is that I'm back at the table with my brothers, and the anger building in me is massive and unruly.

"What's gotten into you? Did you strike out? After all these years, did I finally witness a woman turn down Gabriel Giannelli?" Lucas asks.

I release a sharp laugh. "She didn't reject me. I could have her if I wanted."

"Sooo, you're saying you don't want her?" Marcus tries to clarify.

"I don't feel like talking about it," I growl out.

That wasn't exactly me denying it, and they know it. I see them eye each other with suggestive grins. What the hell has gotten into me? Why can't I get her out of my head? It's only been a week. Surely this will die down soon.

Chapter Eight

Alexis

I've been living in this house for three weeks. That's three weeks of amazing, lighthearted fun with Sienna. Every day that I get to know her, I fall more and more in love with her. I feel such a strong connection to her like we were meant to cross paths in this life.

Aside from my time with Sienna, that's also three weeks of delicious food, learning about *and* tasting amazing wine, and feeling my heart skip a beat every time Gabriel walks into a room. I don't know what the hell to do about it. I've never felt like this before, but it feels massively inappropriate to desire my boss so much.

And I think he may have some kind of attraction to me as well. That is when he's not being a short-tempered, irritable dick.

The way that man can talk about wine is such a turn-on to me. Sometimes when he uses words like sexy, full-bodied, elegant, and smooth, I get confused about whether he's talking about me or the wine. Because when he says those words, he keeps his dark eyes on me, filled with something that looks a lot like lust.

Tonight is a Saturday, and it's my first night off that I'm not going out with Alicia or just hanging out at her place. I'm starting to feel more comfortable in this house, and I'm just too tired to go anywhere. I was hoping that Sienna and Gabriel would be going out, but judging by the laughter I hear downstairs, they are in for the night. I look down at my flannel sweatpants and tank top as I decide how much I care about him seeing me dressed down like this.

Deciding I'm not going to spend the entire summer worried about changing out of pajamas in order to leave this bedroom, I open my door and take slow steps downstairs as I hear Sienna's laughter again.

"Daddy!" She giggles. "That's not fair. Look how many you have."

"I can't help it. I keep asking for the right cards," he defends.

When I enter the kitchen, I look over and see them sitting on the floor in front of the TV. He's wearing jeans and a t-shirt, making the casual look sexier than it should be. He must sense my presence because his eyes meet mine, immediately making my body feel hot. All he needs to do is look at me, and I lose my breath.

Sienna notices me next. "Alex! Come over here!"

I walk into the room and sit down on the couch, feeling like I'm intruding on personal father-daughter time. It's a little too late to just turn around and go back upstairs, though.

"What are you playing?" I ask as I rest my elbows on my knees.

"*Go Fish*! But Daddy isn't being very nice. He keeps getting matches, and it's not fair," she says as she puffs out her bottom lip.

I have to bite my lip in an effort to hide my smile so she doesn't think I'm laughing at her. A quick glance at Gabriel and I know he's trying to fight back his as well.

"Daddy! How could you do that to her?" I feign annoyance.

Sienna gives him a knowing look, raising her eyebrows as she is now confident that she's right since I took her side. What I'm not prepared for is the carefree laugh that falls from his mouth. I'm not used to seeing this side of him. I honestly wasn't even sure it existed.

"Alex, will you play with us?" she asks animatedly.

"Oh, I don't want to get in the way of time with your dad."

"You're not in the way, silly! Right, Daddy?" She looks to him for agreement.

He shrugs his shoulders. "Not at all."

I'm not sure he meant it, but I can't exactly say no to Sienna. Plus, I've missed her. It's only been one day, but I'm used to spending most of my time with her.

"Then count me in." I bop her nose. It's our new thing, and I love the adorable giggle it always produces.

"Okay! Daddy, let's go have that sprinkler party you promised!" She starts jumping up and down.

I can see the shock arise in him as he looks between Sienna and me. "The what?" His voice cracks.

"You said we could have a sprinkler party after we played Go Fish, and I don't want to play anymore cuz you're beating me."

Sprinkler party? I'm not sure what that entails, but if it means seeing Gabriel with his shirt off, my first instinct is hell yes.

The more sensible side of me is saying *oh, shit*, but both sides make valid points.

Gabriel starts to work his neck like he's trying to figure out how to get out of this. "Alright. I did promise you. Alexis," he says, not able to meet my eyes, "you don't have to play in the sprinklers with us."

I'm not sure if he's trying to be nice and let me off the hook, or if he's trying to uninvite me, but either way, Sienna isn't having it.

"Nooooo! She already said she would play with us. Pleassssse, Alex. It's so much fun. Plus, we eat ice cream after."

"Well," I look over at Gabriel, "I can't say no to ice cream."

I stand up with them while Sienna is jumping in excitement.

"Okay, let's all go get our bathing suits on. Alex, will you help me?" she asks with her arms behind her back as she moves her hips back and forth.

Her little act to get what she wants makes me laugh. I stretch my hand out for her to grab it. "Of course, I'll help you. Come on, sweetie. Let's go."

Sienna stands in her room in her pink and gold, one-piece bathing suit, looking like the cutest thing I've ever seen. The entire time I've been helping her find and put on her suit, my nerves have been dancing around my belly. Am I really spending the evening with Gabe playing in the sprinklers with his daughter? If someone asked me how I would be spending the first summer post-graduation, this is not what would have come to mind.

There is this gnawing guilt that keeps telling me to find a real job like everybody else, but I do my best to push it away when it surfaces. Like right now.

"It's your turn," Sienna says.

"My turn for what?" I ask, slightly confused.

"For your bathing suit, silly!"

"Oh, um, I was thinking I would just watch you play in the sprinklers."

"Nooo, that's not the deal. You said you would play with us. Playing means getting *in* the sprinklers."

She grabs my hand and stomps her way out of her bedroom, directing us into mine. Am I really about to let a four-year-old guilt me into this? I look down at her innocent little face, knowing she just wants to have fun with me, and I easily fold like a flat sheet. Not like the fitted sheets. Where I'm concerned, if you know how to fold a fitted sheet, you have some sort of sorcery in you.

I open my drawer and look at the two bathing suit options I have. Both are two pieces. I'm a twenty-one-year-old, of course, I don't own a one-piece swimsuit. I settle for the red one. Even though its color is flashier, it's not a string bikini like the black one, so it offers more coverage.

After I run to my bathroom to put it on, I look in the mirror. There's no way I'm walking downstairs in a freakin' bikini. I scurry over to my dresser, where I grab a pair of black shorts and pull them on. That's better. At least I'm not entirely exposed, and I don't mind if I get these wet. Something about going without the shorts feels too intimate—like I'm something special to Gabe. More than just the nanny.

Sienna grabs my hand, and I instinctively smile. I love the feeling of her chubby little hand in mine. It makes me feel needed in this crazy life. Something I'm not used to feeling.

We walk downstairs hand in hand, and as we walk from room to room, calling Gabe's name, he is nowhere to be found.

"Let's check outside," I suggest to Sienna.

As we reach the stone patio, my lady parts start to rejoice at the sight. Gabe is standing in the grass wearing only his swim trunks with his aviator sunglasses on while bending over with the hose in hand. This man makes the act of attaching the hose to a sprinkler feel like I'm watching a Magic Mike performance. I release Sienna's hand as she charges for her dad while I try to figure out how to pick my jaw up off the ground.

And then, if I wasn't already drooling, he turns around, and I'm greeted by his chest and abs.

Fuck, I've only seen this man eat Italian food and drink a shit ton of wine. How the hell does he look like that? This really is like Magic Mike. But the smile that spreads across his face when Sienna jumps into his arms does something to another part of my body...my heart.

The yard is covered in what looks like an obstacle course of sprinklers. There's a standard sprinkler that is motioning back and forth, but there are also several contraptions of long tubes that wiggle and shoot water out in different directions and at varying speeds. There must be at least three hoses out there hooking these up.

"What do you think, Alex?" Sienna asks with her arms stretched open as if to present the show to me.

I inch closer and think I notice Gabe's jaw clenching tighter as his head visibly looks from my legs up to my face. It's hard to be sure with his sunglasses on.

"It's something," I tell Sienna. "I don't think I've ever seen so many sprinklers set up at once."

"It's our special sprinkler party that Daddy and I do. Right, Daddy?"

"Right, sweetheart."

"Well, come on. We'll show you how we do it." Sienna grabs my hand.

"Is there a certain way to play in the sprinklers?" I ask.

I look up at Gabe, who is smirking at me.

"Sienna used to be afraid of water. I tried so many times to play in the pool with her, and she refused. She was afraid of getting her face wet. So, I started with sprinklers. I thought if I just threw her into it here, she would be fine in the pool. I made a game out of it. Whoever ran through the sprinklers and got the most wet would win an ice cream with all the toppings."

I laugh out loud.

"How do you even judge who got the *most* wet?" I ask.

He smiles. "She always won."

"Is that why she was such a sore loser at *Go Fish*?"

He lets out a small, suppressed laugh.

"Yeah." He scratches the back of his head. "We're working on that. I may have had trouble allowing her to be upset for even a second after her mom left. I'm trying to let her understand disappointment."

My face falls at the mention of his ex.

"Sienna told me her mom left."

His posture turns rigid. "We'll be talking about that later."

"Let's goooo, guys!" Sienna whines below us. "Did Daddy tell you how to play?"

"He did! I must say, I'm pretty amazing at getting really wet," I say, and the moment the words leave my mouth, I regret them. I risk a glance up at Gabriel, and I can sense the anger radiating off him.

Why must I always put my foot in my mouth when I'm around him?

"I'll bet I still beat you," Sienna says, hands on her hips, clearly not understanding the innuendo.

"Bring it on!" I try to deflect.

I stretch my right leg in front of my left in a lunge position.

Sienna giggles. "We aren't racing, silly goose. The slower you go, the longer you stay under the water and the better chance you have of winning. That's what Aunt Mia told me."

"Shhh. Don't give away your secret," Gabriel fake whispers.

I'm relieved to see we've moved passed my unfortunate comment.

"Okay. Countdown, Daddy!" Sienna sings as she dances around in her bathing suit.

"Countdown? Sounds like a race to me," I mutter to Gabe.

He smiles. "Three, two, one...go!"

Sienna takes off for the sprinklers as I wait for Gabe to go first. I want to see just exactly what is happening here. Sienna is standing above the main sprinkler as the water soaks her, clearly no longer afraid.

When I look over at Gabe, he's at the snake sprinkler that is shooting off in several different directions.

Yep, Magic Mike!

I don't even realize I'm still standing here, not participating, as I watch him run through the water, laughing while his body gets wet.

"Alex!" Sienna calls.

I jump, looking around as I realize what I was caught doing.

"Was something distracting you?" Gabriel smiles.

I pay no attention to his comment, even though he obviously knows I was looking at him. Instead, I run into the large sprinkler with Sienna as the two of us start to jump over it together. It's pretty powerful. Within seconds, I'm already a goner, completely soaked.

"Come on, let's go to this one!" she calls.

I follow her to the long tube that has different flowers going wild in every direction while water shoots out. We start to wind our way through the flowers. There's no way to tell which way the flower is going to go. At one point, it blasts me right in the face. I scream at the sudden water invasion as I swat the water away.

Sienna giggles at me.

Damn, this idea of Gabe's could have totally backfired and made this girl terrified of water. Good thing it worked!

I'm lost in my own little world with Sienna when Gabe sneaks up on us and yells. Sienna laughs while I jump and screech like the little chicken that I am.

The gut laugh that comes from Sienna has me following suit. Pretty soon, the three of us are all cracking up as we run through the flower jungle. I'm so focused on not getting blasted in the face again that I don't see Gabe coming my way, and we collide. His arms wrap around my waist, catching me before I tumble back.

I'm giggling like a fool until I realize he is completely still. When I look up, he's stone-faced, and his chest is rising up and down more rapidly. When his fingers dig into my sides, a soft moan escapes me.

Damn, these feelings he's bringing out in me. I don't know whether to follow them through or if my body will fail me again.

The thought is like a bucket of ice water dumped on me. I jump back quickly, turning to Sienna to try to bring myself back to the reason I'm here.

We continue to play in the water with Sienna, and both Gabe and I are careful to keep our distance from each other. I'm wondering if he's happy or disappointed I pulled away. I'm not sure which one I feel.

"Okay!" Sienna yells. "Gather around."

I stop and look at Gabe, who just shrugs at me. We walk to stand in front of this little four-year-old like we are her pets or something.

"The sprinkler competition is over." She looks down at herself. "And I win!"

Gabe and I laugh. I'm relieved to feel the awkwardness has evaporated again.

Once the water is turned off, we all wrap up in our towels and head inside. Sienna is skipping in front of us, knowing that she is about to get ice cream.

"I think your plan to ease her out of always winning needs a few tweaks," I whisper.

He smiles. "Yeah, I created a monster."

Sienna downs her ice cream in record time while Gabe orders a pizza. The evening goes by smoothly as we eat on the couch and watch cartoons. It's oddly comforting, and it's one of the best Saturday nights I've ever had.

Chapter Nine

Gabriel

I put Sienna to bed, snuggling with her long enough to get myself together. I hadn't been prepared to spend my evening with Alexis, but I was even less prepared for how nice it was.

Too nice.

It felt like something I could get used to, and that's dangerous.

When she came outside in that red bikini top, my dick went crazy. And when we collided in the water, her body pressed against mine, I almost lost sight of the fact that Sienna was there and kissed her.

I'm starting to lose this battle with staying away. I don't want to anymore.

When Sienna's eyes flutter closed, I kiss her forehead and walk back downstairs.

The feeling of relief that Alexis is still there should be my first sign to avoid her for the rest of the night. But when did I ever make good decisions where women were involved?

I sit back in my spot on the couch, Alexis on the other end.

"She go down okay?" she asks.

I look over at her. She's so beautiful, sitting there in pajamas, hair in a bun on top of her head, no makeup.

"Didn't take much for her to settle down. The sun and water always does her in pretty good."

"I'm glad she had a good day."

I look over at Alexis. Fuck it, I'm gonna say it. "I did too."

She smiles a genuine, happy smile and says, "Same here."

Stupid! This is stupid. You're being stupid!

But I don't care right now. I can't bring myself to leave and go to my room, even if I know it's safer.

"So, um, about what happened earlier..." she starts.

Oh, crap. Is she going to call me out on putting my hands on her like that?

"Yes?" I question.

"You said you wanted to revisit the topic of, um, Sienna's mom."

Oh, that. I did say I wanted to do that.

"Oh, right." I adjust myself on the couch. "What exactly did she say about her mother?"

My body tenses up at the thought of Angie. At first, she said it was just to get away for a while, six months tops. She would occasionally text to check-in and ask for pictures of Sienna. Last summer was our last point of contact after the divorce was final, and I haven't heard from her since. She said she realized what kind of life she wanted, and being stuck at home with no freedom wasn't it.

I didn't even fight her. I was happy about it. It felt good to just rid her of our life and never have to think of her again. I could have pointed out that getting a job of her own and sending Sienna to daycare could also get her out of the house without abandoning her child, but I wasn't about to beg her to love Sienna. That should come naturally.

"Oh, nothing much. She just said her mom left when she was young. It kind of broke my heart because I could see the sadness in her face."

Well, fuck. I've tried to ease into the conversations and create open dialogue like my therapist advised, but I can tell she's trying to be brave for me. I know she can sense my worry for her and always manages to put on a good front where her mother is concerned.

"I'm sorry I never brought it up. I should have prepared you," I tell her.

"It's alright. The interview and start date were a little rushed. We did the best we could. Plus, I did a good job deflecting the conversation."

I smile. "I'm sure you did. I guess you want to know why she left, huh?"

"Only if you want to share it with me."

She's so easygoing, but I still wasn't expecting her to let me off the hook so easily. I don't feel pressured to do or say anything with her.

"Well, my ex, Angie, left for California two years ago. She said she just needed to get away and think. Eventually, she decided motherhood wasn't for her and filed for divorce. Told me I could keep Sienna full-time."

"She just gave up motherhood like that?" she asks, snapping her fingers for emphasis. "No better reason than it wasn't for her?" Alexis sounds shocked.

The disgust in her voice makes me feel validated. I'm glad I'm not the only person, besides my own family, who finds her decision so repulsive. Sometimes I wonder if I'm not being supportive enough of postpartum depression and what it can lead to. But then I think about all the warning signs from the beginning of my relationship. Everything she did or said exudes selfishness.

"Yeah. And listen, I don't mind being a single parent to Sienna. I love her, she's my world... I just worry about what it will do to her growing up. Will she think it's her fault or always wonder why her own mother didn't want her?"

I'm shocked by the words coming out of me. Aside from my therapist, I've never spoken about this to anyone, not even my siblings. And the only reason I talked to a therapist about it was for the sake of knowing I'm saying the right things to Sienna. Otherwise, I keep these fears of mine locked up.

"Seems like reasonable things to worry about. It's not the exact same scenario, but I can say from my own experience that you definitely don't come out of these things unscathed. It does make you stronger, though, and I think her having a father who cares like you do will go a long way in her confidence in herself."

"Thanks for saying that." I do appreciate her honesty, but I'm stuck on her comment about speaking from experience. "What happened to you growing up? Did you have an absent mother?"

She blows out a breath. "Yes and no. My parent's got divorced when I was young. I was shipped back and forth between the two households. They both got remarried and were distracted with their new families. Don't get me wrong, I love my siblings, but I always felt like the misfit in the family. I was never paid much attention to, and it made me feel like I was just a reminder to each parent that they still had a connection to their ex."

Fuck that.

I hate thinking of Alexis growing up in that kind of environment. It makes me weirdly angry at her parents for making her feel that way.

What kind of parents do that?

Make their child feel like they are not wanted, or worse, like they wish they didn't exist?

"Wow. I'm sorry that was your experience. That isn't fair. Why can't people who have kids learn to grow up and realize it's not all about them anymore? Their words and actions have a real impact on the kids they raise."

Alexis laughs a bitter laugh that I'm not a fan of hearing from her. "I guess parents are just flawed human beings. That's the excuse that's always given, right?"

"That's a cop-out. It's total bullshit. Angie might be a human, but she's a selfish one, and at the end of the day, there's no excuse for abandoning her child."

"Yeah. You're right. Your ex is crazy for leaving Sienna behind. She's the best kid I've ever met. I just love her," Alexis says with a smile.

The words catch me off guard. *She loves her?*

I'm sure she said that off the cuff, but it still does something to me to hear her say those words about my daughter. I'm stuck, not sure what to say next.

"Well, it's getting late, and I'm kind of tired," she says, beating me to it. "Thanks for letting me hang with you guys tonight."

I smile and nod, still at a loss for words. When she walks away, I throw my head back in frustration.

What the hell just happened?

I'm not sure I want to read too much into it. All I know is that the more time I spend with her, the more time I want to spend with her. I need to get my shit together and remember she's off-limits. It's not just my body that is drawn to her, and I think that's the scariest part of it all.

I head to grab a glass of water in the kitchen, and as soon as I enter, I see Alexis standing in front of the sink. She is so deep in thought that she hasn't even noticed my presence yet.

I take a couple more steps, and she jumps back when she finally sees me.

"Sorry, I didn't see you there," she whispers.

It looks like she's been crying. The smart part of my brain would step in and tell me to keep my distance, but I'm too invested. I close the distance between us until I can feel the heat from her body.

She looks up at me, and her face softens.

"Are you okay?"

"I'm sorry. I didn't mean for you to see this," she says as she tries to wipe the evidence of her sadness away.

"Don't be sorry," I tell her. "I'm the one who pushed you on your upbringing. I shouldn't have said anything."

My hand reaches up and wipes away another tear.

"It's not your fault."

I get lost in her eyes as they look up at me with what looks like desire. My body betrays me and steps into her as my hands reach up and cup her face.

"What are you doing?" she asks with a whispered breath.

My thumbs come up and brush her soft cheeks as I look down at her lips. Those lips that have been the object of my obsession at dinners, in the water earlier, on the couch tonight, and basically every other waking moment since I met her. What would it be like to finally get a taste? To delve in and feel that tongue of hers against mine. The same one that pops out to swipe the remnants of wine off her lips.

I have imagined that mouth wrapped around my dick far too many times to count. It's kept me up at night when I refuse to pump my dick to thoughts of my nanny.

But the lines have become blurred, and I can no longer remember a single reason why this would be a bad idea.

My thumb runs across her bottom lip, the same lip I want to bite. When she lets out a soft moan, that's my undoing.

I lean down to finally take what I want.

"Daddy!" I hear called from the top of the stairs, and Alexis immediately jumps away from me.

"Daddy! I had a bad dream!" Sienna calls again.

"I'm coming, sweetheart!" I shout as I take slow steps up the stairs, trying to figure out what just possessed me to try to kiss Alexis in my kitchen.

Sienna is standing at the top of the stairs in her Elsa pajamas, looking scared. I pull her into my arms and squeeze. Right now, I'm just going to focus on trying to cheer up my daughter and forget that moment in the kitchen ever happened.

Chapter Ten

Alexis

Just go downstairs. It's not that big of a deal. You can face him again and not die of embarrassment.

But what if he regrets almost kissing me?

I can't believe we almost kissed. I was so lost in him that I forgot to be nervous. When Sienna interrupted us, my entire body deflated. That's never happened to me before. I mean... I've only ever been comfortable enough to get off when I'm alone. There's this mental block when I'm around a guy, especially after my experience with Trevor.

Okay, let's not go there at the moment. No need to relive that memory.

It's a beautiful Sunday morning. I just need to go down there and pretend like nothing ever happened. Because *technically,* nothing did happen.

I get out of bed and throw on a pair of jean shorts and a floral, flowy tank top. Then, as I make my way from my room to the kitchen, I realize there's no one around. My tense muscles release themselves.

As I make myself a cup of coffee, I grab my yogurt out of the fridge and sit down at the island. Despite walking on eggshells half the time with Gabe and not knowing what the hell is going on between us, I've come to love this house.

The decoration is so homey with warm brown and cream tones, and I appreciate that it isn't all straight lines and muted colors like the latest trends. It feels like a cross between old Tuscany and classic elegance.

Just when I'm finishing up my coffee, the door to the garage opens, and Sienna runs in, giggling.

"Alex! You're awake! What took you so long?" she asks as she barges into the kitchen.

I smile down at her from my stool. "It's only nine, silly."

"We've been up since six-thirty," Gabe says as he walks in behind Sienna.

My body tenses back up as soon as I hear that deep voice of his. He's dressed in dark blue shorts and a gray t-shirt. His muscles poke out from the sleeves, and I'm nearly salivating.

Shit! Whatever energy was floating around between us last night is still there. I know he can sense it, too, because his eyes grow dark as they access me.

"That's pretty early." I try to disregard the sizzling sparks between us and look back at Sienna. "Did you sleep okay?"

"I slept great! But I was sad you weren't here to make me your pancakes this morning." She gives me a pouty face.

"I'm sorry, sweetheart. We can make them together tomorrow."

That seems to cheer her up, and she takes off for her bin of toys in the family room, leaving me and Gabe alone. I try to distract myself by standing up and washing my coffee mug in the sink, feeling his eyes on me the whole time. I sneak a glance over my shoulder, and he is leaning against the island, staring at me while he rubs his jaw.

"Are you just going to stand there and watch me?" I ask.

It looks like my words piss him off because his eyebrows draw together and his jaw clenches.

"If you must know, I'm trying to figure out just how inappropriate my desire to have my way with you is," his cool tone states matter-of-factly.

Wetness pools in my panties.

Holy shit!

That's so damn inappropriate to think, let alone say to me, but my body loves it. Am I equally messed up for wanting him to say more things like that to me?

"What have you come up with?" I hear myself say, not sure where my confidence to reply comes from.

"I think I don't give a shit if it's inappropriate anymore. I'm hanging on by a thread trying to resist you."

This man...this powerful, successful, intimidating man is trying to resist *me*?

I almost can't believe it.

I drop my coffee mug in the sink and turn around, water still running. I'm biting my lip as we both stare at each other, our breaths coming quicker. He takes a step toward me, closing the distance. My heart is beating erratically as I wait to see what he'll do.

Is he going to kiss me this time?

When we're only inches apart, his hand reaches for mine by my side. Our fingers lace together as our eyes never waiver.

"I bet those lips of yours taste better than any wine I've ever had," he whispers.

I close my eyes as I let his words wash all over my body. The way this man makes me feel, it's like my past never existed.

"The way you talk about wine..." I start as I slowly open my eyes. "Sometimes I can't tell whether you're talking about sex or wine."

He smiles. "Wine and sex go well together."

Sienna's laughter rings through the room, reminding us that we're not alone. Gabriel reluctantly releases my hand before he steps away. The loss of his warmth leaves me feeling cold and...lonely.

"I should go join Sienna," he tells me.

I nod my head.

He stands there for a second before he shakes his head and walks away.

Was that regret? Frustration? I'm not quite sure, but it leaves me confused.

I manage to sneak away upstairs to grab my things, desperately needing to get out of the house for the afternoon. I drive to the North Chagrin Reservation Loop and decide on a whim to run the seven-mile trail. I always have a bag of workout clothes packed in my trunk, just in case.

The trail is beautiful and gives me time to think. I'm a month into my time with Sienna and Gabe, which means I only have one month left. If I let something happen between us, am I going to be able to walk away? Is that what he would want?

Would I trust him enough to let something happen between us?

I think back to the last time I had sex four years ago. Trevor and I had dated on and off since my sophomore year of high school. I was too young to give him my virginity, and he was fine with it since we did other things.

Then, we both went to Ohio State together and one night, I decided to finally go through with it. After a couple of times, the pain began to subside, and I was feeling less and less afraid to have sex, but I was far from feeling comfortable or confident in the bedroom. So many thoughts were running through my head.

Am I doing it right? How am I compared to other girls he's been with? Do I smell okay down there? Do I look fat? Is he having a good time? What does he want me to be doing right now?

The thoughts were endless, and it left me feeling stiff and unsure.

I'm not sure if that's what made the sex so...blah, but it just wasn't what I was expecting.

That night, after we had sex, Trevor was being pretty short and snappy with me. I wasn't sure what I'd done, so I guess I asked him one too many times if anything was wrong, and he finally snapped.

"I'm fucking fine, Alex. Leave me alone. Gosh, you're lucky I'm even putting up with you anymore. At first, it was waiting two years to have sex. Now that we're having it, you're like a fucking dead fish. It's boring as hell. You know, a normal girl would enjoy it. Make some kind of noise or move...or something!"

I kicked him out of my dorm and out of my life that night, but that doesn't mean his words weren't going to play in my mind over and over every time I got close to having sex again. In the end, I was too afraid to do it again and risk someone else thinking I suck at it.

Maybe something is wrong with me. Why wasn't it enjoyable for me? The whole experience was just...disappointing. It left me feeling broken and stupid.

I've never told anyone about it, not even Alicia.

I was too scared to hear someone validate Trevor's words. Someone else to tell me I was messed up for not finding it enjoyable. How do other people turn those thoughts off during sex and just *feel*?

Halfway through my run, I come across Squire's Castle, which apparently used to be an old gatehouse in the eighteen-nineties. I spend some time walking around before finishing my run, then I pick up lunch and stop to eat at another park since it's such a beautiful day.

When I get home, I'm able to sneak back into the house. I take a shower and decide to relax and do a bit of Netflix binging for the rest of the day.

I'm two hours into some murder mystery show when I hear a knock on the door.

"Come in," I yell, thinking Gabe will be walking in to tell me he's ordered food or something.

I'm not expecting Mia to stroll in with an older woman following behind her.

I sit up in my bed, feeling weirdly lazy for being caught lounging around.

"Hi, Mia," I smile.

"Hi, Alex! It's so nice to see you again," she replies.

"This is my mom, Patricia."

"Hello, dear. I'm sorry to bother you on your day off. I just wanted to come meet the woman my little Sienna is rambling on and on about."

The energy Patricia gives off instantly puts me at ease, like there isn't a mean bone in her body.

"That's so sweet of her. She's a special little girl. I've really enjoyed my time with her," I tell them.

Both of their eyes light up at my words.

"You should come downstairs and join us. We brought over some pizza and are just hanging out outside for the evening," Mia says.

I'm already thinking up an excuse when Patricia hits me with her words.

"Please. I would just love to spend some time with the woman who's stolen Sienna's heart. It's been so hard not having her around. I've been feeling down lately, but seeing her so happy just makes me feel so much better."

Well, what kind of person would say no to that?

I give her my brightest smile. "I would love to join you. Thank you so much for the offer. Let me get freshened up, and I'll meet you downstairs."

As I put on some makeup and change into a casual summer dress, I try to calm my nerves. I still haven't figured out what the hell to do about this growing attraction between Gabe and me, and now I have to go face his family. What if they all see through my façade, right down to the innocent nanny who can't get her boss out of her mind? I've never been so...pent-up before.

The arousal he pulls from me is unmatched. It's so intense and loud that I may need to take care of myself tonight.

Chapter Eleven

Gabriel

Ma and Mia are walking back onto the deck with huge smiles on their faces as they giggle.

"What's so funny?" I ask them suspiciously.

Mia shrugs her shoulders. "Nothing. Oh, by the way, we just snuck upstairs to Alexis's room. Ma convinced her to join us for dinner. She should be down soon."

I try to swallow past the lump forming in my throat. The thought of being around Alexis with my family here is a bit nerve-racking.

"She's very beautiful," Ma chimes in.

I attempt to feign indifference to her looks. Like I haven't noticed her supple lips and imagined them on my dick one too many times. Or watched her bend over to get something while picturing what it would feel like to slide my dick inside her from behind.

"How are you feeling, Ma? Are you sure you're okay to be out and about today?" I ask, hoping to change the subject from how hot my nanny is.

Ma rolls her eyes at me. "I'm doing fine, honey. You don't need to worry so much about me. So, tell me about Alexis. She seems so lovely."

Before I can respond, Alexis makes her way outside. Just the sight of her makes my heart begin to race, but the sight of her looking so naturally beautiful in a dress has a shiver running through my body.

"Hi, everyone." She waves awkwardly at my family, and I can't help but smile at how damn endearing she is.

"Hi, Alex! Nice to see you again. I see you survived a month with my grumpy pants brother over here," Marcus says as he has the balls to get up and give her a hug.

She seems a bit taken aback by his friendliness. Meanwhile, I'm over here mentally cataloging all the ways I'm going to kill him.

"Come sit next to me," Mia says, motioning for Alexis to take the seat to her right.

Great, so my entire family is going to monopolize Alexis's time tonight. Why does that bother me?

"Alexis, you've met my sister Mia, as well as Lucas and Marcus. And I guess my mother barged in on you, so you know her. This man over here is my pa, Joe."

"Nice to meet you, pretty lady." Pa smiles mischievously.

"Joseph Giannelli, you better leave the young lady alone," Ma warns him.

I roll my eyes while Marcus and Lucas laugh. That's Pa for ya. The man is a classic Italian flirt, and he doesn't even notice that he does it.

Alexis chuckles. "It's so nice to meet you, Joe. I think the real beauty over here is Sienna."

Sienna hears her name and looks up from coloring on Lucas' lap to smile, clearly no clue what was actually said.

"Well, I will have to agree with you there. There's no one more beautiful than my Sienna. *Bellissima!*" Pa agrees.

"Alex, you're here!" Sienna screams as she jumps off Lucas' lap and runs over to Alexis.

"What am I, chopped liver?" Lucas jokes.

I watch Sienna snuggle into Alexis. The two of them look so comfortable and familiar with each other. What is Sienna going to do when Alexis leaves us in a month? I honestly didn't expect them to get along this well.

"So, Alexis, tell us about yourself. What brings you to Cleveland?" Pa asks Alexis.

"Oh, this position, actually. My friend's father recommended me to Gabriel. I'm from Columbus."

"Do you plan on staying here after the summer?" Ma questions.

That question has me on the edge of my seat, waiting to hear her answer. I'm not sure why it matters. I have no intention of seeing her again after the summer is over... right?

"I'm not sure, honestly. I do love it here so far, and my best friend is here," she tells everyone, much to my relief.

"Okay, let's eat some food." Lucas stands up and heads for the pizza sitting on the kitchen counter.

When he walks back out, he's carrying food up to his eyeballs. Pa and I stand up quickly to help him before he trips and spills it all. Marcus, of course, just sits there laughing at him.

"Marcus, you help your brother!" Ma scolds him.

"Come on, Ma. We don't all need to stand up and cater to him. He's got it," Marcus defends himself.

"Do you think you got enough food, Lucas?" Mia asks sarcastically.

As I open the containers of food, I'm realizing she's right. There's red and white focaccia pizza, cavatelli, meatballs, chicken cutlets, and salads. I don't know what the hell all of this is for.

"Shut up! I'm not used to being the one buying the food. I didn't want to run out. I believe what you guys were trying to say was thank you!" Lucas says.

Alexis giggles and I look over at her to see her and Mia laughing together. I'm not sure how I feel about her getting along with my family.

"Oh my gosh, this food looks and smells amazing!" Alexis groans out as she takes in the display.

"So, what's your last name, dear? Tell us about yourself." Ma plates food for Sienna and Alexis before sitting back down herself.

She's not going to let up on this, but I don't understand why she wants to get to know Alexis so much. It's not like she's going to be around for long.

"My last name is Moretti. I just graduated from Ohio State with a major in finance."

"Oh, did you hear that, Joe? She's Italian!" Ma grows excited. "You know, Marcus is our youngest. He's a fine young man. Maybe he could take you out one night to show you around. With you hardly knowing anyone here, it could get lonely. We don't want you to miss out on all the city has to offer."

Marcus winks at me as Ma goes on and on about him. I throw my pizza down on the plate, suddenly losing my appetite. I pick up the glass of wine and take a big sip. For the first time ever, the wine has no taste to me. At the moment, nothing else matters but the thought of Marcus touching Alexis. I'm so fucking angry at the thought, I can't even hear anything besides my own heartbeat pounding in my chest.

Why does she think *Marcus* should be the one to show her around? Just because he's the youngest son? Okay, so he might be twenty-eight to my thirty-five, but Marcus would never know how to soak up every ounce of woman that Alexis is.

The rest of the evening is ruined. After Ma insisted that Marcus give Alexis his number, I sat there in silence until it was Sienna's bedtime. Even taking her to bed to escape the evening was hijacked by Mia asking to take her.

Once my family is finally out the door, I take aggressive steps into my cellar and pick out my favorite *Cabernet Sauvignon* to match my mood. *Cabernets* have tons of tannins which come mostly from the skin of the grapes left in during fermentation, but it offers a powerful kick to the wine. I generally drink this wine when my meal needs a taste to match in both power and strength or when my mood calls for it—like the present moment.

I get out a glass, and then I decide to take the full bottle and head to my study. I don't even bother turning on the lights.

Sitting in my large leather chair behind my wooden desk, I look around the room. There's an entire wall full of books that I've collected, a ton of them I used in my process of studying wine. There's a couch in front of the large window that Sienna likes to lie on while I'm working on the weekends.

I'm not sure how many glasses of this bottle I've had, but my body is starting to feel numb. When I look down at my empty glass I reach for the bottle on my desk. I pour the remainder of its contents, realizing I've been here long enough to polish off the entire bottle.

When I close my eyes, I picture Alexis in her bra and underwear the other day. Instead of walking out or being with Sienna, I see myself walking into her bedroom as I grab her by the waist and slam my mouth to hers. Fuck, I bet she tastes incredible. I would want to taste her pussy next. Fall to my knees, and pull down her lace panties as I demand her eyes hold mine the entire time I make her come on my tongue.

I try to adjust myself in my shorts, my erection full, making it uncomfortable. Maybe I should just take care of myself right here. Just as I'm about to unbutton my shorts, I hear a noise outside my study. When I turn the chair, Alexis is standing there in white pajama shorts and a white tank top.

What the hell did I do to deserve this sort of torture?

"Can I help you?" I bite out.

"Um, I was just checking on you. You seemed off during dinner. I'm sorry if you didn't want me to be there. I didn't want to disappoint your mother," she says nervously outside my study.

Leaning back in my chair, I take a deep breath. My head falls back on the chair as I close my eyes, and as everything starts to spin, I realize I shouldn't finish this glass.

I sigh. "It's fine, Alexis. I'm not mad about that."

"But you are mad about something?" she asks.

I hear footsteps and think she's left, my foul mood not too pleasing to be around. But when I open my eyes, she's standing next to me.

"I hope it's nothing I did," she whispers.

Her voice is so soft, it's soothing to hear, but it also reminds me of exactly what I was thinking about before she interrupted me. When I look down, I realize my dick is still kind of hard. *Does she notice?*

I ignore her question. "Are you going to call Marcus?"

"What?" she asks, sounding confused.

"You heard me. Are you going to call Marcus? It's not a hard question to answer, Alexis."

"No, I wasn't planning on it."

"Good."

"Why does it matter?" she asks, sounding a little frustrated.

Why the fuck does it matter? Does she have any idea what she's doing to me over here? Me drinking by myself in my study like this because my brain is consumed by her?

I look up at her, my eyes drinking her in as they roam down her body until they land on those long, slender legs of hers. I reach out and start to run my fingers up her thigh. Her skin is silky soft.

She sucked in a shuttered breath.

"It matters, Alexis."

When my fingers reach the top of her leg, I run them back down. On their ascent back up, I move further in between her legs. I'm not sure whose breath is taking up the sound in the room, but the energy is intense. We don't take our eyes off each other as I continue to play this game. Will I move them to a forbidden spot that I shouldn't be anywhere near?

Fuck, my dick is begging to be touched.

"Why?" she cracks out.

"Don't ask questions you're not ready to hear the answer to," I demand.

With that, she takes a long inhale and steps away. The loss of her hits me in the chest. We're only separated by a couple feet, but it feels like miles.

She's biting her lip, clearly aroused by our interaction, but there's something else there. It seems like fear. Do I scare her? Before I can ask, she turns around and bolts out of the room.

Chapter Twelve

Alexis

Like a fantom touch that I can't seem to shake, I can still feel his hand on my leg as I stand here in the shower. I've never experienced a moment so electrified, so heated. I was afraid I was going to drip my arousal down my leg.

How embarrassing... I would have been mortified.

Would he think I'm some inexperienced woman who gets overly affected by just a touch to the thigh?

It's been three days, and I've dodged him every chance I can. Dinners have been eaten in the dark, late at night, so I don't have to sit through the torture of his stare. He may desire me, but I'm not who he thinks I am. I will just wind up being a huge disappointment.

I mean, what kind of twenty-one-year-old woman is this scared of having sex again? I'm too embarrassed to even go to therapy. Therapy that I *clearly* need.

I'm sure a lot of this stems from my upbringing. Not feeling good enough for my own parents has transferred over to my love life. All Trevor did was give me the little push that I needed. I mean...would it have killed my parents to just pretend they wanted me as much as my siblings? I would have accepted the façade. Maybe then my heart wouldn't hurt so much; maybe then I would actually believe in myself and my abilities.

The real reason I don't go to therapy, though, is that I don't want to sound whiny. It's not lost on me that I'm still a very privileged person. I was born into a family that took care of my basic needs, I never wanted for anything—not materially, at least. I graduated from a great university with no college debt. I would feel like a spoiled brat going to talk to someone to complain about minuscule things like "my mommy and daddy didn't love me enough."

As soon as I'm done with my shower, I peek into Sienna's room to see her still sleeping. Gabriel is already out the door and at work. He's been going in early since our little exchange on Sunday. Clearly, I'm not the only one who doesn't know how to act now.

I head downstairs to make myself a cup of coffee, sitting down on the couch to read a book until Sienna wakes up.

I know I should be looking for work, but I still feel so lost. What city do I even apply in? Do I go back to Columbus and live near my parents, pretending like they even care if they have me nearby?

Cleveland has Alicia. Could I live in this city knowing Sienna and Gabriel live here but also knowing there would be no reason to see them? After all, I'm just the temporary nanny.

Why does it feel like so much more than that?

The truth is, I do enjoy finance, and I would like to start my career. I just don't know where I belong. It feels like I have no sense of direction, no idea where I should settle down. I guess that's the feeling you get when no one is there waiting for you. I could move to Alaska, and I don't think anybody would care.

Maybe I need a fresh start somewhere else new.

"Hi, Alex," Sienna's angelic voice pulls me from my thoughts.

She's standing in front of me in her purple pajama set with silver stars scattered everywhere.

"Morning, sunshine." I open my arms for her to join me.

This has become a routine for us in the mornings. She snuggles with me until she's fully awake. We talk about what we want to do for the day and just enjoy each other's closeness. It's become my favorite part of the day— when there's nowhere I need to be, nothing else I need to be doing. My brain is silent, and I can just enjoy her.

After she climbs into my lap, I give her a couple minutes of silence before I start our conversation.

"So, what do you feel like doing today?" I ask her.

She looks up at me with her big, brown eyes. "I think we should go to the pool."

"We can do that. I'd have to ask your dad what pool you guys go to."

I try to play it off as if this is no big deal, but the thought of texting him has my heart fluttering.

"First things first: let's have some breakfast," I tell her.

While I made scrambled eggs and toast, I texted Gabe. He responded quickly telling me to go to the country club. It took a while through text to figure out the actual name of the club is *The Country Club*. I kept thinking he was just fucking with me, refusing to tell me the name, like I should have been able to just figure out which one he was referring to.

So, here I am, driving to some fancy schmancy club that I won't feel comfortable at. Are there going to be rich housewives watching me...judging me? Ugh, just the thought of it makes me squirm. When I pull onto the grounds, the large greenery captures my attention and I round up to a large building that looks like a mansion.

"Um, am I at the right place?" I ask Sienna.

She looks out the window. "Uh huh! Yay, I'm so excited! Can I get some ice cream after? It's so yummy!"

I chuckle. "Your dad said you might be asking for that. We're going to have lunch afterward, so I guess ice cream depends on if you eat your food."

She smiles at me. "You know I always eat my food."

"That I do, girl!"

After I park the car, I grab our bag and walk around the building to where Gabe instructed me to go. He gave me his code and told me to just tell them I'm his nanny and I will be taken care of. According to him, his Ma brought Sienna up here all the time, so they should recognize her.

When we get to the pool grounds, I spot the little kid area, and we make our way inside. There are moms everywhere with their kids, but so far, everyone seems to be minding their own business.

Okay, not so bad. Maybe I was overthinking it.

"Okay, sweetness. Let's get your sunscreen on," I tell Sienna once I find two lounge chairs along the edge of the pool.

Even though this girl has a perfect olive complexion, I lather her up in SPF 50. I switch to SPF 15 for myself so I can work on my tan. Once we're both ready, Sienna holds her hand out to me, and we both go to the kid's pool. It's only about a foot deep, but it's up to her knees. I put my feet in and sit on the edge of the pool while Sienna starts to jump under the water and splash around.

It's been over an hour, and as I start to feel overheated, I worry that Sienna is going to get burnt or overdo it.

"Okay, girl. Let's go check out the food here. Maybe see about that ice cream."

Sienna jumps out of the pool faster than I thought possible.

"Yay!" She dances as I wrap a towel around her.

We walk out of the gated pool area to the outside tables. The umbrellas offer a nice break from the sun. I look around at the view of the golf course and feel spoiled that I get to partake in this treatment for my job.

When the waiter comes up, I order Sienna a sandwich and myself a salad.

"Do you come here a lot?" I ask her as we wait for our food.

"Yep. Grandma takes me, Daddy takes me, sometimes Mia takes me. I love it!"

"You're a lucky girl. I hope you know that," I tell her.

"I am? Why?" she asks, looking puzzled.

"Because you have a family that loves you so much."

I see her brain work as she contemplates my words. She looks a lot like her father right now.

"What about you? Don't you have a family that loves you a lot?" she questions.

"I have parents and some half-siblings. We love each other."

"But not a lot?" She looks sad as she asks.

I smile at her. "Well, maybe not as much as what you have. But...I'm still grateful for what I have."

Okay, that's a lie. Well, it's a partial lie, but this is not the setting for this conversation, and she's only four. There's no need to go down that dark path with her.

When the food gets here, Sienna is true to her word and polishes it off quickly. I'm only halfway done with my salad when she's had all her fruit and sandwich.

"Dang, girl! You were hungry." I look at her in shock.

They gave her a full, adult-sized sandwich. I'm not sure where she just put it all, but I'm nervous to give her ice cream now.

"I always get hungry after I swim. Daddy says I eat like a human garbage disposal. I don't know what that means. Do I get my ice cream now?" she speaks emphatically, not stopping to take a breath or gather her thoughts.

I laugh at her pure innocence and joy over something as simple as ice cream. It's kind of contagious.

"You got it, dude. I think I'm gonna have one too," I tell her.

She sits up tall. "Daddy never eats ice cream with me here."

"He probably doesn't want his friends making fun of him. But lucky for you, I don't know anyone here."

I put in an order for two ice cream sundaes, and when they arrive, we both scarf them down without stopping to talk even for a second. We finish at the same time and both lean back on our chairs as we struggle to move.

"I'm so full," she moans.

"Ugh, me too! But you know what?" I ask. "It was totally worth it."

I hold out my fist for her to bump. She knocks hers against mine and we both erupt into a fit of giggles.

An hour later, we are home, freshly showered, and playing in her toy room. Sienna's making me something to eat in her pretend kitchen when I get a text.

Alicia: What are you doing this Friday?

Yes! I need to get out this weekend. This week is slowly killing me trying to avoid Gabriel at every twist and turn.

Me: I'm going out with you! What are we doing?

I haven't felt the need to party and let loose since my early college years. This weekend I'm going to stop thinking about my boss, and I'm going to act like a normal twenty-one-year-old. Minus not being able to calm down enough to be with a guy.

Alicia: We are going bar hopping on 4th Street.

It's like she knows exactly what I need. Now all I have to do is dodge Gabe tonight and tomorrow. *Easy.*

Chapter Thirteen

Gabriel

She's been avoiding me all week. I want to be pissed at her, but I'm too busy avoiding her myself. After I behaved like a drunken molester Sunday night and she ran away from me, I've felt like shit all week. I know my judgment was impaired, but I swear she seemed affected by my touch.

Then why did she run away?

It's already Thursday afternoon. Normally I can't wait to get home to be with Sienna, and I was even starting to enjoy coming home to both of them and having dinner together.

Now, I want to come up with any excuse that I can to work late, but I'm not going to let my bad decisions affect Sienna. What kind of father would I be if I did that?

A knock on my office door startles me.

"Come in!" I shout from my chair.

Marcus peeks his head inside. "Got a second?"

"What's going on?" I ask, waving him in as he unbuttons his suit jacket and takes a seat across from me.

"Not much. Just checking in on you. You've been acting a bit short with everyone this week. Everything okay?"

Is everything okay? If wanting to fuck your fresh-outta-college nanny is okay, then I'm more than okay. I wish I could bounce this scenario off Marcus to see what he thinks, but I'm too chicken shit to breathe the words out loud.

"I'm fine, man. Things are just getting busy around here. I'm gearing up to present the new wine we selected from Italy, you know how it goes."

His eyebrows raise like he doesn't believe me. I wait in my seat to see if he's going to call me on my bullshit.

"It's gonna be a lot of work and a ton of travel to get that wine out there. I'm probably going to need to schedule a night out to release my stress...if you know what I mean?"

Did he seriously just come in here to tell me he needs to fuck to relieve stress? Sometimes I wonder about him. Maybe Pa accidentally dropped a brick or two on his head growing up.

I groan at his words.

"Can we not discuss your extracurricular activities at work? Some of us have class and don't need to strut around airing our dirty laundry."

He inspects his sleeve like he didn't hear a word I said.

"I was thinking of calling Alexis. She seems like someone who would be up for a good time."

I can't tell whether he's serious or not, but I don't give a shit. All the muscles in my body are tense and angry, ready to fight. Unfortunately, punching my brother at our place of work isn't an option. Otherwise, he would already be on the floor.

"Get. The. Fuck. Out," I growl at him.

He starts to laugh like this entire thing is a game to him. Well, I have far too much sexual frustration pent up in me to find anything amusing.

When he doesn't make any effort to stand. I get up and grab his jacket to help him get going, which only seems to make him laugh more. I march us over to my door and throw him out when I hear him yell Lucas's name.

"I did it, Lucas! You owe me a hundred big ones," he yells down the hall.

Well, that's my family for ya. Turning my misery into their entertainment. If only they knew what kind of slow torture the past month has been. I feel like every situation in my house lately puts Alexis into some position that shouldn't make me hard, but damn if my body can control it.

My lungs are gasping for air and, my legs are feeling weak, but I press accelerate on my treadmill and keep pushing myself. It's all I can think to do to ease the mounting tension in my body.

Before Alexis came along, my world was dark, but it made sense. Sienna was my only bright spot, and the rest was just me going through the motions.

Now I'm not sure what to make of anything. I don't like feeling completely out of control every day, but the feelings she's evoking aren't completely unappealing. What would it be like to fuck again and actually feel something when I'm buried deep inside a woman? The problem is with that, comes the danger of someone ripping my heart out again.

And someone breaking Sienna's heart.

I push the increase speed button again. I need these thoughts to fade away...where the only thing I can focus on is the pain.

When I feel like my body can't take anymore, I hit stop and grab my towel. The house is silent early in the morning, so I can go about my routine in peace. No worrying about whether Alexis will be in the next room. I walk into the dark kitchen and fill up a glass of water. The water quenches the dire thirst I was forcing on myself but does nothing for the thirst I'm feeling deep in my soul.

I hear a gasp just as I'm finished slamming down the water.

Alexis is standing in just a T-shirt, hair askew, looking like she was just properly fucked this morning. I'm standing here in just my gym shorts, thinking I had the house to myself.

"Sorry. I was just working out, didn't mean to scare you," I tell her.

There's no denying that she is ogling my body right now. I want to tell her to cut that shit out before I take her right here on the counter, but I'm all kinds of fucked in the head after she ran from me the other night and then proceeded to avoid me all week. I don't know what the hell she wants.

"It's fine. I just came down to lick some water." Her eyes become big when she notices her mistake. "I mean, I came down to drink some water."

"Don't let me stop you." I motion for her to continue.

Was she just picturing licking me? Or was I licking her?

Fuck! There goes my productivity at work today.

Something has gotta give here. I'm not sure what is going on between us, but I need to apologize for the other night and tell her that it will never happen again. I'm not going to make her feel uncomfortable under my roof for the remainder of her stay. Maybe if we just address it and get it out in the open, we can move on from it.

I look down at my sweaty, shirtless body. I'm not having this conversation with her half-naked.

Tonight...after work.

Chapter Fourteen

Alexis

Today was horrible. All I could think about was how insanely hot Gabe looked in athletic shorts, all sweaty and sticky. Ugh, but the fact that I basically admitted to him that I wanted to lick him clean.

I've never put my foot in my mouth like that before. Then again, no man has ever made me feel like this.

But none of that matters because tonight I'm going out with Alicia, and she is going to help me forget all about my humiliating life. It's already eight, and she is going to be here in thirty minutes to pick me up with an Uber. I need to focus on getting my smokey eye makeup right. I've been watching some social media star's video for the last five minutes, trying to understand her technique.

Ten minutes later, I'm looking in the mirror and can barely recognize myself. I used contouring tips from her, and the eye makeup complements it so well. My hair is down in loose waves, and I picked a red dress that is flowy on the bottom but hugs my waist and shows off my chest in a classy way.

Now time to do the dreaded walk downstairs. I know I don't owe Gabe a heads-up that I'm going out, but I am living under his roof, and a part of me still feels like I need to tell him I'm leaving.

I find him in his study wearing glasses as he reads something on the computer.

I didn't know he had reading glasses, but my ovaries can't handle it right now. He looks so stunningly handsome; I actually feel a weird pressure in my chest.

He looks up at me and does a double-take before his eyes look at me from head to toe.

"Going out tonight?" His voice holds a sort of anger to it.

I take shaky steps closer to his door, stopping right outside his office. I'm reminded of what could have happened in here if I hadn't stopped it. I didn't want to, everything in me was telling me it was going to be amazing, but that fearful part of my brain took over, and it got loud. Too loud for me to ignore.

"I am. I wanted to let you know I was going to be gone most of the night. Depending on the time, I might just spend the night at Alicia's."

His jaw tightens.

"I see. Any special occasion you're so dressed up for?" He looks back at my dress.

I look down at myself. "Oh, not really. Alicia just told me to get dressed up because we were going out."

"You look beautiful," he tells me.

My heart skips a beat at his compliment.

"Thank you."

We hold each other's eyes for what feels like an eternity. So many unspoken words are drifting through the air, waiting for someone to admit the truth between us.

Not able to stand here in silence any longer, I nod my head and turn around to walk away.

"Alexis," his voice rings.

I turn around and see him standing from his seat, getting ready to chase me if he needed to.

"Yes?" I answer.

His shoulders sag as I see a slightly insecure man in front of me for the first time.

"I've been meaning to apologize to you for the other night. I had too many glasses of wine, and I crossed a line. I'm sorry if I made you feel uncomfortable."

He didn't make me uncomfortable in the way he thinks. I don't know whether to let him go on feeling bad about it, thinking he misread me, or to put him out of his misery and tell him it was me, not him. Neither response is free of complications.

"There's no need for an apology. I..." I stumble on my words. "The thing is—it's not that I wasn't uncomfortable, I was...but not for the reason you think," I say.

"Shit. I'm sorry, Alexis. I was completely out of line. I hope you know I won't let something like that happen again. The last thing I want is for you to feel unsafe here."

Those words coming out of his mouth are like a dagger. He won't let it happen again? What if I want it to happen again?

Do I want it to?

His phone rings, interrupting our conversation. When he looks at his screen, he releases a frustrated sigh.

"I'm sorry, Alexis. I have to take this."

I nod my head and walk to the kitchen to grab a water.

By the time Alicia arrives, I'm waiting outside and all shaken up from my talk with Gabe.

"Damn, you look sexy," she tells me as I hop in the back seat with her.

"Thanks." I force a smile as the driver moves forward.

As we're pulling out of the driveway, the car passes the bay window in Gabe's study. I catch him standing there on the phone as he watches the car drive away.

"Okay, spill the beans. What's gotten into you lately?" Alicia's muffled voice barely registers.

"Huh?" I look back at her. "Oh, sorry. I was just distracted by a conversation I had. No biggie. So, tell me...what's going on with that guy from your new job?"

Alicia's face lights up at the mention of his name. "Craig. I can't get a read on him, but he is so damn fine. He's a bit older. I never noticed how sexy older men are when they can afford to dress and smell so damn good."

She's got that right. Gabriel puts the guys at my college to shame with his fancy suits and designer cologne. My body gets goosebumps whenever he walks by me, and I get a trace of his scent.

I laugh as Alicia tells me more about Craig. The girl can get infatuated pretty easily, but it sounds like she's smitten with him.

Once we arrive downtown, we get dropped off right outside the first bar. It has live music, and the nightlife has already started to form. We push our way to the bar, where we order our drinks.

"Let's go find a spot in the back. I need to get some drinks in me before we dance," she shouts.

I gesture my head in agreement and duck around a group of girls that may have already had one too many drinks. A flash of Sienna and Gabe snuggling on the couch watching a movie hits me, and a twinge of jealousy hits.

I wish I was with them right now.

It's a completely ridiculous thought. There's no room for me to be taking part in those little family moments... I'm the nanny.

We find a high-top table closer to the entrance, which gives us a nice separation from the craziness of it all.

"So," Alicia starts after she takes a sip of her martini. "Tell me more about what it's like working for Mr. Hottie!"

Ugh, she has no idea the can of worms she's opening with that question. I've been reluctant to tell Alicia about the sexual tension occupying the space in the house.

"It's been amazing working with Sienna. She's the best," I smile as I think of her.

Alicia gives me a skeptical look. "What aren't you telling me?"

"What are you talking about?" I try to come off as casual and cool.

"Well, you got noticeably uncomfortable when I brought up Mr. Hottie, and you blushed. You also completely avoided my question."

She's right. I'm trying my best to avoid any topic involving Gabe. It's wearing on me, and I need somebody to talk about it with. My shoulders sag in defeat.

"You got me," I tell her. "I'm totally trying to dodge this topic. It's just...I don't even know what's going on myself."

"Wait a minute! Is there something going on between you and Mr. Giannelli?"

"Alicia! Don't call him that. It makes this whole thing feel weird. And...I don't know if there's something going on. Kind of. It feels like there is."

She looks confused. "Okay, you need to give me more than that. Have you and Gabe had sex?"

"No, nothing has happened between us. Well, one night, I think it could have happened. And he has mentioned how attracted he is to me. I just...I'm nervous to go there with him. It's so inappropriate."

"Why the hell would you say that?" she raises her voice.

"Because I'm the nanny! It's like the classic stereotype. Sexy dad gets caught in bed with the younger nanny."

"Sometimes the classics are the best. Like watching *Dirty Dancing* or *Friends.*"

I laugh at her comparisons. I'm not sure sleeping with my boss is like watching a movie or TV show. I take another sip of my martini, needing some more liquid courage for this conversation.

"What about Sienna? I don't want to hurt her in any way."

Alicia considers my words. "Well, this is a temporary position. I can see how that would make sense if you were going to stay her nanny. But if this whole thing has an expiration date anyway, I say have some fun!"

She winks at me and turns around to get a view of the band, leaving me a minute to ponder over her words.

She does have a point. There is an expiration date, so we don't have anything to lose if something did happen. The question is do I want something to happen?

Like some kind of fate, my phone vibrates with a text from Gabriel.

Gabriel: I'm sorry we got interrupted. Once again, Alexis, I'm so sorry for making you feel uncomfortable.

I look up at Alicia as she dances in her seat to the music. The band here is really good and I can tell that her one martini is already kicking in. I look down at my now empty glass and realize I may be feeling it as well. That may be the reason for my next text.

Me: The only thing that made me uncomfortable was my stupid insecurities.

Shit, I said it! My hands are shaking as I clutch my phone for dear life. What happens if he asks me to elaborate?

"This band is amazing!" Alicia turns to me and smiles as our next order of martinis arrives at our table.

I smile at her, pretending like I'm just as into the show as she is. "I know! What a great spot to come to tonight!"

I take a big sip of my drink as I wait for his text. I'm about to give up on him when my phone vibrates in my hand.

Gabriel: What the hell do you have to be insecure about?

A bitter laugh escapes me as I think about my entire life. Maybe the fact that I've never been enough for anybody.

Me: I don't know. Maybe the fact that the only person I ever had sex with told me how bad I was at it. The fact that I haven't had sex since, and that was years ago. The fact that no man has ever made me come, because I can't settle my brain enough to relax and enjoy the moment. That I'm broken and bad at sex, and I don't want to disappoint you.

The words come out fast and full of emotion. Obviously, I'm not going to send it, but it feels good to have typed them out. I move my thumb to hit the backspace button when all of a sudden, the text disappears from the box.

What? Where did it go?

I look up at our thread and see my text sitting there with *delivered* written below it.

Holy shit! NOOOOO!

That did not just happen. Oh my god! Did I just text my boss and tell him I can't get off with a man? My entire body is shaking. What the hell do I do? Do I text back and just say I was joking?

I see three dots appear on the screen before disappearing. This happens over and over for the next ten minutes before they disappear for good.

Shit, of course, he has no idea what to say to that! I probably scared him.

"Girl, you look like someone just kicked your puppy. What's gotten into you?" Alicia screams over the music.

I look at her, trying to decide my next move. I decide it's too humiliating to tell her what just happened, so putting on a brave face is my only option.

I smile at her. "Sorry, I was just thinking about something. Do we need another round?"

She looks down at our drinks. "We haven't even finished our second one yet, but I'm game!"

The night goes by quickly after my third drink. We move close to the band as we dance our worries away, literally choosing dancing over focusing on what just happened a couple hours ago. I decide I will just pretend it never happened and avoid him entirely for my remaining month.

Easy enough, I can do that.

Chapter Fifteen

Gabriel

I'm standing in my kitchen, drinking a glass of whiskey. I need something strong for the tsunami of emotions running through me. I'm not sure if I'm interpreting her message correctly, but from what I can tell...there's an ex-boyfriend's ass I need to kick and an orgasm I need to give.

How is it possible that she has *never* had an orgasm before with a man? I always take care of my woman, and making sure she's satisfied is my top priority. Stupid fucking college guys that only care about themselves.

It's getting late, and just as I'm starting to worry that she decided to spend the night at her friend's place, I hear a car door shut outside.

The front door opens, followed by the sound of her walking up the stairs to her room.

This is it, my last chance to come to my senses and leave her alone. Then I think about her upstairs in her bedroom all alone, never having experienced pleasure like she deserves, and my anger and determination are back.

I take the final swig of my whiskey. Here goes nothing.

The steps are quiet underneath my feet as I take slow, careful strides upstairs. When I get to her bedroom, I tap gently on her door.

Her door opens slowly. "Hi," she whispers when she opens it.

She's still in her red dress, but all her makeup is removed. It leaves me with the view of a naturally beautiful face that never needed makeup to begin with.

"How was your night?" I ask.

Her head leans to the side as I see the look of confusion on her face. She's wondering what I'm doing at her door at one in the morning. Hell, part of me is wondering the same damn thing.

"Umm, it was good. Is everything okay?" she questions me.

I start to walk into her room without permission. With each step that I take forward, she takes one back.

"No. For the last couple hours, I've been playing your text message in my head over and over again."

Her head falls into his hands as she shakes her head. "Oh my gosh, I'm so humiliated. I can't believe I sent that. I'm so sorry. Please just forget I—"

"I wasn't done talking, Alexis," I say with an edge.

She peeks out from her hands.

"I don't know what kind of *boys* you've been with," I bring my hand out to caress her cheek, "but I can't let you go another second without showing you that there's not a damn thing you could do to disappoint me. And that you not getting off is not a you problem. That's a man's job. And instead of the guy owning up to the fact that he doesn't have the slightest clue what a real woman like you needs, he decided to make you feel bad about it."

Her eyes look at me curiously.

"Are you going to show me?" she whispers.

"Do you want me to show you?" I ask, desperate for her reply.

She nods her head quickly.

"Go lie down on the bed. I'm going to show you that you can relax enough to enjoy what I do to you."

She releases a breathy gasp that makes my dick hard. *Down, boy. Tonight is not about you.*

"You want me to...lie down on my bed?" she stutters out. "What if...I...I...*can't* with you either?"

"I'm not going to be the one getting you off tonight. I'm just going to show you that I can make you feel good. No pressure. When I feel like I've accomplished that, I'll leave the room and you can either finish yourself off or not. But I'm damn well going to start to change your mind about what a man can make you feel. Now...I'm not going to ask again. Go. Get. On. Your. Bed."

I know she wants me, but I also know that if I don't push her, she'll continue to write this narrative about herself that is complete bullshit.

She takes small steps until she reaches her bed. I watch her start to shrink in on herself as her chin hits her chest and her shoulders sag.

"Do you trust me?" I ask her, pulling her chin up until her eyes meet mine.

I wait with bated breath for her answer, wanting desperately for her to say yes.

"I do," she finally answers.

"Good," I respond hoarsely, trying to get my emotions in check. "Now, lie back. I promise I'm going to make you feel good."

She sits on the bed, then scoots back before lying all the way down. Her ragged breaths put emphasis on her significant breasts as they rise and fall. With her brown hair splayed across the white comforter and her red dress hugging her body, I realize I've never seen anything so beautiful.

"Spread your legs, Alexis. I need to get a look at your pretty pussy."

Her eyes open wide at my words. I can tell no one's ever talked to her like this before. She's never been with a man who will take control and tell her exactly what's on his mind. I'm going to show her how easy it is to get out of her head.

My hands come up to her knees before they head down the inside of her thighs. I reach up to her hips and grab her matching red underwear, slowly sliding them down her legs until I toss them on the floor. With my hands back on her knees, I push her legs open to reveal the sexiest pussy I've ever seen.

Fuck, my dick is begging to slide into that slick warmth right now.

With a featherlike touch, I skim my fingers down the outside of her legs until they reach her hips. Then I work my fingers over her stomach and down her sides, back to her waist.

"Just focus on my touch," I whisper to her.

She closes her eyes as she takes in the connection of our skin. I continue my movements, getting closer and closer to her clit with each pass. Eventually, her hips lift off the bed every time my fingers get close as she tries to force my fingers to brush her clit.

"Do you want my touch, baby? It seems like you want me to touch your pussy," I ask her.

Her eyes open, and as soon as she meets my gaze, she bites her lip and nods her head up and down quickly.

I lie down on the bed so my side is touching hers. I want to be close to her when I finally sink my fingers into her.

"Keep your eyes on me," I command.

With that, I bring my free hand back to her hips and drag my fingers over her clit. As soon as I make contact, a gasp escapes her.

I smile down at her. She's sensitive. She won't have a problem getting off, not with me.

My fingers run several slow circles around her clit before they drop down to her entrance, where she is soaking wet.

"Fuck, baby. You're soaked. That's so damn sexy."

I see a slight blush appear on her cheeks.

"Nothing to be embarrassed about. There's nothing sexier than a woman who is desperate for her man to touch her."

I realize I just referred to myself as her man. It should bother me, but all it does is make my dick twitch in excitement.

Her breasts are calling for me. I reach for the top of her dress and pull it down with her bra until her breast is exposed. I lean down and take her nipple into my mouth. She moans as I suck and lick at her, my hand going back to her entrance, where I push in one finger. It's my turn to growl into her breast as I feel her tight walls on just one finger.

Shit! She would squeeze the fuck out of my dick.

I try to start slow so she can adjust to me. Once her moisture is coated everywhere, I add a second finger. I stop sucking on her breast so I can look at her.

Her face is mixed with pleasure and surprise. I don't think she was expecting it to feel like this. It's new for me, as well. I didn't think I was going to feel so unhinged and desperate for more.

I push my fingers all the way in and keep them there as I shake my hand up and down, knowing I'm hitting her spot. She lets out another moan, followed directly by whimpering, her jaw falling open.

"Does it feel good, baby?" I ask her.

She nods at me with vigor. My thumb moves over her clit and starts to rub circles as my fingers continue to work her. As I feel her wetness increase and her walls start to twitch, I know she's close.

As much as it kills me, I pull my fingers out and stop, keeping true to my promise that I wasn't going to get her off.

"Why did you stop?" Her voice sounds tortured.

"I told you I wasn't going to get you off. I just wanted you to see I could make it feel good. No pressure."

Her mouth is hung open as I pick myself up off the bed. Her perfect pink pussy is glistening at me, and I have to adjust my dick.

"Now I'm going to leave this room. If you want to finish yourself off, you are free to do so. Or you can just go to bed. I think you should get off, baby. You deserve it."

I manage to get myself to her door and close it behind me. That took herculean effort to walk away, but I didn't want to push her. I can't help it, I put my ear to the door and listen, hoping to hear something. When I hear soft whimpers and ultimately a louder finish, I know she just touched herself.

"Good girl," I whisper and turn around to walk downstairs to my bedroom.

I go straight to my shower and strip off my clothes. As soon I'm under the water, my hand is on my dick. Images of Alexis on her knees as she takes me into her mouth, her lying back on the bed while I feast on her pussy, are floating through my head while I pump myself hard. It doesn't take long before I'm blowing ropes of cum onto the shower floor.

What am I going to do with this attraction to my nanny? We've already crossed a line. Now I have to wait until tomorrow to see how she acts around me.

One thing I know for sure: I've gotten my taste... and I want more.

Chapter Sixteen

Alexis

Sunlight flickers through my window as it casts a warmth that envelopes me like a blanket. I open my eyes and look to my left and right as I come to, images of what happened last night flooding my mind.

Oh my god! I can't believe that was real. It wasn't a dream.

Gabriel came into my room last night and made me feel better than any man has with just his fingers.

And his words...they hit me hard, making my entire body ignite. For the first time, the thought of him stopping was devastating to me. I wanted more from him, so much more. I'm sure if he continued, I would have come.

Instead, I got myself off within seconds of him walking away.

Never did I think that a tipsy text was going to result in the single best sexual experience of my life.

But now...how do I act around him? Was that just a one-time thing, or is it going to happen again? Are we going to do more? *God, I want to do more!*

Knowing it would be embarrassingly obvious if I hide upstairs all day, I crawl out of bed. Coffee is a must for me in the morning. All I manage to do is go to the bathroom and brush my teeth. Before I leave the room, I look in the mirror right by the door.

The woman looking back at me looks different. I *feel* different. I don't know exactly what the difference is, but it's liberating. I feel like I could go outside and run a marathon.

I find Sienna sitting on the island while Gabe is next to her, mixing something in a bowl. He looks so handsome with his disheveled hair and white shirt with black athletic pants.

I stand by the wall to get a glimpse of this secret *daddy and daughter interaction.*

"No, Daddy! That's not right. That's not how Alex does it. The sprinkles disappeared, and now it's just a gross brown batter. It looks like poop."

I try to contain the giggle that wants to burst out of me. He must have used the crystal sugar in what I'm assuming is pancake batter. It dissolves into the mixture and turns colors. Although, I'm not sure why it's brown.

"I don't know what I did wrong. How many different ways can there be to add sprinkles?" he responds, looking down at the bowl.

"I don't know, Daddy, but I don't think I want to eat that," Sienna suggests.

He puts down the spatula and looks up at Sienna. "I'm not making this again."

I take that as an indication for me finally enter the room. Sienna turns her head, and Gabe looks up. He looks me up and down, and I suddenly feel shy. This man's fingers were inside me last night, and there's something different in his stare this morning. It's like he isn't trying to hide his appreciation, and that's doing things to my body.

"Alex!" Sienna screams in delight. "Daddy doesn't know how to make your pancakes. It looks like poop!"

I let out my suppressed laugh. "Nobody wants to eat poop. Let me see."

I peer into the bowl to find a dark brown mixture. It almost has a hint of gray to it. I look over at the bottle of sprinkles and see he used green, blue, and red.

"Ahhh, I see the problem. Well, you used the wrong sprinkles."

He looks down at me, and I see a hint of a smirk splay across his face.

"I already told her I'm not starting over."

I chuckle. "It's okay. We can just add some cocoa powder and chocolate chips. They can be chocolatey pancakes; that way, the brown color makes sense."

"Ooh, I love chocolate!" Sienna claps her hands.

Gabe puts his hands up in defeat. "Do what you gotta do."

He winks at me, and my body takes notice. It's like he has a manual to my lady bits and knows exactly how to make me come alive.

I do my best to ignore the growing need between my legs and move around the kitchen. Gabe is leaning against the island next to Sienna, watching me as I revive the sad batter into a chocolatey dream.

"There we go," I exclaim after I put the chocolate chips in. "I think this will be a fun creation. Plus, I added pink sprinkles so it still has some color."

"Yay! You're the *best*, Alex," Sienna cheers.

I smile up at her, and can't help but notice Gabe watching our interactions thoughtfully.

"I think I can take over from here," Gabe says with a spatula in his hand. "Thanks for saving the day, Alexis."

"Not a problem. I'm just gonna get some coffee and sit outside for a bit."

I watch the two of them laugh together as my coffee brews. My heart is exploding at how cute they are together.

After a cup of coffee and a shower, I'm back outside on a chair as I dive into my book. It doesn't take much before I'm lost between the pages in a world that's not my own. I don't come back to reality for two and a half hours, when my stomach growls and reminds me that I skipped breakfast.

When I walk inside, it's unusually quiet for a Saturday afternoon. I'm wondering if they left to go somewhere for the day. I'm proven wrong when I enter the kitchen, and Gabe is making a sandwich.

I give him a shy smile. "Hi," I manage to get out.

Ugh, I'm so damn awkward.

Gabriel stops what he's doing and drinks me in. He does that every time I'm in the room with him, assesses me from head to toe. He gives me a slow, wicked smile.

"Hi, yourself."

"Um, I just came in here for lunch."

He bites his bottom lip as he watches me. "I'm making a sandwich. Would you like one?"

I'm a bit taken aback by his offer. "Oh, um, sure. Thank you."

"Take a seat, Alexis."

I let out a nervous laugh but manage to take a seat without further embarrassing myself. I put my hand under my chin and watch him continue his process. "You don't have to use my full name. You can call me Alex."

"I like it when you call me by my full name. I've noticed you only do it when you're speaking directly to me. If there are others in the room, you use Gabe."

I shrug my shoulders. "I guess when it's just you and me, it feels more...intimate. And Gabriel is such a sexy name."

Did that just come out of my mouth?

I can't believe I just admitted that to him. It must be the orgasm doing funny things to my brain.

His eyes turn dark. "Never stop using my full name with me."

It feels like an order, but once again, my body likes it. I nod my head because I think my voice would give away my reaction.

He plates the sandwiches, places them on the island, and joins me on the other side.

"Thank you. You didn't have to do this," I tell him, feeling bad he went through the trouble to make me lunch.

His head tilts to the side while he studies me. I squirm in my seat, feeling unsure about the attention.

"Do you ever relax and let someone do something for you?" he asks.

The sandwich is halfway to my mouth but is completely forgotten with his words. No one has ever asked me something like that. Honestly, no one has ever really done anything for me. I'm used to riding through life in the shadows.

I shake my head back and forth. "No," I rasp.

"It's a shame," he says as his hand reaches out and tucks a stray piece of hair behind my ear.

The gesture is so small and yet so tender, like I'm precious to him. I gulp down the feelings rising to the surface.

"What about you?" I ask him.

"What about me, Alexis?" His eyebrows raise at my question.

"Who takes care of you?" I clarify.

He seems surprised that I turned the tables. Maybe even equally illuminating to him as it was to me. I get the feeling that he doesn't let his guard down easily for someone to take care of him.

"I don't need anybody to take care of me. You have to trust someone to let them take care of you," he finally answers.

"And you don't trust anybody?"

"Nobody but my family," he says.

Feeling like the conversation has gotten too serious for a lunch, I nod my head and take a bite of my sandwich.

I think I need something crunchy with my food, or maybe just some space from this overwhelming conversation and man.

"I'm gonna get some chips," I tell him as I scoot off my chair.

I walk inside his massive pantry and let out a breath I didn't even realize I was holding. He sees through me, down to the deepest parts of me. Not only that, but my mind can't stop replaying what it felt like to have his fingers inside me last night. Watching him make the sandwiches, seeing the sexy veins on his hands and forearms.

I'm so lost in my thoughts about Gabriel that I barely register what food is in front of me. A hand appears on the shelf in front of my head as I feel the warmth of his body only inches from my back.

"You're taking a really long time to find chips," he whispers in my ear.

I take in a shaky breath.

"I...couldn't decide which kind I wanted."

His other hand is on my hip. "You're not going to find anything standing here in front of the bread."

I look up and realize I'm nowhere near the chips. When his hand reaches over to my stomach, I close my eyes.

"Turn around, Alexis."

I spin around to find him looking down at me with indisputable desire.

"What are you thinking about?" he asks.

I can't lie to him, and I don't think I want to. Not after what he made me feel last night.

"I was thinking about last night."

While one hand is still on the shelf behind me, the other hand on my hip is now moving down to my behind as he moves me closer to him.

"What about last night? Were you thinking about how it felt to have me finger fuck you, or how it felt when you rubbed your clit until you came after I left?"

"Your fingers inside me."

"Good girl. I haven't been able to get the feeling of your pussy out of my mind all day. Do you want to know what I did as soon as I left your room?"

"What did you do?" I ask as I rub my thighs, trying to ease the ache between my legs that this man's presence creates.

"First," he whispers with his mouth only a fraction away from mine. "I listened to you make yourself come. Then, I got into my shower and fucked my hand to thoughts of your mouth wrapped around my dick."

I let out an involuntary moan. Hearing him admit that he touched himself to thoughts of me is almost too much.

"Please," I beg, not sure what I'm even asking for.

"Tell me what you want right now, Alexis."

"Kiss me. Touch me. Make me feel like you did last night," I brazenly ask, too in the moment to be fearful.

He lets out a growl before his lips come crashing down on mine. The moment we come together, overwhelming sensations go straight to my chest. His lips work over mine with such intensity as both his hands come up to my face. He steps into me until my back hits the shelves.

Food falls to the floor around us, but neither of us let up. I wrap my arms around his neck and go up on my tippy toes so I can give as much as he is.

The moment our tongues meet, we let out a simultaneous moan. Our tongues mix and course each other, like this is our only moment, and we need to make the best of it.

"I need to taste you," he whispers into my mouth.

I'm too worked up to really take in what he's saying. He unbuttons my jean shorts and then shoves them down with my panties. When he starts to kneel before me, a wave of panic hits me.

"What are you doing?" I blurt out.

He tilts his head to the side. "I'm going to taste you. Is something wrong?"

I look down at the ground, feeling slightly ashamed that I'm feeling so self-conscious at the moment. At least he is in tune enough with me to know there's something wrong. Most guys just go for it, doing it to move the process along until it's their turn.

"It's just...I always worry that I'll take too long when a guy is down...there. I get in my head and can't..." I trail off.

He rubs his hands up and down my thighs in a soothing motion. "There is no amount of time too long for me to get to taste you. I would do it forever if I could."

"You actually *want* to do it?"

He smiles. "It's been running through my head since I met you. I've been dreaming about getting the chance to fuck you with my tongue."

Fuck, his words again. They turn me on like nothing I've ever experienced.

He winks at me. "You like when I talk to you like that, don't you?"

I bite my lip and nod my head.

"How about this? If you feel like it's not working, tap me out and I'll finish you off with my fingers. Or fuck...I'll watch you finish yourself off. It would be an honor to witness that."

"Okay."

"Good girl."

He gets right in front of my pussy but doesn't make a move to lean in. Instead, his hands come up and his thumbs spread me apart. He kneels there as he just takes me in.

"Fuck, baby. You have the most beautiful pussy I've ever seen." He drags a thumb over my clit and I shudder at the sensations. "Look at how much it's already glistening with your arousal."

I look down at myself and am surprised at how sexy it is to watch his movements as he runs his hands along me. It makes me even more wet for him. He looks up at me and leans in to give a small kiss to my center, then opens his mouth and takes a slow, deliberate lick from my entrance up to my clit. My eyes roll in the back of my head at the intensity of it all. I'm shocked that the first swipe of his tongue feels as good as it does.

Maybe I can come like this.

His tongue starts to focus on my clit as he makes fast motions back and forth, up and down, then circles around. When his lips wrap around me and suck hard, I start to lose focus on what the hell is even happening in my body. All I can do is beg him not to stop.

"Fuck, please. Oh, god. Please, please, Gabriel."

His eyes hold mine when I say his name and he groans into my pussy. He inserts two fingers and beings to pump in tune with this mouth.

Unable to do anything but feel, I close my eyes and let my orgasm rip through my body. It's like an eruption that starts in my center and shoots all over, even into my toes and fingers.

When I come down from the high, I realize I'm clutching onto his head and pushing it into my pussy.

"Shit! I'm so sorry," I tell him as I let go.

He pulls back and wipes his mouth with the back of his hand.

"Fuck, you are so damn sexy when you come," he says as he gets back to his feet. "I could do that every second of every day and die a happy man."

I can't believe he enjoys doing that to me so much. I also can't believe I just had my first orgasm with a man. He made it seem so easy, like he had a road map to my body and knew each twist and turn to take to blow my mind.

I notice his dick is pressing firmly against his jeans, and I realize that never in my life have I wanted to please a man so much in my life. Giving head has always been just for the guy, but it feels like me wrapping my lips around him would be for me.

When he stands up, I reach out for his pants and grab his belt, gently pulling him toward me. He looks down at my hand and then back up at me.

"You don't have to, Alexis."

Well, if that isn't the sexiest thing in the world. It only makes me want to please him more.

"I want to," I whisper.

I get up on my tippy toes and kiss his soft lips while I unbuckle and unzip. The kiss turns abrasive, momentarily distracting me from the task at hand. Just as my hand is reaching into his pants, we hear a shout from upstairs.

"Daddy! Where are you?" Sienna's voice carries through the house.

We both jump away from each other as the moment turns from heat to panic.

"Shit," Gabe mutters as he works to get himself buckled back up.

He runs out of the pantry to find Sienna, and I spend the next couple minutes cleaning up the mess we made on the floor while trying to pull myself together.

Chapter Seventeen

Gabriel

"Daddy, how long is Alex going to stay with us?" Sienna asks me while I lie next to her.

After nearly getting caught in the pantry with my pants down, Alexis and I scarfed down our lunch before she disappeared upstairs, and I haven't seen her since. Now I'm putting Sienna to bed and hoping like hell Alexis will be downstairs when I'm done.

I just want to talk to her. I want to make sure she's okay after what's transpired in the last twenty-four hours.

"Until the end of summer," I tell her.

"How much longer is that?" she asks.

I do the math in my head, wondering how time has gone by so fast. My chest feels tight at the thought of saying goodbye to Alexis.

"Three weeks," I tell her.

"I don't want her to leave," Sienna says with a crack in her voice.

It breaks my heart. I didn't think she would cling so tightly to a nanny within such a short period of time, but I also never expected Alexis to come in and fill the void in our home. She brings so much joy and energy to our lives. It's going to be hard without her here.

"Neither do I, sweetheart," I admit.

I snuggle closer to Sienna while her eyes get heavy. What are we going to do without Alexis? I know I should cut off whatever has started between the two of us. If it's this hard to even think about a goodbye, I can't imagine what it will feel like if things continue down the path they're going. I've already had one woman choose to walk away from me. Can I bear it happening a second time?

When I get back downstairs, I notice I'm alone, and disappointment floods my body. This is getting ridiculous. I told myself I would never feel like this after Angie left. I need to get my shit together.

I need a glass of wine. When I walk into the cellar, I stand there for a second as flashes of this afternoon come flooding back. Fuck, she was going to suck me off in the pantry. What would her mouth feel like wrapped around me?

Dammit! My dick is hard. I grab the Vivino Antinori Tignanello, before I open the bottle, grab a glass, and make my way into my bedroom. There's nothing like drinking by yourself to remind you just how alone you are in life.

I place the bottle and glass on my nightstand. Reaching behind my head, I pull my shirt off and rid myself of my belt. After I pour myself a glass, I prop myself up on my dark, wooden headboard. The first sip goes down gracefully and showcases its silky tannins. I rest my head on the headboard and close my eyes.

A sudden light tap on my door startles me.

"Sienna?" I call quietly.

She normally just opens my door and barges in if she's had a bad dream or is sick.

"It's me," Alexis' silky voice echoes through the door.

I quickly jump up from the bed and place my glass on the nightstand. I take long strides to my door and open it up. She's standing there in a pair of pink silk shorts and a white tank top. I can see her nipples through her shirt, and I already want them in my mouth.

"Is everything okay?" I ask her.

She nods her head up and down. "I just couldn't stop thinking about you. You've...ummm...helped me out twice, and I haven't...at all with you," she says nervously.

I bite my lip in an effort to hide the smile that my body wants to display. It's absolutely adorable that she's so damn worried about making me feel good. She really has been with some assholes if she thinks it's more important to please me than to worry about herself.

I want to do it again for her. Making her come is addicting.

"I told you I didn't do any of that expecting anything in return."

"What if I want to do it?" she says with a small smile forming on her face.

Fuck, how does a man say no to that? I don't think I have it in me, but I don't even have time to respond because she takes a couple steps forward and reaches up on her toes, pressing her lips to mine.

I stand still as our lips slowly slide over each other. Something in me snaps, and I grab the fabric of her shirt and slam her body to mine. I need to feel her soft body against mine. I wrap my arms around her and lift her up, kicking the door shut behind us.

I move us over toward the bed, but when I try to lay her down, she stops and pulls away from me as she shakes her head at me. Without speaking any words, she drops to her knees.

My dick is as hard as a rock at just the sight of her on her knees.

She reaches up and unbuttons my jeans with steady hands. I fucking love the fact that she seems eager to please me. It's hot as hell.

After she unzips me, her hands come up to the top of my jeans, and pulls them down with my briefs. My dick pops out and bounces in her face. I notice her eyes open wide as she takes me in.

"Everything alright down there, princess?" I ask.

Her eyes blink rapidly before landing on me. "You're bigger than anything I've ever..." she trails off.

A slow, wicked grin takes over my face. "It'll fit, baby."

She reaches up with a hesitant hand. I wonder how long it's been since she's touched a man like this. The thought of her with someone else brings up this boiling sense of rage. I quickly squash the thought and focus on watching the beauty in front of me.

When her hand finally wraps around me, my entire body tenses at the sensation. I could blow in seconds; the sight alone is enough to do me in.

Then she starts to slowly move her hand up and down with the perfect grip. She opens her mouth and places my tip on her tongue, and moves her tongue back and forth over the bottom. Her mouth hangs open the entire time while my dick just sits at the entrance of her mouth. It's the sexiest fucking thing I've ever witnessed.

Until precum dribbles out of my dick onto her tongue, and she moans as she pulls away and drinks it up.

"Holy. Fuck. Baby. Do you like the taste of me on your tongue?" I growl at her.

She nods her head at me. "I want more," she tells me before she moves forward to take more of me into her mouth.

My head falls back in complete and utter euphoria as she starts to work her way up and down my shaft.

Why the hell did I think she was going to be this shy and inno-cent woman in the bedroom? This is downright fucking dirty, and she doesn't even know it. It's the pure joy that she is exuding that makes it so damn filthy.

She hollows out her cheeks and really starts to pump me. I can't help but grab her hair and aggressively tug at it to try to regain some semblance of control, even though she is completely own-ing me right now. The tingling inside of me starts at the base of my dick. Shit, I'm about to blow.

I pull her hair back as I try to get her off of me so I don't blow in her mouth, but she isn't having it. She must know what I'm trying to tell her because she shakes her head and just goes at me harder.

"Fuck, I'm coming!" I almost shout at her as my orgasm rips through me.

Several ropes of cum shoot down her throat as she works my entire load from me. When she pops off me, she wipes her mouth with the back of her hand.

I pull her off the floor and slam my mouth down on hers.

In between kisses, I thank her. "That was amazing. I don't want to know where the hell you learned to do that, but thank you."

She smiles. "I've never enjoyed doing it before...until now."

Fuck. Satisfaction runs through me at her words.

"Your turn again," I whisper into her mouth as my hands start to run up her body.

I start to trail kisses down her neck as she lets out a low moan. I feel her start to pull away, and I catch her line of sight as she stares at the wine.

"Wine in the bedroom?" She smiles up at me. "Makes sense. You always make wine sound so damn sexy. It seems fitting here in your room."

I begin to run my fingers up her arms before they glide over her chest.

"Wine is sexy. Although, it has nothing on you."

I lightly move the straps of her top off her shoulders as I watch them slide down to her elbows.

"I don't know about that," she whispers as her breasts expose themselves to me.

I make a low groan at the sight of her perfect tits. "Baby, look at you."

"The way you talk about wine. I could never imagine you talking about me like that," she breathes.

I look over at my glass of wine then back at the beauty in front of me who thinks I can't make her feel as sexy as my passion. Challenge accepted.

"Lie down on my bed, Alexis. I'll prove to you how damn sexy you are."

She takes a step back and lifts herself up onto my bed before lying all the way down.

"Good girl. We need to get rid of these." I gesture to her clothes as I pull her top down. "They're just gonna get in the way for what I have planned for you."

When her top reaches her waist, I pull down her silk bottoms as well until she is completely bared to me. I throw her clothes on the floor and reach for the wine glass, then climb on top of her until I'm kneeling over her thighs.

I bring the wine glass up to my nose and inhale.

"There are nine characteristics that make a wine great, that make it the best thing you've ever put in your mouth. Distinctiveness is one of them. Sometimes you try a wine, and it's no different than a hundred others before them. It doesn't spark any real difference that makes you stop in your tracks and know that you have something special in front of you," I tell her as I drag my fingers down from between her breasts down to her belly button.

I can feel her body shudder underneath my touch. My fingers ascend back up and swirl around each nipple.

"The moment I saw you, I knew you were distinct. Everything about you draws me further into your orbit. And looking at your body, I know I'll never see a sexier woman in my life."

I squeeze a nipple between my thumb and finger. I want her to be with me in this moment. I want her body aware of what I can do to it. Her back arches at the pain, and she releases a slight cry.

I sit back up and take a sip of the wine.

"Mmmm. The perfect balance, which is another characteristic. You, Alexis, are the perfect balance between beautiful and sexy. Shy and bold. Innocent and sinful. Sweet and sour. You're everything mixed into one."

"Do you want a taste? It's a *Vivino Antinori Tignanello.*"

She nods her head, but when she makes an effort to sit up, I stop her.

"Don't move. You'll get a taste when I decide you're ready," I tell her.

I lift the glass just above her stomach and let it drip down into her belly button. The red wine sits there waiting for me, and I begin to kiss and lick around her belly button as she squirms in an effort to stay still.

"The next one is complexity. A great wine doesn't just reveal itself all at once. It tells a story over time, reveals itself more as you continue to taste it. Now...open your mouth."

I move my mouth over to the wine and suck it into my mouth, then I crawl forward with the wine and release it into her open mouth.

"Leave it on your tongue for a second, then swallow."

She listens to my instructions, and I watch her throat as she gulps down the contents.

"As much as I love this wine and its complexity," I whisper as my mouth hangs just over hers, our lips brushing as I talk, "it's nothing compared to you. I could spend forever trying to memorize your body." I kiss her lips.

"Its reactions to my touch."

Kiss.

"And just when I think I've figured everything out, you'll be there to throw me for another loop."

I move my mouth to kiss her neck.

"But more than the complexity of your body, there's your mind and heart. They are just as sexy and layered as your body."

"Gabriel," she whispers as her hand lands on the back of my neck.

I continue to trail kisses down her collarbone until I reach her breasts. I grab both of them in each hand and begin to knead, leaning forward and wrapping my lips around one of her nipples. Fuck, she tastes so damn good. I need to taste her again before I lose my mind.

I scoot down the bed until my face is exactly where it wants to be. I use one hand to move her thigh over so I can get the view I want.

"Length is another one," I tell her before my tongue takes a long swipe up her center. "The better the wine, the longer the flavors last on your tongue. I could taste you for hours today after my face was buried in your pussy."

She lets out a gasp when my lips wrap around her clit and suck. When I put my fingers inside her and feel her wetness dripping down them, my dick twitches.

"Gabriel," she begs. "More."

I moan into her clit as I quicken my strokes, and she starts to pant. She grabs me by the hair and pulls my head up, and as soon as I look into her eyes, I see pure desire.

"I want more. I want you inside of me."

I rise up onto my hands. I wasn't expecting to have sex tonight. For some reason, foreplay was always the only thing on the table for me. I'm used to only sleeping with random women that mean nothing to me since Angie left. Sleeping with Alexis feels dangerous, but right now, the thought of burying my dick inside of her is too tempting. And the possibility of hurting her feelings when she's asking me for something so monumental for her would be too much.

I move forward until our lips are together, and our tongues stroke each other. She moans into my mouth.

"Mmmm. I taste myself on you. I've never tasted myself."

"What do you think?"

"I like it. We'll see how long it lasts on my tongue," she whispers before she reaches up and brings our lips back together.

Fuck! She doesn't even realize how dirty that is.

"Damn, you keep talking to me like that, I'm not sure if I'll be able to hold back."

She smiles shyly at me. "So, do you have condoms?"

I sit up and grab a condom out of my nightstand. Before I begin to open it, I move myself on top of her and look into her eyes.

"Are you sure you want to do this?" I ask her. "I know you've only done it with one person, and I don't want to pressure you."

"You're not pressuring me at all. I want this, but I might not be able to..." She raises her eyebrows suggestively.

I bite my lip as I smile down at her. "I doubt it, but if that happens...I'll go right back down there with my tongue, baby. I promise as long as you're with me, I'll take care of you, and I'll never make you feel bad about it."

I lean down and offer a chaste kiss before pulling away to get back on my knees. I grab the condom off the bed and tear it open, Alexis watching me intently as I roll it down, her intense stare making my dick jump in excitement.

"How long has it been for you, Alexis?" I ask, feeling oddly nervous, like it's my own first time.

"Four years," she speaks softly. "But you're extremely big compared to the other guy."

Knowing the dipshit who made her afraid of sex has a small dick makes me oddly happy. Maybe I don't need to find him and beat the crap out of him. He has a lifetime of only giving women inadequate sexual experiences.

"This is gonna sting for a bit," I tell her as I lay my body on top of hers.

I don't make any move to line myself up yet. I want to get her warmed back up so she's completely ready to take me.

Putting the weight on one arm, I use the other to run my fingers over her breasts and then down to her pussy. I place two fingers inside her and curl them up to repeatedly hit her in her most sensitive spot. I reclaim her lips as I crush them to mine, my tongue exploring the recesses of her mouth.

I pull back and watch her jaw fall slack when my thumb starts to rub over her clit. She's so wet that I can hear the slapping sounds each time my hand hits her walls. She is squirming beneath me, and it's tempting not to make her come right here.

"I think you're ready for me. I remove my hand and roll back over her.

Once I line myself up, I grip one of her hands above her head with mine before I inch forward. She hisses as the first couple inches of me enter her. I wait for her to adjust for a second before sliding the rest of the way in.

"Holy shit," she screams, squeezing my hand.

"I'm sorry, baby. I'm all the way in now." I offer kisses to her cheeks and neck. "Tell me when I can start to move."

She wiggles and adjusts herself underneath me, which makes my dick want more, but I wait patiently for her.

Chapter Eighteen

Alexis

The burn that came over me the second he pushed himself inside me was intense. It feels like losing my virginity all over again. Only this time, the man inside me makes me feel so damn sexy and confident.

I don't know what got into me tonight.

I was tossing and turning in bed, thinking about how much I wished we hadn't been interrupted this afternoon, and then I just...decided to go for it.

He's already made me feel so alive in the past forty-eight hours.

The pain starts to diminish, and just looking up at the man inside of me, feeling him stretch my walls, makes me start to feel excited.

"Okay. You can move," I urge.

He starts out slow, seemingly not wanting to hurt me again. His jaw is tight while he concentrates on moving carefully. With each thrust in, he does this circular motion that hits my clit and sends waves of pleasure to my core. I open my legs wider as all my defenses fall away.

"Fuck, Alexis. You feel amazing, like you were made for me," Gabriel states as he continues to move.

"Oh, god. Please don't stop. Keep moving. I need...I need..." I try to get words out, but each time he thrusts back inside, I lose my train of thought.

My hands run up his back, and I feel how defined his muscles are. When they reach the top, my fingers squeeze his shoulders in an effort to hold onto something.

"Tell me what you need, Alexis," he growls, which gets my attention.

"More. Go harder," I tell him.

He pushes from his elbows to his hands and starts to increase his speed and his power. I can feel myself getting wetter and wetter as my body starts to lose it. The thing that has me completely thrown for a loop is his eyes on me. He refuses to look anywhere but directly into my gaze, and it's this thrilling feeling that makes my stomach flutter. To have this man's sole attention feels incredible, but it's more than that. His eyes hold something in them, and I feel like they're trying to communicate with me.

The combination of the intimacy mixed with his movement brings me right to the brink of release. I feel my walls start to close in around him, which only intensifies the pleasure.

"Shit, baby. You're about to come already, aren't you? God, it feels so damn good."

His words are the final encouragement I need. My orgasm shoots through my body. I'm not sure what noises I'm making, only that I'm not the only one making them. We are both a mixture of growls, moans, and curse words.

After what feels like a slow-motion orgasm that goes on forever for both of us, Gabriel collapses on top of me. His face is tucked in the crook of my neck as we both work to catch our breaths. Neither of us makes any effort to move a muscle. I can feel his dick start to soften inside of me, and it makes me feel so close to him.

I was never close enough to Trevor to notice something like that. I actually can't remember him staying with me. Immediately after *he* came, he was out of me and cleaning himself up.

Could it be that all this time, it wasn't me that had the issue? Was I just with the wrong kind of guys?

It certainly feels that way lying here with Gabriel.

He lifts his head and starts to lightly kiss my neck. It makes me feel like I'm special to him, a dangerous feeling.

"How are you doing?" he asks before leaning up to look at me.

"I think I feel really freakin' good, actually." I smile up at him.

The grin that spreads across his face is bigger than one I've seen him give, and it makes me shiver.

"Me too," he says.

"But I didn't retain anything you taught me about wine," I joke.

He throws his head back and lets out a carefree laugh.

"Then we must keep educating you until the information stays put." He kisses my lips before pushing himself off me and pulling out. The loss of him filling me up, coupled with the warmth of his skin, leaves me instantly wishing I could have him back.

"I'm just gonna go take care of the condom. You stay put," he tells me as he scoots off the bed.

I move my head to the pillow and pull the covers over me. His bed feels amazing, and it smells just like him. As he exits his bathroom, I can't help but watch his body as he heads toward his dresser. His muscles are so distinct, mesmerizing me.

He pulls out a pair of black boxer briefs and steps into them before he comes over to join me under the covers.

"Damn, you're so fucking sexy, Alexis. I'm getting hard again already," he says before pulling me into his arms.

When I tiptoed down here tonight, I didn't think it would result in the two of us cuddling at the end of the night.

I move my hand to his chest and wiggle around until I feel comfortable. Being like this with him feels oddly natural.

"How could you possibly be getting hard again?" I laugh into his chest. "You've already come twice in the last half hour."

"Maybe it's because I've literally fantasized about you every day for the last five weeks."

His admission has me lifting my head to look at him. "Have you really?"

He tucks some stray hair behind my ear. "Can you blame me? You know you're beautiful."

I'm not sure how to reply to that, so I lean in and kiss his lips. What was supposed to be a peck turns into long slow kisses with lots of tongue.

"Want some wine?" he asks, reaching for the glass after we pull away from each other.

"Sure." I take the glass from him and take a sip. "Mmmm...tastes different when it's not given to me directly from your mouth."

"I think I like drinking wine like that. It should be the new way you taste test." He smirks at me.

We spend the next hour sharing the remaining wine and talking. I tell him more about my upbringing, and he tells me about his. He has such a close-knit family, and his parents are very involved. I hate the stab of jealousy that gets exposed when I compare what others have. What would it be like to have a mother that was so in your business that it was borderline overbearing? Some people may complain about it, but I long for it.

My own mother hasn't even called me once while I've been here. Alone in a new city with a new job, she doesn't even seem to be worried. If something happened to me, how long would it be before she realized I was missing?

I curl into Gabe's arms to try and get rid of the depressing thoughts. His warmth and slow breaths calm my racing mind, making my eyes start to flutter closed.

Chapter Nineteen

Gabriel

Last night didn't go how I thought it would. What was supposed to be a new experience for her turned into something new for me. Sex has never felt like that before. Shit, I don't know what was in the air, but it felt different. Looking into her eyes, I felt hypnotized and exposed. And she was so damn tight; the grip on my cock had me ready to blow the entire time. I was only able to hold on because I *needed* her to come.

I look over at the clock on my nightstand. This is the first time in years that I've skipped a morning workout, but with her lying sound asleep in my arms, I didn't want to wake her up. Now it's getting close to when I have to be at work.

I nudge my shoulder against hers and whisper her name.

She moans and stretches her arms before she leans up on her hands and looks around. She looks adorable as I watch her face contort in confusion, trying to figure out where she is.

My eyes travel south, and see her perky breasts hanging right in front of me.

"Morning." She smiles at me, and my heart skips a beat.

I lift my eyebrows as her nipples harden.

"It's a very good mornin'. Especially waking up with these," I tell her as I massage her breasts and then pinch her nipples.

She giggles as I move her thigh over my stomach and seat her on top of me. She wiggles her ass on my cock, and this time, she's the one with raised eyebrows.

"I swear waking you up was innocent," I tell her. "I need to go to work. But then you flashed me with your tits, and now I'm thinking about other things."

"Like what?" she asks in a sultry voice.

"Like how I need to sink my cock deep inside you right now. I need that virgin-tight cunt to get me off this morning," I say as my hands run up and down her thighs.

I can feel the moisture gather on my briefs, proof that she isn't as innocent as she thinks she is. You don't get turned on by those words unless you have some naughty in you.

She surprises me by reaching over my shoulder and opening my drawer for a condom. I pull down my briefs and kick them off while she rips the foil open with her mouth before rolling it down my shaft.

"How are you feeling this morning? Are you sore?" I ask her, remembering how long it's been for her.

"I'm definitely sore, but you're also super sexy and tempting." She bites her bottom lip shyly.

"Are you okay riding me this time?"

My thumb reaches for her clit and starts to rub circles. It's the sexiest thing to watch her face reveal just how much she likes it.

"I've never been on top before," she admits.

"It's okay. I'll help you along," I tell her.

She nods her head, but I can tell she's a bit nervous. I grab my dick and line it up. With my hands on each side of her hips, I pull her down slowly.

Shit, I'd already forgotten just how good it feels to be inside of her, even just a couple inches.

I let her decide when she's ready to take all of me as I let my hands rest on her hips. Her hands lean down on my pecs as she slowly sinks all the way down until her ass is resting on my balls.

Without my direction, she lifts herself back up and slams down. Her head falls back and her hands reach for her breasts.

Fuck, it's hot watching her find her own sexuality.

She starts to increase her pace, and when she lifts her head, her jaw is slack and she looks like she is on the verge of coming.

"This feels so good," she whispers as she continues, only this time when she bottoms out, she moves in circles as her clit drags on my stomach.

"Fuck, baby. You're a natural at this," I tell her.

She starts slamming down on me so hard that my headboard starts to hit the wall. I'm no longer able to hold back my orgasm. I dig my fingers into her thighs and curse out my release.

Thankfully, she isn't far behind me as I feel her walls squeeze my dick.

She's glistening in her own sweat, and I've never seen anything sexier. She falls down on top of me.

"I can't believe I never knew it could be like this," she whispers into my chest.

Her words fill me with pride. I can't believe I'm the lucky bastard who gets to be with her.

Three hours later, I'm standing in the breakroom at my office. Alexis and I agreed to go shower separately after our morning fiasco. I didn't want to risk getting caught by Sienna. She normally sleeps in, but you never know what can happen with a four-year-old.

The pot of coffee brews in front of me. While I wait, my mind drifts off to the last couple days. My mind and body have been consumed with Alexis. What started out as me trying to help her relax and enjoy herself sexually has turned into something I don't think I can control or slow down. Like now, I can't wait for work to end so I can get home and see her.

"What's gotten into you?" Lucas interrupts my thoughts as he walks into the room.

"Just waiting for coffee," I tell him.

The pot is ready, so I grab it and pour myself another cup. I turn around, and Lucas is leaning against the fridge with a strange look on his face.

"What?" I lean my head to the side to try to figure him out.

He pushes off the fridge and grabs a mug to pour himself some coffee, and then he faces me.

"You've been in an increasingly better mood lately, but this morning is a whole other level," he says with a smile.

"I don't know what you're talking about," I rebuke with irritation.

I try to walk out of the room, but he stands in front of me.

"Come on, admit it! For two years, you've moped around this office, ready to blow up at anyone who even looks at you the wrong way. Now, I walk in on you waiting for coffee with a smile on your face like it's Christmas morning and you're five years old."

"I wasn't smiling," I defend.

Was I? It doesn't sound like me to just smile out of nowhere.

He takes a sip of his coffee. "Dude, your mouth couldn't stretch any bigger than it just was. What gives? Could it be your pretty nanny making you Mr. Sunshine?"

"That's none of your business," I reply, then walk around him and straight out the door.

I hear his laugh echo through the hall as I do my best to escape back to my office.

Not much time passes before I hear a loud knock on my door. I don't even get a chance to respond to the knock before my door is opening, and all three siblings are filing in.

I glare at Lucas, who seems rather happy with himself at the moment.

"So, I hear congratulations are in order." Marcus slaps my shoulder, then moves to the couch on the far end of my office.

"Stop messing with him, guys." Mia defends my honor. She takes a seat across from me with a sweet smile on her face. "Is it true?"

I take that back, she's just as bad as my brothers. She just does it with class.

"What are you talking about?" I respond as I drag my hand through my hair.

She smiles at me. "Are you sleeping with Alex?"

"I don't see how that's any of your business."

"So you are. Good for you," Marcus shouts from the couch.

I look over at him and glare. He lifts his hands up and shrugs like he has no idea what I could be offended by.

"She's a really sweet girl, Gabe. Be careful," Mia warns.

Anger scatters through my body at her warning. I don't appreciate her acting like I'm a bad guy who would treat Alexis poorly.

"Why the hell is it *me* who has to be careful? I'm the one who got my heart stomped on by my ex-wife, not the other way around. I'm the one raising a four-year-old by myself."

"Easy there," Lucas says. "I think she just means don't lead her on if this is just a summer fling."

Is this just a summer fling? What's going to happen when her time is up in three weeks? Is she going to leave this city behind, and Sienna and me will just be a distant memory she sees as a pit stop in her life? She's so young and has her whole life ahead of her.

This question sits with me for the rest of the day, but I try to shake it as I'm driving home from work. It was one night...there's no need to analyze anything.

When I walk into my house, I hear music playing loudly through the kitchen. As I walk in, I'm hit with Sienna standing on her stool next to a sexy-looking Alexis in pink cotton shorts and a baggy gray sweatshirt. They're dancing around and laughing while mixing something in a bowl.

I'm not exactly sure what it is they're making, but Alexis pulls the spatula out of the bowl and licks the contents. My dick twitches in my pants at the sight. Fuck, that damn tongue of hers has some serious skill.

Alexis leans the spatula down for Sienna to get some. They both smile and groan over how good it is.

"Okay, let's get these babies rolled out onto a baking sheet and pop them in the oven," Alexis says.

When she turns around, she screams, and the spatula flies right into her chest.

"Oh my god! You scared me!" She puts her hand to her heart.

"Daddy!" Sienna screams and runs into my arms.

"Hi, sweetie! What are you two baking over here?" I ask as I pick her up and kiss her cheek.

"Chocolate chip cookies!" she bellows.

"Can't wait to try one," I tell her as I put her down.

She runs off, screaming that she has to go potty. The girl always waits until the last second before it's almost too late. It drives me insane.

I stuff my hands in my pockets and glance back at Alexis. She is wiping some cookie dough off her sweatshirt. At closer inspection, I see a lacrosse stick across the front. Call it instinct, but I know she doesn't play lacrosse.

"What's with the sweatshirt? You didn't play lacrosse, did you?" I nod to her chest.

"Huh?" she asks with confusion as she looks down at her sweatshirt. "Oh, no, I never played. Some guy just left it at my apartment after some party."

Possessive jealousy comes over me at the mention of some other guy. I don't know if they were ever romantic together, but I don't give a shit. All I know is that I want her out of that sweatshirt *now*. She should be wearing something of mine.

I step into her until I can almost taste her. Grabbing the front of the hoodie, I pull her against me.

"I want you *out* of this damn thing right away. Go take it off, and then throw it away. You don't wear another man's clothes around me," I growl out.

She bites her lip and swallows. "I didn't realize it would bother you."

"Well, it does. I want you to go into my closet and pick something of mine. From now on in this house, if you're cold, you wear my sweatshirt. Got it?"

She nods her head up and down.

"Good. Now go...get that off and come back in something of mine."

She places the spatula on the counter and walks toward my room with a little sway to her ass. I lean against the counter and cross my arms across my chest. I don't know where that anger and passion came from, I've never felt such overpowering jealousy in my life. Seeing her in that hoodie made me feel like she could never be mine, and I just snapped.

She comes back out a minute later in my gray Italia hoodie that I got on a trip when the weather turned a bit colder than I had planned.

Fuck, that's what I like to see. I feel like a gorilla who wants to pump his chest with pride.

She smirks at me when she gets back to the kitchen.

"Is this better, sir?" she says with a bit of mischief in her tone.

I can't tell if she's playing with me, but it makes me want to grab her hair and force her on her knees. Before I can say anything, Sienna comes barreling back into the room.

She jumps around in front of Alexis. "Can we finish the cookies now?"

"Of course, let's get rolling," Alexis tells her.

"Hey, that's my daddy's shirt," Sienna says as she points at Alexis.

"Oh, um," Alexis starts while she glances at me. I offer a smirk in her direction, interested to see what she's going to say. "I got cookie dough on my other one. Your daddy let me borrow his."

Sienna shrugs her shoulders at that response and gets back on her stool.

Alexis glares at me as she walks over to the counter, and I can't help but let out a small laugh.

Chapter Twenty

Alexis

Once Sienna figures out how to roll the cookie dough, I steal a glance at Gabriel. He's looking thoughtfully at Sienna and me, and I wonder what he's thinking.

He's in such a good mood today, though. I don't know if I've ever seen him smile this much, and I want to believe I have something to do with it, but the thought seems kind of ludicrous. When have I ever made someone that happy? My own parents don't even get that much joy from my presence.

"How am I doing?" Sienna interrupts my thoughts.

I look down at a huge hodgepodge of shapes and sizes.

"Oh, wow! Look at you. Good job, honey!" I tell her with enthusiasm.

"What do you think, Daddy?" She looks up at Gabe.

He gives her a pat on the head. "They look pretty awesome. I can't wait to taste them."

We both look at each other and smile, knowing the cookies look like a disaster. They are going to cook completely unevenly with all the different sizes on the tray. But that isn't what matters. We're baking them for fun, not for perfection.

"I'm gonna get started on dinner," Gabe tells me as he moves towards the fridge.

Great, I get to spend the next half hour watching him roam about the kitchen. It's like porn for women. He likes to roll up his sleeves, exposing the muscles and veins in his forearms. Not to mention the fact that his ass in work pants is divine.

Over the next hour, I try to keep my head down while Sienna and I finish the cookies and then clean up our mess. I manage to stay pretty distracted, minus the stolen glances and touches. Gabriel seems to keep finding reasons to rest his hand on my lower back.

Whether it was to peek over my shoulder and take a look at the finished cookies or to get something from the drawer I was in front of.

It's massively distracting and making me feel really hot. I'm going to need a shower tonight to cool me off.

After dinner, Gabe takes Sienna upstairs for her bath and bedtime routine. I do what I can to clean the kitchen, then decide to head up to my room to read for a bit. Dinner has me feeling all sorts of weird emotions. Between Sienna gushing over our time together, Gabe's sexy looks, and the laughter we all shared, I'm starting to feel like my heart is in jeopardy.

I'm leaving in two and a half weeks. What is going to happen when my time is up? Am I just going to leave these two behind and never see them again? I still need to start thinking about where I want to settle down and find a job.

I open my book and try to get lost in the pages of someone else's reality. It only helps for a minute, and then my brain is back to thoughts of Gabriel.

I reach for my phone to call the one person I know will be able to talk some sense into me.

"You've been dodging my calls. Something is going on," Alicia answers.

I roll my eyes. She is too perceptive; I can never get anything by her.

"How could you possibly know that?" I ask.

"Because you always go quiet when you have something to say but don't know how to say it."

Damn, I know I do that. I just wasn't aware it was that obvious.

"So, what's going on? You still trying to deny the hotness of your boss? Is it driving you mad?" She laughs at her own jab.

I sigh into the phone. "There's no denying anything between him and me anymore."

I swear I can hear her fumbling with things in the background, completely caught off guard by my admission.

"What the hell does that mean? Did something *happen* between you two? Oh my god! Did you guys have sex?"

"Yes! I'm so screwed... I went and had life-changing, earth-shattering sex with him, and now I'm starting to feel things."

"Like love kind of feelings? Are you falling in love with him, Alex?" Her voice raises in question.

I roll over to my side and groan into the phone as I bring the blanket up to my face. "I don't know. This is all so new for me. I've only ever really dated one guy, and you know that didn't end well. I mean, if it's not love now...I can see it getting there quickly. Am I an idiot for sleeping with him?"

"Fuck no! You're human. I would've done the same thing. Has he told you how he feels?"

"Yeah, right. He just stopped being a dick to me a couple days ago. He doesn't talk much about his feelings, if ever. Plus, I'm his nanny. I'm probably just another notch in the belt for him. A funny story to tell his friends when they're out for drinks."

Oh, God. I would die if that's all this is to him.

"Oh, come on, Alex! Give the guy more credit than that. If he was that big of a dick, I don't think you would find him so attractive. You're not like that. You don't like guys strictly based on their appearance. I know this! I've lived with you for three years now."

"What am I supposed to do? My job is over in a couple weeks. Should I look for a job here in Cleveland to stay near them? Do you think that would sound desperate if I told him that I wanted to do that?"

The line is silent for a minute. I think I've lost connection with her when I hear her sigh.

"Honestly, I don't know if I would recommend taking a job in a city for a guy you've been with for a couple days. You need to think about yourself right now. I've watched you take a backseat to everybody else's life and happiness for years with your family. I don't want to see you do it again. If this guy isn't confessing his love openly and begging you to stay with him, I wouldn't plan my life around him. You deserve the world. Don't settle for anything less."

"I don't know what it's like to put myself first like that. You know I struggle with it," I whisper as I try to hold back tears.

"I know you do, but you need to learn how. The more you do it, the more you will start to believe that you're actually worth it. You have to do one before the other will come."

I blink quickly to try to fight off the tears. I don't want to cry right now. I've wasted too many tears in my life feeling sorry for myself.

"Thanks, Alicia. You know how much I love you, right?" I ask her.

"I know, girl. I love you too," she replies. "I have to ask, earth-shattering sex? I need more details on that ASAP!"

I laugh. I guess I brought that on myself. You can't admit that to her and not expect her to request more details.

"Yes, earth-shattering. It was just sooo...I don't know. There are really no words to describe it. It's like he knew exactly what to do to get me there. And he is so into it. Like...he seems to really enjoy getting me off in any way possible. It's like for the first time, I can just relax and enjoy it."

"Damn, girl. Good for you."

I smile. "Yeah. It's unlike anything I've ever experienced. And I like pleasing him, it makes the experience even better for me."

She whistles. "Okay, well, here's what you're going to do. You're going to fuck like horny little teenagers for the next couple weeks and just enjoy the time together. Then you are going to say goodbye and come live with me while you figure out your next move."

Just hearing those words eases the anxiety I've been as feeling. I had a lot of panic attacks my freshman year of college, and Alicia was always there to help me through them.

I think I've been avoiding job searching because the thought is overwhelming, and the familiar panic starts to rise whenever I think about it.

"Thanks for the offer. I might have to take you up on that. I hope you won't mind if I'm a ball of emotions with a broken heart in a couple weeks."

"Not at all. We'll just eat sweets and drink wine. The cure for heartache."

I laugh. "I like the sound of that."

"But seriously, just enjoy the next two weeks. You've got someone worshipping your body and making you feel good. We'll figure things out together after."

I take a deep breath, knowing I can do this. She's right, I do deserve to enjoy this time. She doesn't even know the extent of my sex deprivation.

"Thanks. I love you," I tell her.

"Love you too, girl."

As soon as we hang up, I decide to jump in the shower. After I discard my clothes, I put my arm into the stream to make sure it's warm enough. As soon as I step in, I close my eyes and let the heat relax the tension built up in my body. I'm not sure how long I stand under the water with my eyes closed, letting my brain float off to another world, but it's long enough to miss the sounds of my bathroom door opening.

It's not until the shower door opens that I jump and open my eyes.

Gabriel is stepping into my shower with nothing on his body. I'm speechless as I watch him walk towards me. My eyes follow his every move until I have to tilt my head up to keep my eyes on his.

"What are you doing here?" I whisper.

He wraps his hand around my waist and pulls me into his arms.

"I've been waiting downstairs for you. You never came," he says with a hint of anger.

"I didn't want to just assume that you wanted me down there," I admit.

His hand travels down to my ass and squeezes a cheek. I can feel his dick hard against my stomach, and my body clenches in anticipation. I want to feel him slide inside of me again.

"From now on, always assume I want you down there with me. I want you whenever I can have you," he says.

My heart skips a beat at his words. *Just remember this is for fun*, I remind myself.

"You want to know what I can't get out of my fucking head?" he asks, and I angle my head in question. "You calling me sir while wearing my sweatshirt. It made me want to grab you and own your mouth. Make you work my dick until I shoot into your mouth."

His words are so dirty and dominating, not to mention border-line offensive, but they make me feel excited. I like that he has such wild thoughts about me. I reach for his hand and kiss his palm. He moves it to my cheek and rubs up and down. We both lean in for a kiss. It's slow and unhurried as our tongues take their time moving with each other.

I pull back to look at him and move his hand to the back of my head. When he doesn't understand what I'm trying to say, I know I have to use my words which is kind of scary. I'm not used to being this brave.

"Grab my hair," I tell him.

He looks at me with a bit of confusion.

"Grab my hair and make me work your dick," I continue.

His eyes grow wide when he realizes what I'm telling him to do. I feel his fingers squeeze around my hair like his control is about to snap.

"Alexis, I didn't mean it literally. You're so inexperienced, and I... I don't want to make you feel uncomfortable."

"I am inexperienced, but I want to experience this with you. I want to feel what it's like when you completely give in to your desires. This is for me too, seeing you like this..." I explain.

His fingers grip my hair tighter, and my jaw falls slightly at the pain, but it only spurs me on more. It shows me that this is exactly what I want.

"Fuck, Alexis. I'm not gonna be able to hold back when you talk like that," he growls. "My dick is so hard for you it hurts."

"Don't hold back. I want it all. Right now. Please," I whisper as my body leans in slightly until it's right in front of his dick.

His other hand grabs more hair, and he pulls back, my head following as it exposes my mouth to him. He moves until his tip is lined up with my face. With the circle of his hips, his precum starts to paint my lips.

"Fuck. You're going to be the death of me, Alexis. Look at your mouth covered in my cum. Lick your lips, I want you to taste me."

I do as he says and slowly drag my tongue in a circle around my lips, making sure to get every last drop. It tastes salty and bitter, masculine, just like Gabriel.

"Good girl," he tells me. "Now open your mouth for me, baby."

I do as I'm told, pride filling me at being called a good girl. When he pushes his hips forward, the first couple inches of him enter my mouth. I roll my tongue around the bottom of his dick before I wrap my lips around his length.

His hands fist my hair again while he starts to move his hips back and forth. He goes slow at first as he allows me some time to adjust. When he thinks I'm ready, he starts to fuck my mouth. I mean, really fuck my mouth. Tears start to spill over my eyelids as he relentlessly moves.

"There you go, babe. Your mouth feels like heaven. Fuck! Wrap those lips tighter around my cock," he demands.

I follow his instructions and strain my lips while keeping my tongue out for his dick to glide over.

"Shit... just like that, baby. Oh, god!"

His head falls back in ecstasy. The arousal between my legs becomes uncomfortable, and I reach down to run circles over my clit, eliciting a moan.

He brings his head back down, and when his eyes catch my hand on myself, they turn even darker.

Without any warning, he rips me off his dick and brings me to a standing position. I'm breathing hard and fast as I try to catch my breath. Both of us stand together as we gasp for air in the thick steam.

"Why did you make me stop?" I question.

"I can't fucking watch you so desperate to come that you start touching yourself. It's my job to make you feel good. Change of plans, I'm going to fuck you from behind in this shower. Please tell me you're on birth control," he begs.

I nod my head up and down.

"Can I fuck you like this? I'm clean."

"Yes," I rasp.

He slams his lips on mine, then pulls away.

"Put your hands on the wall behind you," he instructs.

I do as I'm told and look over my shoulder and see him staring down at my behind.

"Shit. You have the best ass," he says as he grabs each cheek with a hard grip and spreads them. "One of these days, I'm going to show you the pleasures that come with this."

He grazes his thumb over my opening which makes me squirm. I wouldn't think that would ever turn me on, the thought of being touched there, but when Gabriel does it, my body reacts.

He wraps his hand around his dick and lines himself up before pushing in. The force of it throws me forward, and I have to lock my arms to keep myself from slamming into the wall. It takes me a minute to adjust to his size.

"Holy. Shit. Your pussy feels amazing like this," he says, and I feel his forehead hit my back.

When he can feel my body relax and adjust to him, he starts to pump in and out. His hand comes back to grab my hair and gives it a tug.

I let out a loud moan, knowing we can make noise while in the shower.

"Fuck, you like being dominated, don't you? We're going to explore that more, baby," he tells me.

I don't know what it is about his control that turns me on so much. I think part of it is knowing that I don't have to think about what I need to do next or if he likes what I'm doing. I just do what I'm told, and he uses his words to tell me how much he loves it.

The sound of our bodies together in the water echoes throughout the bathroom.

"Oh, god... Gabriel!" I cry out.

I know how much he loves me saying his full name. This time is no exception as it draws out a growl from his throat.

"Fucking take it. I feel that pussy squeezing me," he remarks.

His words make my body clench, bringing me closer to orgasm.

This time when he pulls out, he stops for a minute, then slowly enters back in with a quick thrust at the end. He reaches around my waist and starts rubbing circles around my clit.

"This is mine to play with. You ever feel the need to come, you tell me. You got it?" he asks.

I nod my head, unable to formulate words. He continues the circles and the slower thrusts. That's all it takes for me to come apart at his touch. My body convulses as the strongest orgasm I've ever felt rips through me. At the height of its spiral, he picks up his pace again as he chases his own release.

He's all cuss words and dirty remarks as he pumps his own release inside of me.

He pulls out and kneels down behind me. I'm not sure what he is doing until I feel his thumbs part my lips.

"Squeeze for me. I want to see my cum drop of out of your pussy," he says.

HOLY SHIT.

Chapter Twenty-One

Gabriel

I know this is caveman shit, but that's how I feel when I'm with her. I've never in my life wanted to make somebody mine in every way. And the good girl that she is, she clenches her pussy for me. Watching my cum start to spill out of her makes my dick jerk with excitement.

"Fuck, just like that, Alexis. You look so damn sexy filled with my cum."

I use one thumb to hold her lips open while I insert two fingers into her channel, my fingers instantly coated in my release. As I push them back in, it starts to dribble down my hand.

She looks over her shoulder with hungry eyes. When she sees the evidence on my hand, she does something that will be seared into my brain forever. She spins around and kneels down with me as she brings my hand to her mouth and proceeds to lick it off my hand.

"Alexis," I growl.

When she's tasted every last drop, I bring her mouth to mine in a hungry kiss. How can someone so inexperienced blow my mind like no one else has before? I grab her chin and mold our tongues together. When we both pull away, the air is charged with our rekindled desire.

"Let's clean up and get out of the shower. I still have plenty more I want to do to you tonight," I tease.

She nods her head and takes my extended hand to stand up to move us under the water. I put in a large water tank when I remodeled this house, so the water is still running hot. I grab her shampoo bottle and squeeze some into her hands before doing the same to mine.

"I guess I'm going to smell like your rose petal shampoo tonight," I tell her as we both begin to massage the contents into our hair.

She giggles at me, which makes me smile down at her. When she starts to tilt her head back to rinse, I have the strangest urge to help her.

Instead of overthinking it, I give in to temptation.

"Let me help you," I whisper as my hands reach her hair and start to work the shampoo out.

She closes her eyes and lets me continue. The act feels intimate and very domestic, and it occurs to me that I never did anything like this with Angie. We lived such separate lives.

After our shower, she grabs pajamas, and we both make our way to my bedroom. I set my alarm early enough so that she can sneak out before Sienna wakes, and then I bring her into my chest for another kiss.

This morning, my brothers cornered me at the office to tell me that we were all going out for dinner and drinks at TOLI in Little Italy tonight. Ma is feeling much better, and she has been going on and on about how much she misses her granddaughter, so her and Pa are going to watch Sienna.

At the end of the day, Mia pops her head in my office.

"Hey," she says. "Just wanted to stop in and tell you to invite Alexis tonight. You guys both have the night free, and I want to get a chance to spend some more time with the woman who's stolen both my niece's and big brother's hearts."

She walks away before I have a chance to respond.

I pack up my things and get into my car. As I'm driving, I think about Alexis. We've spent every night of the past week in each other's arms. I've completely lost control of the situation. My heart is so completely involved at this point, I'm not sure there's any going back. I've been watching Sienna and Alexis together, and I've thought about what it would be like if we were all a family.

Is that something Alexis would ever want with me? Am I crazy for even thinking it's a possibility?

I want to bring her out with me tonight. It would be nice to be out in the world with her, but I'm afraid of leaving our little world that we've created in my home.

Would people judge our age difference? I know I'm not old and grey, but I'm not twenty-one anymore, either.

I pull into the driveway and notice my parents' car sitting in the front, even though I told them I would drop Sienna off. Seems pretty fitting for Ma to do things her own way.

When I open the door, I hear laughter echoing through the hall. It's an unfamiliar feeling, one that never occurred when I was married. Angie never cared to put in an effort with my family.

I walk into the kitchen and see everyone standing around a box of Corbo's baked goods. Sienna is sitting on the counter eating an Italian cookie with rainbow sprinkles, my father standing next to her. Alexis and my mother are on the other side of the island laughing as they eat what looks like coconut bars off their plates. I stand and observe in private before anybody notices me.

My mother is beaming at Alexis as she animatedly tells a story. I'm not even sure what she's saying, but even I'm drawn to Alexis as I watch her. Ma's head falls back in laughter and I can't help but smile.

Is it possible that I've already fallen in love with this brave, confident, thoughtful woman? Standing here in this moment as I watch her, it feels like it.

I clear my throat, and everyone turns their head my way as I finish walking in.

"Oh, hi, sweetie!" Ma greets me. "Now, I know you said you would drop her off, but I couldn't wait. We've already packed her things, so you don't have to."

I smile as I approach her and offer her cheek a kiss.

"I can't say I'm all that surprised. You never can let any of your children do something to make your life easier."

Pa laughs. "She's as stubborn as a mule. That's what I've always told her."

"Nothing wrong with her being excited to see her granddaughter," Alexis defends with a smile.

Pa points between Ma and Alexis. "You better watch out for these two. Two peas in a pod. They're dangerous together."

I chuckle and look down at the treats in the box, grabbing a cannoli. "And I see you brought over some treats as well?"

"Something's different about you," Ma analyzes me as I continue to eat.

I look down at myself. Same old as always.

I shrug. "I haven't changed anything. Same haircut, same suit."

She gives me a look up and down and shakes her head. "No, nothing like that. You seem...happy."

Pa looks between Alexis and me. "That's what love will do to ya. L'amore è bello."

Alexis starts to choke on her dessert at Pa's words. "Sorry," she croaks as she pounds her chest lightly. "Coconut flakes down the wrong pipe."

"Oy." Ma rolls her eyes at Pa. "Stupido uomo. Come on, Sienna, let's head back to Nonna and Papa's house."

"Can I have more cookies?" she asks excitedly.

"We'll see, mia bella. I have gnocchi waiting for supper. You eat good...you get a treat," Ma tells her.

I walk them to the front door and give Sienna a big hug and kiss goodbye. I open the door, but Sienna doesn't take a step to follow my parents out. Instead, she turns around and opens her arms to Alexis.

"I need a hug from Alex first, Daddy."

Alexis seems surprised but recovers quickly and walks over to Sienna. She brings herself down to Sienna's level and gives her a big hug. Ma and Pa watch on with a look of curiosity.

My heart starts to beat erratically at the obvious love between the two in front of me.

"Bye, Alex. I love you," Sienna's innocent voice exclaims.

"I love you too, Sienna."

When I close the door, I can't help but make a move straight into her arms. I grab her face and kiss her lips. They taste like coconut and chocolate. My mouth moves quickly over hers like I can't control the hunger inside of me. We both groan into each other.

"Come out with me tonight," I blurt out as we pull apart.

"Where are you going?"

"Out with my siblings for dinner and drinks. They specifically requested your presence."

She smiles. "Did they? That's sweet of them."

I don't mention the fact that they know about the two of us. I don't want to scare her or further complicate things.

"Afterward, we'll have this entire house to ourselves. I plan on fucking you on every single surface of this house, so save your energy."

She giggles. "I'll do my best. Don't keep me out too late."

"Trust me," I lean in for a kiss. "I have no intention of sharing you for too long. Now go get ready, I'll meet you down here in half an hour."

She runs off to get ready, and I jump in the shower real quick. I dress in casual gray shorts with a dark blue shirt and give myself a quick spray of my cologne. I'm embarrassed to admit that I feel nervous to hang out with my family and Alexis tonight. These feelings are new to me and slightly unwelcome. I'm supposed to be protecting myself so that no one can reach into my heart and rip it out again.

I walk out into the kitchen to find Alexis standing there in a white dress that fits her figure perfectly. Her hair is down in waves, and her makeup looks a bit darker.

"Damn," I say as I approach. "If you wanted me to be able to keep my hands off you tonight, wearing this was not a good idea."

I wrap my arms around her waist and kiss her cherry lips that I've come to adore.

"Who said I wanted your hands off of me tonight?" she taunts, giving me a smirk.

"Don't tempt me. Come on." I give her ass a little slap. "Let's go before I decide to keep you here to myself all night."

I grab her, and we walk to my car, hand in hand. I open her door and see she's wearing a funny look on her face.

"What?" I ask as I gesture for her to get in.

She shakes her head. "Nothing, I just don't think a man has ever opened a door for me."

She finally sits down, and I walk around the car as I take in what she just said to me. What kind of adolescent dickheads has she been out with? This girl has not been treated right her entire life. First by her parents, then her boyfriend. It brings out this boiling rage inside of me. I want to be her armor through life, protecting her from the people who don't appreciate her like they should.

I start the car and begin to drive toward the bar. TOLI has great food and drinks with a fun atmosphere, so the outside patio is always a great place to hang out in the summer.

After I park the car, we walk the short distance to the bar. Lucas texted me on the way to let me know they are sitting at a table on the patio. Alexis grabs my hand as she follows me, and I feel her squeeze a bit tighter as we spot my family.

"Hey guys," I greet my siblings.

I pull a chair out for Alexis and see that taken-aback look again. She better get used to it. When she's with me, she gets treated like the treasure that she is.

"Alexis! I'm so glad you came," Mia, who is sitting to the left of her, says.

"Thanks for inviting me. It's nice to get out and enjoy this weather before it goes away," Alexis says.

"Ugh, don't remind me about the good weather leaving us," Marcus groans. "I'm not ready for winter, winter, and more winter in Ohio."

We all laugh because anybody who's lived in Ohio knows the pain of living through so many months of winter. It helps if you're into winter sports, but that has never been an interest for my family or myself.

"So, what's good here?" Alexis asks as she peruses the menu.

"Everything!" Lucas emphasizes. "We always start with the drunken mussels and fried calamari."

"Sounds yummy!" Alexis replies.

The waitress comes around and takes all our orders. Alexis decided to try their spaghetti aglio e olio based on Mia going on and on about it.

When our drinks come out, Marcus raises his beer in the air.

"A toast, to overcoming our past and to new beginnings." He looks over at me and winks.

I sigh, hoping Alexis doesn't catch onto Marcus's inability to not overstep boundaries. Everybody raises their glass, knowing exactly what Marcus is doing.

Once the food is out, conversation is flowing, and I feel myself finally relax.

Mia and Alexis are deep in conversation while Lucas goes on about pre-season football. Alexis has stolen glances at me here and there, like she isn't sure if she wants me to hear her conversation. It may be all in my head, but I'm getting a weird feeling.

The crowd is really starting to gather in the back as it slowly turns from restaurant to nightlife. The music is a bit louder, the crowd younger, and people seem thirstier as they wait in line at the outdoor bar.

Our food has been taken away, and our drinks refilled. I've already had two, so I switched to water.

Mia stands from the table. "I need another glass of wine. Alexis, you wanna join me at the bar?"

Alexis gives her a genuine smile. "I'd love to," she tells her, then turns me. "I'll be right back."

"So, how long are we gonna have to pretend like we don't know about the two of you?" Marcus blurts out as soon as Alexis is gone.

"Maybe give us longer than a week before you force her to answer any of your idiotic questions," I snap back.

"Do you know what you're doing?" Lucas asks me. "Isn't she done watching Sienna in like two weeks? Have you guys talked about what happens after? Does she even want anything more? She is fresh out of college, after all."

"Like I said, it's only been a week. Give me a break."

"Just be careful. You still haven't totally dealt with Angie leaving, and now you're jumping into something that's got complicated written all over it," Lucas pushes.

"Just fucking drop it," I shout and slam my hand on the table.

"Fine. Don't say we didn't warn you," Lucas responds, which just pisses me off more.

Who is he to tell me whether or not I've moved on from my divorce? He's never been married. He can't pretend to know anything about what it's like.

All I know is that being with Alexis makes me happy. Maybe it's selfish and stupid, but for once, I just want to feel good and enjoy myself.

I'm waking up content again and going to sleep satisfied. These fools have been begging me to get back out there, and the second I do and I actually feel something real, they shit all over it. I'm feeling pissed off and on edge.

Realizing Mia and Alexis have been gone for a while now, I look around the patio in search of them. When I spot them at the bar, they are both laughing at something a guy is saying. Him and his friend are standing awfully close to them.

I know guys, and these two are interested in what they see. What I don't understand is why the hell Alexis is standing there smiling with them when she should be sitting here with me?

The anger I was feeling toward my brothers has multiplied as I sit here and watch the guys keep my girl grinning like a fool.

Before I've even consciously made the decision to intervene, I'm out of my chair and taking quick strides toward the bar.

As I approach, I hear one of the guys talking about his sailboat that he takes out on Lake Erie. *My intuition was spot on.* No one brags about their damn sailboat to a chick if he isn't trying to impress her or get in her pants.

I stand next to Alexis and wrap my arm around her waist, pulling her into my chest.

"Excuse me, just checking in on my girl. What's taking you so long?" I speak to Alexis loud enough for the crowd to hear me.

She gives me a funny look.

"Um, sorry. We just got our drink a minute ago," she replies.

I notice she didn't answer my question as to why the hell she is still standing here talking to these guys after she already has her drink.

My hand squeezes her hip tightly.

"Are these guys bothering you two?" I ask protectively.

Mia gives me a look that, if I'm interpreting correctly, is saying, "tread carefully, big brother."

"No, Gabe. They aren't bothering us. We were having a perfectly pleasant conversation before you showed up," Mia answers back.

"I'm sorry. I didn't mean to cause any drama here. It was nice meeting you ladies. Have a good night," one of the guys says before they both turn and walk away.

"What the hell was that for?" Mia raises her voice at me, then storms off back to our table.

"Are you okay?" Alexis asks with concern.

All I want to do right now is get her back to my house and claim her as mine.

"Let's just get out of here. I'm feeling kind of tired. Long work week," I lie.

She nods her head hesitantly and grabs my extended hand as I lead us over to the table to grab our things.

"Where are you going?" Lucas asks.

"Feeling kind of tired. We're gonna head home," I say.

Mia glares at me. "Yeah, I'll bet you're pretty tired. Hey, by the way, thanks for scaring off the cute boy who owns a boat."

Lucas and Marcus look at each other.

"What the hell is she talking about?" Marcus asks. "What cute boy with a boat? Was some dumb asshole trying to hit it and quit it? I'll kill 'em, I swear."

Mia groans with frustration. "Okay, idiots. How many times do I have to tell you to leave me alone and let me date like a normal person? I can handle myself. Besides, Gabe was not shooing these boys away for my protection."

I cut her off before she can continue. "Alright. Well, it was nice seeing you guys tonight. Thanks for inviting us out."

I turn to Alexis. "You ready?"

"Um, sure. Bye, everyone." She smiles at my siblings. "It was nice seeing you again."

It's silent on the walk back to the parking lot. When we get to my car, I open her door for her again and help her in.

"So," she starts as I pull out of the lot. "Are you okay?"

I grip the steering wheel.

"I'm fine."

We sit in silence for another couple minutes.

"Are you sure? You seemed...jealous back there," she says.

"Well, you were flirting with another man. I mean, call me crazy, but I thought you were a one-guy kind of gal."

She gasps.

"Excuse me? What are you implying?"

"I don't know. Maybe this whole innocent thing was an act. Something to trick me into bed. What the hell do I know?"

I feel a jolt to my arm when she punches her fist into me.

"What the hell was that for?" I shout.

"That was for being an idiot!" She matches my decimal. "How dare you accuse me of faking something so scarring for me! That was such a hard time in my life, and you just acted like it was all a lie. For what? To get you into bed? Excuse me, but I don't think I needed a whole backstory to accomplish that."

"Sounding a little cocky there," I mutter to myself.

"Just stop talking," she tells me as she crosses her arms across her chest.

She looks out the passenger window the rest of the ride, refusing to acknowledge me.

I feel a twinge of guilt as we approach the house. I'm not sure why I felt so jealous and possessive watching her talk to another man. I have no right to those feelings. We've been sleeping together for a week now, and I've said nothing to make her feel like this isn't just a momentary fling. Hell, I'm not sure I know what I want myself.

I open the door from the garage, and Alexis storms past me. When I enter the kitchen, I hear her stomp up the stairs and close her bedroom door.

I know I need to apologize, but I also wonder how she would have felt if my brothers and I went off with a group of girls and flirted the night away with them. There's no way she wouldn't be angry about that.

I knock on her door lightly. It flies open, and I'm greeted with a still angry Alexis, only now I'm slightly turned on by it. She's cute when she's pissed off.

"What do you want?" she asks.

"Can I come in?"

She folds her arms across her chest again. "Are you done being a dick?"

I shrug my shoulders. "I thought it was part of my charm."

I see her fight a smile as she opens the door for me. Hopefully that's a good sign.

I step into her room but notice she doesn't make an effort to follow me in. It's not until I take a seat at the end of her bed that she walks cautiously in my direction, stopping for a seat on the ottoman diagonal from me.

"I think I owe you an apology," I admit.

Her eyebrow raises. "You think?"

I sigh. "It wasn't right of me to suggest you were ever lying about your experience level. I know that's a difficult subject for you, and it was wrong of me to use it against you."

"Okay. Yes, it was a dick move. What else?"

"What else what?" I ask her.

"Do you have anything else to apologize for?" she drawls out.

I look at her skeptically. What else does she want me to apologize for? Am I supposed to apologize for being jealous? Seems a little overboard since I'm sure she would have felt the same way if the roles were reversed.

"You're not suggesting I should apologize for being jealous, are you? Because I think that's a little— "

"It's not about being jealous, Gabe," she cuts me off. "That's a natural feeling for anyone to have. It's about how you handled it. You treated me like something you owned and had to claim right in front of those guys. I'll have you know, I'm no one's property."

Her words piss me off, and I stand up to take a step in her direction.

"I don't share, Alexis. Don't ask me not to protect what's—" I cut myself off.

"What's...? Go ahead, finish that sentence," she urges, clearly frustrated with this conversation. "What's yours? Your own family doesn't know about us, so why would you think I'm yours?"

"My family does know about us. They figured it out the day after we slept together," I shout.

She stands up. "What? They *know* about us? I was the only one not included in that piece of information tonight. Why the hell didn't you tell me?"

"I didn't want to put any pressure on you!"

"Too late for that!"

"Can you just—" she starts, but I'm now standing in her space, and all I can focus on is her lips.

Without thinking, I grab her and smash our lips together. The kiss is punishing and angry as I ravish her mouth with a sense of cruelty. My tongue reaches for hers to explore the recesses of her mouth. I can't control the passion and desire that have surfaced from our argument.

When I pull back to take a breath, she looks up at me with a sense of bewilderment as her eyes take me in.

Then, she pulls me back down on her lips and takes her own anger out on me. I can feel the push and pull as we both fight with our mouths. It's sexy as hell.

We walk backward until we both fall onto her bed. She straddles my hips, and I groan into her mouth. This is going to be a quick and hard fuck. There's so much urgency between the two of us.

I flip her over and kneel by her legs as I unzip my pants, then I take control and use my anger to fuck her into three orgasms.

Chapter Twenty-Two

Alexis

I wake up in his arms as I recall what transpired last night. The night out with his family, the fight, the best sex of my life.

Gabriel, when he's pissed off, is a force to be reckoned with. My muscles feel weak and sore, yet thoroughly pleased with the orgasm parade I had last night. It was one after the other.

I still feel a bit weird about not finishing the fight. Why did me talking to another man cause so much rage in him? It wasn't even for me. Mia was the one doing the flirting. She was interested in one of the guys. I made no attempt to be part of the conversation. I just smiled and nodded along when it felt appropriate.

He starts to move around as he stretches an arm above his head. I take this time, before he's fully awake, to watch him. His biceps bulge as he flexes and unflexes. It's a sight to behold, watching this man in the morning. His hair is disheveled, and his beard is more than just a bit of scruff. He's all man, and it's so much more of a turn-on than I had expected.

He opens his eyes and looks over at me. When he realizes where he is, a big smile crosses his face.

I'm still getting used to being the one to put that smile there.

When I met him, he was all groans and scowls. Not to say he doesn't still have some of that, but he has become lighter and happier in the last week.

"Good morning, beautiful," his raspy voice says.

I smile. "Good morning, yourself."

He makes a move to stretch again, and I see a wince cross his face.

"What's wrong?" I ask him.

"My muscles are a bit sore. It must've been all the crazy sex I had last night. I feel like I was in the push-up position for hours."

I do a little stretch myself. "I'll make us some breakfast."

When I look back at him, he's biting his lip, and his eyes have turned more aggressive.

"What?" I ask.

"Your tits are hanging out the side of your tank. I'm trying to decide if my body needs a break or if I have enough in me to go another round this morning."

His contemplation of his dilemma makes me burst out in laughter.

"How about I make some breakfast first? My body aches as well. I might need a hot bath today to soothe my muscles," I tell him as I pull off the covers and get out of bed.

He does the same, and I realize he's completely naked, and his dick is hard. I chuckle at how ridiculous it looks. I'm not used to being this intimate with someone that we wake up and walk around naked so casually.

"What's so funny?" His arms open as he asks.

"I'm sorry." I giggle again like the innocent woman I am. "I'm just not used to waking up with a guy, let alone with that," I say as I point down.

A look of pride takes over his face.

"What can I say? He knows when a beautiful woman is around," Gabe jokes.

I roll my eyes and smile all the way downstairs as I cook us breakfast.

We don't get Sienna back until dinner time tonight. After we eat breakfast and shower, we decide to have another cup of coffee outside on the patio.

It's a beautiful afternoon. The sun is out, and the humidity is oddly low for this time of year. There's a gentle breeze that sweeps through every so often, providing the desirable relief from the heat.

"What do you want to do the rest of the afternoon?" Gabe asks.

I try to think about if there's anything I have on the agenda this weekend. Aside from looking for jobs, which I'm still actively avoiding, there isn't anything I can think of.

I shrug my shoulders. "I don't really have anything I need to do."

We sit in silence for a minute.

"What do you enjoy doing during your free time?"

I have to think about that for a second. What do I usually do with my spare time?

"I like to bake. Don't worry, I'm not gonna suggest we actually do that. I wouldn't want to make you feel inferior to my amazing baking skills."

He chuckles. "Woman, you have no idea the skills I have in the kitchen."

"I mean, I've seen your cooking skills, but I don't think those will translate over to baking."

He sits up straighter like I just challenged him. "Oh, yeah? Tell me, what is your specialty?"

"Hmm. I make a mean cheesecake."

He throws his head back in laughter. "Cheesecake is my specialty."

I give him the side eye. "Funny how your specialty is the first thing I say I do well."

"Care to put your skills to the test?" he says mischievously.

"What do you mean?" I ask.

"I bet you my cheesecake is better. How about we each make one and see who really does come up victorious?"

"You mean...like a bakeoff?" I ask suspiciously.

He chuckles. "If that's what you wanna call it. I was thinking more of a bet."

"I didn't realize you were looking to lose to a girl on your day off," I say confidently.

His smile shows off the lines forming at the corners of his eyes, reflecting his age. They look sexy as hell.

"You're going down, Moretti." He stands up from his seat.

"Where are you going?"

"We are going to the grocery store," he says.

I stand with him. "Like, right now?"

"Right. Now."

"Wait...you said it's a bet. Who judges? And what does the winner get?"

He starts walking backward with a smile as I follow.

"Sienna judges tonight at dinner. Winner gets..." He rubs his chin as he thinks. "To pick the location of our first date."

I almost stumble. Date? He wants to go on a date with me?

"A date?" I breathe out.

"I think you deserve to be wine and dined. What do you say? I'll get one of my siblings to come over and watch Sienna one night this week."

"That sounds great." I smile.

"Okay. Now you better let me win because I know all the great restaurants in the city."

I laugh. He's not wrong about that. Although, if I win, I'm going to be calling up Mr. Albertini for suggestions. Shit, I can't exactly tell him I'm going on a date with his... friend. That sounds so weird. But Gabe is so much younger than Mr. Albertini, it's not like they're friends from school or anything.

After we get back from the grocery store, we eat a quick lunch before he insists we get started. Thankfully he has a double oven, so we can each set our own temperature and don't have to worry about baking separately.

I told him he wasn't allowed to see my ingredients and copy me, so I checked out alone. He claimed I was being dramatic and that he didn't need to copy me.

I get started on the graham cracker crust just like Gabriel is doing right now. I look over at him, and he gives me a panty-melting smirk followed by a wink before he gets back to focusing on his crust.

The next step is to make the cheesecake. My secret is that I not only use cream cheese, but I also use ricotta cheese and add some heavy cream. It still has the heavy density of the New York style but has a light airiness to it from the ricotta and heavy cream.

I've never made this for someone without getting several oohs and aahs. Like Kevin from The Office says of his chili, it's what I do best.

Alicia and I spent way too many hours watching episodes of The Office instead of going out on the weekends.

I'm in the middle of mixing my ingredients when I feel Gabriel's hand reach around my stomach as he grabs a spatula. Instinct has me pushing my ass into his groin.

He grunts in my ear. "Don't start something you don't intend on finishing, baby."

A couple minutes go by, and I realize I need to find some parchment paper. I like to put a strip around the edges to guarantee it stays intact when you take the springform pan away.

Gabriel is standing in front of the drawer holding the paper. I tap his hip to get him to scooch. He sticks his ass out so I can open the drawer. I reach for the paper, and my arm grazes a hard bulge.

My brain forgets everything it was doing as my hand reaches for him. His dick hardens completely under my touch.

"Fuck, baby. Are you trying to distract me, you little cheater? It's working..." he growls before he swings around and brings me into his chest.

A laugh takes over me as he peppers kisses down my neck.

"I don't even know what made me do that," I say through a fit of laughter.

"I'm not buying it." He brings his mouth to my ear. "I think you want me to pound the fuck out of you right here on this island."

Shit... I think I do. My body has erupted into goosebumps. My underwear is now damp. The things this man can evoke from me with just a few words...

His mouth claims mine in searing kiss. I part my lips and raise myself to meet him. He continues with a savage intensity, one that I can't easily match, and I drink in the sweetness of his kiss.

He turns us around and lifts me on the counter, in between both of our bowls.

I don't care, I need him now.

He lays me down to my elbows, then unbuttons my jean shorts and works them down my legs.

His eyes remain on me as his hands explore the soft lines of my waist, my hips. His finger grabs the material of my underwear and brings it to the side.

"I'm gonna eat this beautiful pussy," he says, then takes a long, hard swipe up my center. He moans. "If your pussy was part of the bet, it would win. It's, without a doubt, the best-tasting thing I've ever had on my tongue."

I shudder as waves of pleasure roll through me. He doesn't take his time with me. His tongue is ravenous as it feasts on me with all it has. I shout when he starts to suck on my clit with the most amazing amount of pressure and suction.

"Wait for me, baby," he growls as he sheds his pants.

He grabs onto his long shaft and starts to run his tip up and down my entrance. We are both watching our bodies in awe, his jaw falling slack as he continues rubbing his dick on me.

He pushes forward an inch then pulls back.

"I'm gonna paint this pussy and this underwear with my cum," he tells me.

Moisture falls out of me. It feels like a lifetime ago that I was this scared, innocent woman who thought sex was something she couldn't enjoy. Now I crave it all day, every day. He's brought out this little vixen, and I love it.

He finally slides himself all the way inside of me and bottoms out, hitting my G-spot. I moan at the sensations. My body still needs to adjust to his size, and I wonder if that will ever change.

"You're so thick. It still makes me stop for a second each time and wonder if I can handle all of you," I say.

"Oh, you can handle all of me. I'll make sure of it," he says, quickening his pace.

He grabs my thighs for leverage and hits me hard with each thrust. I can't control the outright cry of delight as my body edges closer to release.

"Are you gonna come for me, baby?" he growls at me.

At my nod, he urges, "Good girl. I want your pussy to clench and your juices to pour out of you."

I can sense his thrill of arousal as he is in the moment fucking me and watching our bodies join together. His eyes are dark, and his mouth is open.

My body starts to tremble as an orgasm begins to erupt.

"That's it, Alexis. Let it happen. I need your pussy to squeeze the fuck out of my dick. I want it to strangle it," he says.

The orgasm goes off like fireworks as my eyes roll in the back of my head.

"Open those fucking eyes right now, Alexis. I need you to watch me come all over you," he demands.

I do my best to lift my head and open my lids. When he's satisfied that I'm watching, he pulls out and strokes himself as thick, white ropes shoot out. He lines himself up, so it hits all over me. My clit, my panties that are scrunched to the side, my entrance.

I'm covered in his release, and it's sexy as hell. I'm rooted in my place, frozen at how much I enjoyed what I just witnessed. My eyes can't pull away from my body.

When they finally do, his eyes are watching me.

"Did you like watching me coat your pussy with my cum, Alexis?" he asks.

"I loved it," I tell him truthfully.

"That's my girl." He smirks.

We both look around ourselves at the mess scattered about the kitchen. My hands are inches away from our bowls. It was pretty reckless to do this right here amongst all the food.

"Well..." I look around at our food. "I don't think we can give this to Sienna. It feels kind of wrong at this point," I say.

His eyes survey the room once more.

"Yeah, I guess you're right. I mean, it's not like we did it *on* the food, but it still feels kinda icky to make her try them now."

"Well, I'm still gonna bake mine and eat it. It's too yummy not to!"

He smiles. "Jury's still out on whose will be better."

"Now, how are we gonna settle it?" I hop off the counter and grab my pan to pour the cheesecake into.

"How about my siblings?" he suggests as he continues working on his dessert.

I ponder it for a second. They like we could trust them to make an impartial decision.

"Yeah, good idea. When would they try it?"

"I'll bring it to work on Monday."

"Okay. You're on, Gabriel." I smile at him.

Chapter Twenty-Three

Gabriel

"What's all this for?" Lucas asks.

I have three paper plates laid out on the breakroom table, each plate containing a slice of each cheesecake. Alexis and I both tried each other's cakes yesterday after they cooled in the fridge for twenty-four hours. Hers was annoyingly delicious. I was watching as she baked and noticed that she uses ricotta cheese in hers, which is actually kind of brilliant.

"Alexis and I need you guys to settle a little bet we made," I tell them as they shuffle into the room.

"First, you're all smiles with this girl, which hasn't happened in years. And now you're baking together..." Marcus says. "You've got it bad, man."

This is not news to me. Alexis is changing me, making me feel like there's a possibility for me to have a second chance at a happy life. I'm not ready to admit those words to anybody else, though. I've barely admitted them to myself.

"Just try the fucking cheesecakes," I snap at him.

He smiles like my reaction to him only confirmed his suspicions, which just pisses me off.

"I could go for some cheesecake," Mia grabs her plate. "So, what's the deal here? I just take a bite of each and tell you which one I like better?"

"Congratulations, Mia. Thanks for stating the obvious," Lucas bites out sarcastically.

"Fuck off, Lucas. I just wanted to make sure we weren't judging on certain categories or if it's just overall taste."

"Just tell me which one you like better," I suggest.

Marcus takes a bite of mine first and chews slowly. I watch as Mia and Lucas do the same. They move on to the other cheesecake, Alexis's, and I notice a visible delight on their faces.

Damnit!

"This one is really frickin' good," Lucas states as he points to her cheesecake with his fork.

"Which one are you talking about?" Mia leans over to see his plate. "Oh, yes! That one is definitely my favorite. It's so light, and yet, I don't know how to describe it...heavy at the same time. Does that even make sense?"

"Makes total fucking sense," Marcus agrees as he devours the last of Alexis' cake.

I sigh. Well, it looks like I'm eating at a restaurant of her choosing. I really wanted to do something special for her. What if she picks a horrible place? Do I tell her that or just keep my mouth shut?

"I'm guessing by your reaction that we didn't pick your precious cheesecake." Mia smiles as she takes another bite.

"Whatever. I don't care about that part," I lie, hating that my food isn't the best.

"You suck at lying," Lucas states. "So, what does Alexis get for winning?"

"She gets to choose where we go for a date this week," I tell them.

"You're going out on a date? Does that make you two official?" Mia asks curiously.

I don't know what the hell we are. It's confusing and unnerving, not knowing if we're on the same page. I know I need to get it over with and ask her where her head's at.

"Not sure."

"So, how does it feel to lose to your girl?" Marcus smiles at me.

I shrug but think about the fun we had baking the cheesecakes. It was worth it. Who knew baking with a woman could be so fun? Alexis is so damn adventurous and reactive. It's a shame she was made to feel anything but the sex goddess that she is.

On the other hand, there's something so satisfying about being the only man to ever get her this way.

"What's that face for?" Lucas asks.

"Nothing. I'm cool with losing. We had...fun making these together."

"What the hell kind of *fun* are you referring to?" Marcus looks at me eagerly. "Dude, did you two fuck on these cheesecakes?"

"No, of course not," I say, and they look relieved. "I mean...not *on* them."

"Ugh, gross!" Lucas puts his plate down. "You guys had sex while baking these? Were they at least in the oven when that happened?"

I place my hands in my pockets and look at the ground.

"Disgusting! You two are animals!" Marcus states on his way to the garbage can, where he throws his remaining food in the trash.

"Seriously, you could have warned us." Mia gives me an accusatory look.

"Well, would you have eaten them if I'd told you?" I defend.

It's not the best argument, but it's all I've got.

"Don't ask stupid questions," Marcus states. "No, we wouldn't have eaten your sex cheesecake if we had known."

"Well, at least Alexis won," Lucas folds his arms across his chest.

I find the entire situation hilarious—I can't help it. Only with Alexis in my life would I get myself into a situation like this. A fit of laughter escapes me as I think about the absurdity of the situation.

Eventually, the four of us are cracking up together. It feels good...it feels normal. Like it's been ages since I've been able to be this way with them.

Mia has tears running down her cheeks and can barely get the words out as she says, "I... can't... believe... you... did... that."

When I pull into the driveway, I feel the familiar flutter of excitement in my stomach. I'm going to miss this when she leaves next week. Fuck, we really need to talk about what we're doing here. There's no way she would just pick up and leave us for good... would she?

I don't mean she needs to continue to be Sienna's nanny, but I would like her to stay in Cleveland. Maybe we can give this thing a shot.

"Hello," I yell as I walk through the door.

When there's no answer, I wander through the first floor but see no signs of the girls. As I begin to climb the stairs, I hear voices and giggles coming from Alexis's room. I approach the bathroom, where I see the light glowing on the carpet.

When I peek inside, Alexis is standing between Sienna's legs, who is sitting on the counter as she swipes a brush around Alexis's face.

"Just like this?" Sienna asks in her sweet little voice.

"Just like that. It goes on the cheeks," Alexis instructs.

I lean on the doorframe and cross my arms. "What's going on in here?"

Sienna's face beams with delight. "Hi, Daddy! Alex is letting me do her makeup."

"I see that." I laugh. "How did you trick her into letting you do this?"

Alexis smiles. "There was no tricking involved. Sienna said she's never seen anyone do makeup. I told her she could watch me. One thing led to another, and here we are. Right, sweetheart?"

Sienna giggles as she dabs the brush in the powder and glides it across Alexis's eyelid. My heart flutters as I watch the two of them, struck by how much they look like mother and daughter. It also reminds me of the things Sienna will miss out on because of Angie leaving... I never thought about something as trivial as watching your mother put on makeup.

It might not seem like a big deal, but those moments help you learn and grow. And here Alexis is, gladly willing to step in and show Sienna. Not even just show her; she's letting her try it out on her.

It's in this moment right now, I know for sure I'm in love with Alexis. How could I not be?

She's *everything*.

She's beautiful, smart, brave, kind-hearted, and she loves my daughter. It's so evident in the way she is with her.

"What's that look?" Alexis asks as she looks at me through the mirror.

"Huh?" I stand up straight, realizing I've been caught in my thoughts. "Oh, nothing. I was thinking about work."

"How was your day? Stressful?" she asks.

"Well, there was one bad thing that happened." I sigh.

"What is it?"

"My siblings ate our cheesecake..."

"Did something happen?" she asks with concern.

I laugh. "I'd say so. For one, they know we had some *extra* fun around our baked goods. They didn't take to the idea so kindly."

Alexis makes an audible gasp. "Oh my gosh. Gabriel! You told them?"

"Told them what?" Sienna looks between the two of us.

"Don't worry about it, sweetie," I smile at her, appreciating that she's pretty good at understanding when it's an adult conversation.

"And I didn't tell them, they guessed."

Alexis gives me a skeptical look. "Really? They guessed? They were sitting there eating the cheesecake and just knew what we did."

"Okay, Miss Sarcastic. I may have alluded to it," I admit to her as I rub my chin.

"Why on earth would you do that?" she says with a hint of anger to it.

Too bad I just find it adorable and not intimidating in the slightest.

"Not sure. I think it was when I lost the bet that I may have said something, then Marcus guessed it."

A small smile crosses her face. "They liked my cheesecake better than yours?"

"Whatever. They were probably just hungry. It was lunchtime, they were ravenous. It doesn't mean anything."

She doesn't gloat. She just stands in place with her smile intact while Sienna continues her process.

"Sweetie, I talked to Aunt Mia. She's going to watch you tomorrow night," I tell Sienna while watching Alexis's reaction through the mirror and giving her a wink.

Her cheeks blush, and I wish I could take her in my arms and kiss her.

Chapter Twenty-Four

Gabriel

I check myself in the mirror. My hair is done, I have on a dark blue suit with my brown leather shoes, and my cologne is sprayed.

Alexis still insisted on picking the restaurant tonight, but when she told me she was going to text Allen, I left the room and called him. It was a little strange to have to admit to him that Alexis and I were an item, but it felt kind of nice to speak the words out loud.

He gave me a protective father kind of talk, which I actually appreciated. I didn't realize he looked at Alexis like a second daughter.

In the end, he agreed to suggest the restaurant I want to take her to—Marble Room. The downtown venue is set in an old bank with marble walls, hence the name of the restaurant, and large Corinthian columns adding to the Renaissance style of the room. It's a pretty spectacular area to dine in, with the rich history oozing from every direction your eye takes you.

I convinced Alexis to let me pay for the evening so we don't have to worry about prices or expenses. The winner of the bet gets to pick the restaurant, not pay for the evening.

When I get to the kitchen, I see her wearing a gold dress that has long sleeves and shows off her killer legs. She's laughing with Mia as they lean against the island.

She looks up at me and smiles.

"Wow," I tell her. "You look...stunning."

I kiss her cheek. When my hand reaches for her lower back, I notice that I don't feel any material. I steal a glimpse and find that the dress is backless all the way down to her ass.

Fuck me! I'm gonna be hard all damn night.

"Thank you." She blushes as she glances shyly between Mia and me, hopefully not noticing how quizzical Mia looks.

"Thanks for watching Sienna tonight," I tell Mia.

"No problem. You two get out of here and have fun. Sienna and I have some trouble to get into."

I smile but give her a stern look so she knows I'll be less than amused if she does anything I wouldn't approve of.

As we drive downtown, I start to think that tonight might be the perfect night to tell her that I'm falling for her. Maybe even tell her I want her to stay here with me. It may be sudden, but it feels right.

After I give the car over to the valet, I take her hand and lead her inside.

"This feels weird," she says before we enter. "I won the bet and picked the restaurant, but you're the one who booked the reservation and knows where to go."

I smile and turn my back to the door as I stop.

"Confession," I tell her.

Her eyebrow lifts as she waits for me to continue.

"I may have called Allen and told him what restaurant I wanted him to refer you to."

Her eyes open as wide as saucers. "Gabriel Giannelli. You are one sneaky man."

"And I'm not sorry. I wanted tonight to be as special as you are."

She lifts herself up and kisses my mouth. "Thank you."

"Also, you don't get a reservation the night before at a place like this without knowing somebody." I wink at her before opening the door.

She rolls her eyes at me. "You're sweet, but not modest."

"I'm just saying, I may know a few people because of what I do. One thing I can promise you, you're gonna love the wine."

"I'm sure I will." She licks her lips.

I know that look she's giving me. She's thinking about our first night together.

"Behave," I whisper in her ear with my hand on her back. "If I know you're having those thoughts while wearing this dress, I'm not going to be able to contain myself."

"I don't think I want you to contain yourself," she says flirtatiously.

"I've created a monster," I chuckle.

I give the hostess my name, and then we are being led to a booth off to the side to give us some privacy. I watch Alexis's eyes gaze around the room as she takes in the columns, marble walls, and the grand ceiling which adds to the luxurious feeling the place gives off.

"This place is incredible," Alexis says in awe as she takes a seat in the booth.

I follow and scoot in close to her, my body never wanting to be far from hers.

"It's the best indoor dining view you're gonna get in the city," I tell her. "But the architecture is only half of what makes this place so wonderful. The food is out of this world."

"Gosh, I can't wait. Thank you so much for picking this place." She beams in delight.

I look at her until she realizes what she just said. When it dawns on her, we share a laugh.

"Thank you for being overbearing and a control freak and making me pick this place," she corrects herself.

"It's my pleasure. I just didn't want you to miss out on this place," I admit. "So, I'm not going to be some controlling prick who tells you what food to order, though I'd be happy to offer my opinion if you'd like, but would it be okay if I picked the wine for the evening?"

"I appreciate you asking, but *of course,* you can pick the wine."

"Great, it's a Bordeaux," I tell her, then give the waiter our order.

"So, tell me something I don't know about you," she requests.

"Hmmm, that's quite a question to start the night," I say.

"I want to know more about you."

I lean back and rest an arm on the back of the booth as I think about what I could tell her.

"I wanted to be a professional baseball player growing up," I finally admit.

She leans in. "A baseball player, eh? I can get behind that. You certainly have the butt for it."

My head falls back in laughter. "Thanks. That's the only reason I wanted to. To show off my ass."

"Did you play baseball in high school?"

"I did. I actually played in college, too. But that's when my passion for wine and starting a business began. In the end, I knew I would prefer to have a more stable life. The constant traveling I would have to do in the league just started to appeal less and less to me."

"I can respect that. Do you ever wish you went for it?"

"Not at all. I have Sienna, and she wouldn't be here if I went another direction."

"Sienna is worth everything," she agrees, grinning at me.

Those words spoken out of her mouth are just confirmation that telling her tonight is the right move.

We stop our conversation for a minute to look at the menu, and she asks, "What do you prefer here?"

"I like to get a steak and add lobster."

"Mmmm. I don't know if I'd have room for dessert if I had both. I'll stick with the bone-in rib eye."

"Excellent choice. I'm gonna go for the bone-in New York strip with lobster. Care to share some sides with me?"

"Only if we get the potatoes au gratin for one," she replies cheekily.

I chuckle. "Yes, ma'am. And they are to die for, nice choice. Are you good with the crispy brussel sprouts for the other side?"

With her approval, I put the order into the waiter as he pours our wine for us.

"Cheers." I hold up my glass to her. "To an amazing summer."

"Cheers." She clinks me.

"My turn for a question," I tell her. "Where do you see yourself in the future?"

She looks at me thoughtfully.

"I guess that's been the question of the summer for me. I've struggled with the answer. I just get so in my head. Honestly, my whole life has been a battle of getting somebody—anybody—to love me...to pay attention to me. It's hard for me to think only of myself."

I know we've had this conversation, but that was before she and I started sleeping together. Before I fell in love with her. It feels bigger now. It's hard for me to believe that someone as amazing and selfless as Alexis can struggle to see herself as important enough to decide her future for herself.

"Did spending time with Sienna give you the break you needed to take the pressure off?" I ask.

She sighs. "It definitely took the pressure off for the summer. I suppose I got so distracted living your life with you and her, that I forgot to think about what I need for myself. I know I still need to make that decision. It's looming in the background every second, but I'm still putting it off for some reason. I don't know why."

Her answer is like a stab straight to my heart. She's been living my life for me, not one for herself.

Am I holding her back from making a decision?

I know I am. How could I not be? She basically just admitted it.

"Why do you think it's so hard for you to make that decision?" I ask, my heart racing as I wait for her answer.

The food comes and temporarily distracts us.

"This looks amazing." She eyes her steak appreciatively.

I know this conversation isn't over, but I also know I don't want to ruin our meal by forcing it to continue, I let it slide. I try to keep the conversation as light as possible while we eat, but I have this looming feeling hanging over me that this night will no longer be ending the way I had originally thought it would.

"I'm stuffed," Alexis places her napkin on the table and leans back, "but that was incredible."

"I'm glad you liked it."

"I loved it." She smiles at me.

I pay the tab, reaching for her hand to help her out of the booth and not letting go until we have to separate at the valet to get in my car.

"Thanks for an amazing evening," she says in a silky voice.

"It was my pleasure, Alexis."

As I drive, I think back to the question still lingering in my brain.

"You never answered my question," I say in a hardened voice.

"What question?"

"Before our food came," I remind her. "I asked you why you think it's so hard for you to make decisions for yourself, with just your happiness in mind."

I steal a glance at her to find her worrying her lip.

"Who really knows why they do things? It could be because I just don't really know what I want to do. Or maybe it's because of my family."

"Have you always wanted to stay in Ohio?"

"No, actually. For a while, I thought about California," she says carelessly.

California? The state my ex left me for to pursue a happier life. And if I ask Alexis to stay with me, how long before she changes her mind and takes off for the golden state?

I think I fucking hate that state. Why do all the women in my life want to move there?

What does California offer that makes my love and commitment not worth it?

There's no way the two of us could work. Even if I asked her to stay and she agreed, would I want to be the reason Alexis didn't go for her dreams? *Absolutely not.*

Whether I want to admit it or not, Alexis is special to me. I do want her to be happy, and I'm afraid if I tell her how I feel, she'll stay and go against what she really wants to do. She deserves to make a decision for herself and her own happiness.

I owe it to her to let her have that clarity without my responsibilities weighing her decision down.

"Are you okay?" she asks.

"Huh?" I look over at her concerned face. "Oh, yeah. Sorry. I was focusing on the road."

I know she doesn't totally buy my response, but she doesn't say anything further. The rest of the ride is quiet as I think about letting her go on Saturday.

Three more days together.

Although I know this is the right decision, anger starts to grow. By the time we are pulling into the garage, I'm gripping the steering wheel until my knuckles are white as I try to suppress the fury.

I'm on autopilot as I thank my sister for watching Sienna and usher her out the front door. When the click sounds, I look up at Alexis before taking calculated steps in her direction and catching her off guard when I wrap my arm around her with force and drag her body against mine.

My mouth slams down onto hers as I ignore the end of the evening. Right now, I just want to feel her in my arms, feel her lips against mine, hear her breaths of pleasure when she comes on me.

This kiss...it's powerful. My mouth claims every bit of hers as my tongue finds its way into every crevice of her mouth. When I pull away to take a breath, she looks up at me.

"I thought you were angry with me," she tells me.

I don't respond. I just take her in my arms and carry her up the stairs and into her room. I already know I can't bear to have her sleep in my bed again without it being too much for me.

When we get into her room, I close the door with her still in my arms before I place her down on the bed.

"Tonight, I'm going to take you hard, Alexis," I warn her.

She bites her lip and nods her head in agreement.

"Now take your dress off for me," I demand. "I want to see those perky tits."

As she reaches for the bottom of her dress and starts to pull it up her body, I grab my belt and start to strip.

There's no time for undressing each other or making this romantic.

She sheds herself of her dress, and I get the view I wanted of her breasts. She's lying in front of me in nothing but her white underwear.

I get rid of my shirt so I'm only in my boxer briefs.

"Touch yourself, baby," I growl. "I want to watch those delicate fingers slide inside your wet pussy."

Her jaw falls at my words. I step forward and let my finger graze her hip until it comes down to one of her knees. I bring my hand behind it and lift her leg up and to the right so she's spread wide, revealing an already wet spot on her underwear.

"You fucking want to touch yourself, don't you?" I accuse her. "Look how wet you are, you're soaking through your underwear. You can't wait to show me how you like to touch yourself. I'll show you how I like to touch myself too. Do you want that, Alexis?"

"Yes," she breathes out.

I use my finger to pull her underwear to the side. Her pussy is glistening, and part of me wishes I could just push my dick inside.

"Let me see it," I tell her.

Her hand comes down to her pussy. She runs her fingers through her folds then brings them up to her clit where she starts to rub circles. When her fingers slide inside of her, I'm gone. I drop my briefs and pump my dick.

It only takes a minute before I know I need to feel her.

"Get on your hands and knees. I'm going to fuck you from behind."

She follows my command and is in position in an instant.

"Good girl," I encourage as I step close.

I glide my dick around her slickness and slide inside. I pump inside of her as my fingers grab onto her hips, squeezing hard as thoughts of this possibly being our last night together start to form.

The more those thoughts haunt me, the harder I fuck her. If this is possibly my last time with her, I want her to remember me.

Chapter Twenty-Five

Alexis

He's gone. I just woke up from our first date night together, and there's an empty spot next to me. Usually, he'll at least nudge me to tell me he's leaving for work.

It's not like we've been together very long to have a reference point of what our *routine* is, but still.

Our date last night started out amazing. Sometime during dinner, I feel like something happened. He was still sweet enough and being very thoughtful...but he seemed slightly on edge. Then, on our drive home, I swear it shifted to anger.

And though I loved how rough he was last night in bed, even that felt different, too.

Maybe I'm just overthinking things.

What I really want to know is what's going to happen to us when I leave on Saturday. I've already told Alicia I need to stay with her for a week or two while I figure things out. But as the days continue to pass with no acknowledgment from Gabriel, my fears start to grow.

He wouldn't just let me leave his house without talking about us first, would he?

Surely this is more than having some fun in the sheets for both of us. I thought we were more... I thought we were falling in love.

I know I am.

I drag myself downstairs for a cup of coffee. As I sit on the couch, I think about what I should do. Do I talk to him tonight and just come out and ask him what we're doing? Do I ask him if he wants to continue to see me after my nannying gig is up?

And Sienna. How am I going to leave her in just a couple days? I have fallen in love with that girl. She is the sweetest and strongest kid I've ever met. She has already been abandoned by her mother. What is she going to think of me leaving?

We've already talked about it a little bit together. She's looking forward to time with her grandparents again, but she's sad that I have to leave.

I promised her I'd come visit, but that was when I thought her father and I were possibly going somewhere.

"Morning," a little voice greets me from the other side of the room.

Sienna is standing there in her pajamas with wild hair.

I smile at her. "Morning, sweetie," I greet her as I open my arms for her to come snuggle. "Did you sleep well?"

She nods and rests her head on me. Tears start to form in my eyes at the realization that these mornings are almost over. I've come to love our morning cuddles.

"What are we going to do today?" she asks.

"What do you want to do?"

She sits silently for a minute. "I just want to spend the day here. Don't tell Daddy, but Aunt Mia let me stay up late last night."

I try to hold back my smile. Mia is a sneaky little one. I wonder if she also gave her all the sweets that Sienna always asks for.

"We can hang here. Maybe we can put the sprinklers on and play around in the backyard."

"Yes! Let's do that."

"Deal. We can change into our suits after breakfast. Just let me finish this cup," I tell her.

She knows the drill. I need my coffee before I start our days together or I'll run out of energy.

"I don't want you to leave," she whispers.

The tears I thought I had successfully gotten ridden of start to form again.

"I don't want to leave either, sweetie," I barely get out.

Thankfully she doesn't look up at me as tears fall down my cheeks. My lips are trembling as I desperately try to keep my emotions under control.

"Why do you have to leave? You don't want to, I don't want you to, and I know Daddy doesn't want you to."

"How do you know that?" I ask.

"It's so obvious. He's always smiling and happy when you're around. He wasn't like that before you got here."

"I know it's hard to understand. I was only here to help out until your grandma was better, and now that she is, you guys don't need me anymore. I have to find a new job."

"I think we still need you," she says.

I can't finish the conversation without crying and getting caught in my grief. I remain silent, and she doesn't push.

We spend the day doing our favorite things. Baking, playing outside, and ending with more snuggles.

By the time Gabe gets home, I'm exhausted.

Sienna runs into his arms. As they talk about their day, I remain on the couch and watch. It's not until he puts her down that I notice he won't look me in the eyes.

"How was your day?" he asks as he focuses on untying his tie.

"It was good. She really enjoyed the sprinklers," I tell him.

Instead of looking at me, he looks back at Sienna and smiles.

"How about we order in some pizza tonight?" he suggests to her.

She jumps up and down, confirming that his choice is a hit. I know he always insists on me eating with them, but I don't feel like I'm very welcome at the moment. Maybe everything I thought was only in my head is actually true. I must have done something wrong last night.

"I'm going to go rest for a bit," I say, excusing myself.

He nods his head at me, barely acknowledging my words.

I think about what it is I could have done to cause this distance he is clearly putting between us, but I'm drawing a blank.

I try to read a book, but my mind is racing, and can't focus on a single sentence.

An hour passes before I realize I dozed off, and as soon as I'm awake, my stomach is growling.

When I stroll downstairs, I see Sienna and Gabe sitting at the table.

"Alex, pizza is here!" Sienna shouts. "Come sit next to me!"

At least her presence will be a much-needed distraction from the awkwardness in the air.

I take a seat next to Sienna and grab a slice of pizza. I'm not really in the mood to eat, my appetite suddenly vanished as dread now fills my stomach.

"Daddy, I think we should do a special dinner for Alex on her last night. Like we did on her first night here," Sienna says sweetly.

I look up at Gabe, who, for the first time today, meets my eyes. He offers me a small smile that doesn't reach his eyes like it usually does, then turns to Sienna.

"I think that's a great idea, sweetie. We will definitely do that, and you can even pick out the food," he says to Sienna.

She claps her hand and cheers. "Yay! Don't worry," she leans into me, "I'll pick something you love!"

I smile at her. "I know you will. Thank you."

Dinner continues with more of the same. Both of us talking to Sienna, our own conversation non-existent. When we're done, the two of them head upstairs for their usual bath and bedtime routine.

I do the dishes and pour myself a glass of Chianti. As I'm sitting on the couch, I remember the first night Gabriel ever taught me about wine. How he patiently instructed me, talking so passionately about it.

What a world of a difference it was from that night to our dinner tonight.

I finish the glass and stay seated on the couch. I'm hoping that when he comes back downstairs, we can talk a bit about what is happening. Maybe I can apologize for whatever happened last night that brought on this sudden change in his mood.

I hear his footsteps as he comes down the stairs, my nerves instantly dancing in my body as he gets closer.

He rounds the corner and starts to walk toward his room when he spots me.

"Oh, hey," he says.

"Hi." I smile.

"Um..." He scratches the back of his head. "I'm actually completely exhausted. I think I'm just gonna head to bed tonight if that's alright."

My stomach sinks. If there was any chance that I thought I was imagining his change, there's no doubting it now.

He's clearly blowing me off. I should say something, I *need* to say something. He can't just treat me like this after the night we had last night. Not after the last two weeks we've spent together.

Instead, I find myself saying, "Okay. That's fine. Goodnight."

"Goodnight," he says, then walks away, leaving me alone.

I'm not sure how long I sit in silence on the couch, frozen in place. I don't even know what to think about what just happened. Who is he? This is not the man I met nor the man I fell in love with. This is someone entirely different.

Or maybe I never really knew him to begin with.

Chapter Twenty-Six

Gabriel

Two miserable days without being able to sneak in a hug or kiss. Without having her in my arms at night. Now it's her last day here, and I'm no closer to having a damn clue how to say g   o   o   d   -
bye.

I know I need to. She deserves it. What we have deserves a proper goodbye. But every time I try to open my mouth, the words get stuck in my throat. The truth is, I don't want to say goodbye. I'm afraid if I see her cry or get upset, I'll cave and beg her to stay.

But I know this is the right thing to do. I can't be selfish and take away her chance at finally doing something for herself.

Sienna told me she wants me to make the same thing we had for dinner the first night we ate together with Alexis: chicken marsala with pasta. Apparently, I have a sentimental child on my hands. I was surprised at how thoughtful it was of her to remember what I cooked that first night.

Now here I am in the grocery store after work, collecting all the ingredients that I need for dinner. I texted Alexis to tell her I would be home early to get started on dinner.

When I think back to that evening, our first night together, I remember how enamored I was with her. She had me hooked from the moment I laid eyes on her. It started out as infatuation, but somewhere along the way, it became something more powerful than I knew I could feel.

These last few days, it's been hard to even breathe as I prepare myself to say goodbye.

As I pull into the driveway, I try to take some deep breaths to calm the nerves that are forming in my body.

I can do this. Tonight is about having a nice evening and saying goodbye. It's not about keeping my distance to protect my heart. My heart is already broken. The least I can do is give her a proper send-off.

Carrying the grocery bags into the kitchen, I notice that the house is silent. I catch a glimpse of them outside playing in the backyard as I unload the food. It gives me a sense of relief that I can have some time to cook alone, though part of me wonders if Alexis is just hiding outside to keep her distance. There's no doubt she's confused as to why my attitude has changed in the last two days.

I walk into the wine cellar and grab the bottle of Chateau La Conseillante. It was the first wine that we drank together at our first dinner. I'll never be able to drink it without thinking about her full lips on the wine glass as she tried to listen to my instructions on how to taste wine.

In that moment, I didn't know whether I wanted to taste the wine or Alexis's lips more.

Shit, combining both of them on our first night together in my bedroom... How will I ever drink wine again without thoughts of her swirling through my senses?

I'm almost done preparing the meal when the two of them come giggling through the sliding door.

"Daddy! You're here!" Sienna comes running into my arms. I pick her up and try to focus on the sense of calm her presence normally creates for me. Sienna opens her arms to Alexis. "This is your goodbye dinner, Alex! I told Daddy we should eat the same dinner we had together our first night."

I think I notice Alexis's eyes get misty as she takes in the meal in front of her.

"Sienna, that is so thoughtful of you," Alexis tells her before turning to me nervously. "Thank you for doing this."

"It's my pleasure," I tell her. "I wish there was more I could do. You've been everything to us this summer."

She looks away quickly as her eyes rapidly blink. I have to turn away and clear my throat to contain my own emotions. I'm fucking this up so badly.

"Come on. Let's eat!" Sienna shouts excitedly, thankfully serving as our icebreaker for the evening.

"Okay. Dinner is served," I announce as I lay the tray of food in the center of the table.

"Smells amazing." Alexis smiles, though I can tell it's not her normal infectious one that I've come to love.

It's guarded like she isn't sure how to act at the moment. Neither of us does.

"Would you like some wine?" I offer as I hold up the bottle. "It's the same Chateau we had that night."

"I'd love some," she agrees.

I pour each of us a generous amount, then hold mine up for a toast. Sienna loves to toast. Her pink cup is in the air before Alexis can grab her glass.

"A toast," I begin. "To the best nanny we will ever have the pleasure of knowing. Thank you for putting a smile on my daughter's face every day. I will forever be grateful that you were the one who walked through my office that day. Cheers."

"Cheers! I love you, Alex! I'm gonna miss you so much," Sienna adds.

"Cheers. I love you too, Sienna," Alexis croaks out as tears begin to run down her cheeks.

We clink our glasses together. Both Alexis and I take a huge sip of our wine. I normally don't chug wine, as it's meant to be sipped and enjoyed, but this evening might call for more alcohol, and quickly.

Twenty minutes later, the entire bottle of wine has been drunk, and I think it's starting to kick in. I'm feeling loosened up.

"Tell me what your favorite Sienna memory has been so far?" I grin as I swirl the remaining contents of my wine around in my glass.

Sienna has already given up on us, claiming we were taking too long, so she's playing with her dollhouse.

Alexis leans back in her chair with a lazy smile on her face.

"I think it's gotta be our first time baking together. She tricked me into letting her do most of the measuring and cracking eggs on her own, telling me she did it all the time. I learned very quickly that she was not telling the truth and needed some assistance. A couple ruined batters later, we did it together. But she was trying so hard to crack those eggs and pour the vanilla in without spilling."

I laugh as I think of Sienna trying to do those things on her own. Gentle and patient she is not, so I imagine things got pretty messy. It sounds like her to try to tell a little lie to do things on her own, though.

"I didn't know about that one. If she wasn't so cute..." I trail off as I shake my head.

We both share another laugh together.

Sienna walks up to us with a look I know all too well. It's the one she wears when she's trying to get what she wants.

I raise my eyebrows at her. "Yes, Sienna?" I question.

"I was just wondering," she sings, "if the *two* of you could put me to bed tonight. Pleasssssssse. It will make me feel better about saying goodbye."

She hits us with a pouty lip.

I sigh. "Honey, I don't thi—"

"I'm okay with it," Alexis cuts me off, "if your daddy is."

Both girls are looking at me like I'm gonna be the bad guy if I say no. Everything about this idea seems dangerous. Sienna getting it in her head what it would be like to have two parents tucking her in at night; me having a vision stuck in my memories of what it would be like to have Alexis be a mother to my child. But I know I can't say no to these two.

"Fine," I agree.

Sienna jumps up and down. "Okay, Daddy. I'm ready for my bath."

"I'll clean up down here. I'll meet you two upstairs after the bath. Just let me know when you're ready," Alexis tells us.

As soon as I have Sienna bathed and in her jammies, she shouts from the top of the stairs for Alexis to join us. Sienna jumps into bed just as Alexis appears in the doorway.

My heart begins to beat out of my chest as I watch her step quietly into the darkened room, glowing softly from the nightlight.

"Come on this side," Sienna suggests as she pats the other side of the bed.

It's only a twin bed, so it's going to be a tight squeeze. Alexis lies down on the other side as she snuggles up to Sienna. We are only inches apart.

"How does this normally go?" Alexis asks us.

"Sometimes we do a bedtime story. If it's a workday, we talk about each other's day. Other times, we just talk about random stuff, maybe make up stories," I tell her.

"What do you want to do tonight?" Alexis asks Sienna.

"I just want to talk," she says.

"Okay." I go to rest my hand on her belly but find Alexis's hand there.

I'm a weak man. I choose to hold onto Alexis as the three of us lie here and talk about our day. Sienna continues telling me more about what she and Alexis did until her eyes start to get heavy.

I look over at Alexis. When our eyes meet, it feels electric. I can't take my eyes off her. The way she looks in the soft light, cuddled up to my daughter, my hand resting on hers.

I want this. Why can't I have it?

As soon as Sienna's eyes are shut, Alexis and I climb out of her bed and tiptoe out of the room.

I watch as Alexis starts down the hall, and my strength breaks. I catch up to her just before her room, grabbing her hand and walking backward as I tug her into her bedroom.

My lips are on hers in an instant. I put everything I feel and everything that I have into this kiss. It's slow and thoughtful, so I can memorize exactly how it feels to have my lips on hers.

I push her back to the bed where we fall down together. I don't let go of her, I can't. I need her near me.

I feel the passion between us rising like the hottest fire, clouding my brain. Nothing else matters but being with her.

I slowly peel down her tank top and take her breast into my mouth. My tongue swipes across her nipple which is now swollen to its fullest form, then I move over to her other nipple and give it the same treatment.

Her breaths are loud in the deafening silence as I tenderly play with her. I look up into her eyes, and the desire to feel her lips on mine against wins out.

We both undress each other through our kisses as they grow more and more intense. By the time we're both naked, I'm hard as a rock and need to be inside of her.

She spreads her legs as an invitation, letting me know we're both ready for it.

As soon as I sink into her, my body gives out and falls on top. My weight must be crushing her, but instead of saying anything, she grabs my face and brings my lips back to hers.

No words are necessary in this moment.

I start to rock back and forth on her body as my dick slips in and out. I can feel my stomach rub against her clit, giving her extra friction to enjoy.

Her mouth remains on mine, even through the slow thrusts. I've never felt like this before; like I'm a part of her. Like wherever she is, I am, and where I am, she is. My heart is part of her, and hers a part of mine.

I start to feel her walls close in on me, and I know it's time for me to let my own release go.

We both come at the same time, our tongues still working together in sequence. We kiss all the way through the orgasm until there is nothing left.

When we pull apart, our bodies are trembling.

I try to find words for what just happened between us, but there are none. Nothing can describe what we just experienced.

It becomes pretty clear to me that I'm irrevocably in love with her. She has brought every fiber of my being back to life. Parts of my soul that I thought were lost forever, have been found now that she is back in my life.

As goosebumps begin to spread across her body, I roll over and maneuver us until we are under the covers.

We lie on our sides, looking at each other.

I'm still racking my brain for words to say because goodbye feels impossible. How do you tell the woman who brought you back to life goodbye? How do you explain that you are saying goodbye *because* you love her?

Before I know it, her eyes grow heavy, and she falls asleep as our hands hold each other's in the middle of the bed.

I lie awake for most of the night, tossing and turning as my mind races. I can't seem to come up with the right words for tomorrow.

Around four o'clock in the morning I give up on sleep and crawl out of the covers, tip-toeing out of her room and downstairs to my room. I throw on jeans and a t-shirt and make a pot of coffee. Hoping the caffeine will somehow provide the jolt I need to come up with something that won't break her heart, even though I know it's breaking mine as well.

Chapter Twenty-Seven

Alexis

I stretch out in bed as the sun hits my face. It takes a bit of time for me to remember what happened last night. The magic that I felt in his arms. It was far beyond anything I could have imagined.

I look over to the other side of the bed, finding him gone again. I must have fallen asleep right after. I've spent forty-eight hours in a constant state of dread as I've watched Gabriel pull further and further away from me.

Maybe he really has just been busy and preoccupied with work. Maybe he's been sad I'm moving out and doesn't know how to talk about it. But after last night, there's no denying what is happening between us.

I can't leave today without confronting our love. It's too big, too powerful to walk away from.

I climb out of bed and dress in jeans and a t-shirt. When I open the door, I smell coffee, grinning at how much.

I love our weekends together. It's just so...peaceful.

As I walk downstairs, I catch a glimpse of Sienna's closed door, meaning she's still sleeping.

When I turn the corner into the kitchen, Gabe is sitting at the kitchen table with his hands in his hair. He looks pretty rough, unlike I have ever seen him before.

He must hear me because as I approach, he lifts his head.

"You alright?" I ask.

He shakes his head back and forth. It looks like he might cry. Oh gosh, I hope everybody is okay.

"Why don't you get some coffee?" he croaks. "We need to talk."

"Okayy," I reply.

This doesn't sound good. I wonder if it has anything to do with why he's been acting so weird lately. I walk over to the counter and pour myself a cup of coffee, my hand trembling slightly.

I walk back to the table and settle in the seat across from him. We sit in silence for several minutes. I blow on my coffee as I wiggle in my seat, trying to find a comfortable position.

"I've been thinking about us," he begins. His hand wipes over his face, like he can barely get out his next words. "It all started when we were out to dinner the other night. You were talking about how you've never done anything for yourself before. How all your life you've been making decisions based on making others happy, and how their decisions were never about your own happiness. It just got me thinking. You're so young, you just graduated college, you have your whole life ahead of you. I don't want to be the one to hold you back. I've got a daughter that I have to put first. We're just going to hold you back."

My stomach feels like it just dropped, like I'm on a rollercoaster ride and just went down the biggest hill of my life. I feel tears pricking my eyes and I try to hold them in.

"You don't want to see where this goes with us?" I say with a shaky voice.

He sighs like he isn't even sure what the hell he wants anymore. "Of course I want to. That's the problem. Alexis, the things you've made me feel this summer. I don't want to lose that. But this isn't about what I want, it's about what is best for you."

A cynical laugh escapes me. "What are you my father now?"

"Alexis, I know this isn't what you want to hear. It's killing me to do this, but I feel like it'll kill me to beg you to stay. Because..." he stands up and starts pacing right in front of me "fuck, that's exactly what I want to do. I want to get on my knees right here and now, I want to beg you to stay with me. But that's not fair to you." He kneels right in front of me as tears begin to roll down my cheeks. "Alexis, you are the most incredible, selfless, beautiful, kindest person that I've ever met. And you deserve to figure out what will make you the happiest in the entire world."

I look down at his hands that are now holding mine. "What if that's you and Sienna?"

"What if it's not and you'll never know because you stay here and don't experience life? Then you'll wake up one day and resent me for asking you to stay. I can't be that guy who does that to you. I'm so sorry."

I nod my head. Sounds about right. I'm great, I'm kind, but not worth fighting for. It's the story of my life.

"So, this is it?" I whisper.

I think I see his eyes start to water. He looks away from me and coughs before looking back at me.

"This is it."

"Will I get to see Sienna again?" I ask.

"Of course. You two have a bond, I wouldn't take that away from either of you."

"What time should I leave today?"

"That's up to you. Sienna is prepared for it, she knows what's coming."

My heart physically aches at the idea of saying goodbye to Sienna, but I think I need to get out of here as soon as possible. I feel like I can hardly breathe.

"I think I'll go pack. Maybe I can have breakfast with Sienna and then say goodbye."

"Of course," he replies. He stands up and kisses my forehead. "Take all the time you need. I'm sorry, Alexis. I wish it didn't have to be this way."

I can't respond, so I just get up and walk quickly upstairs until I get to my room. When I close the door, I run to my bed and fall onto it as my tears come stronger and more fiercely. I just want to scream at him for doing this to me, to us. I thought we were more than this. Why can't he just let me make my own decisions instead of making one for me?

His words sound sincere, and I trust that he really does feel this way, but something about it seems wrong. It's like he was triggered that night at dinner, and I don't know what it was. But I have enough pride to now get on my knees and beg him to change his mind.

I grab a tissue from the nightstand and blow my nose. That's it, I'm not going to walk out of here crying. Sienna deserves better than that. This next hour, I'm going to put on a brave face for her.

I get changed and ready for the day, pack my things as fast as possible, and walk downstairs with as much as I can carry.

Gabe is standing in the kitchen with Sienna sitting on the counter.

"We're making eggs and toast for breakfast," she says as she smiles at me. "We're sad that you're leaving, and want to cook for you."

Don't cry, don't cry, don't cry.

I smile. "That's so sweet of you. Let me just put these things in my car and I'll be right back in."

I load up my car and am back within minutes.

Sienna is now sitting at the table where there are plates and drinks already set.

"Take a seat," Gabe tells me. "I'll serve you two up."

I notice there are only two plates. He's not going to eat with us, this is my time to be with her. I'm grateful for it.

"Here you ladies go," he says as he scoops up some scrambled eggs and puts it on our plates. There's already toast and fruit sitting on our plates.

"Thanks, Daddy," Sienna says.

He gives her a kiss then walks away, giving us our space.

We have our usual morning discussions about how we slept, what we're going to do today. Only this time, our agenda's aren't the same. She's going to her grandparents house today. I'm so happy she has something to be excited about today, so me leaving won't be too hard on her. She's still young, so she'll bounce back quickly.

"Well," I look down at our empty plates. "I think it's time for me to go."

She looks thoughtfully at me. "Daddy says I'll still get to see you, and that I can call you if I miss you."

I wipe away the tear that escapes. "Absolutely! You better call me. I'll be waiting to hear from you."

She smiles, seeming satisfied with my response. Gabe walks back into the room.

"Thanks for breakfast," I tell him as I stand up.

He nods his head. "Do you need help with your stuff?"

"No. I'm just gonna grab the rest of the bags and I'll be on my way."

"We'll meet you at your car."

After I grab my bags and walk outside, I see the two of them hanging out by my car like he promised.

I throw the remaining bags into my trunk and close it shut. The three of us stand there, a bit of awkwardness growing in the moment.

"Well, I guess this is it." I bend down and open my arms. "Can I get a hug?" I ask Sienna.

She runs into my arms and I squeeze her tight. There's no chance at holding my tears back now, so I let them go. When I stand up, I notice Gabe wipe away his own tears.

He opens his arms and I walk into his.

"I'm so damn sorry," he whispers.

I don't know what to say back. I don't want to say it's okay, because it doesn't feel like it. I pull away and look down at her Sienna then back up at him.

"Bye, guys."

"Bye, Alex! We love you," Sienna says as she waves.

"I love you," I reply as I walk to my car door.

I open it and sit down. I start the car and look in the rearview mirror to see the two of them standing next to each other.

As I pull away, they start to wave and I give them one last wave then drive out of sight.

It's likely not a smart idea, but I drive to Alicia's through my tears. It may not be safe, but I have to get out of here.

When I pull into her parking lot, I head straight for her front door, deciding to worry about my bags later.

"Oh my god. Are you okay?" Alicia says as she opens the door, instantly pulling me into her arms.

"I don't think so," I cry into her shoulder.

She doesn't need to ask who or get any more information from me right now.

"Come here," is all she says, and it's exactly what I need.

Chapter Twenty-Eight

Gabriel

"Why the hell did someone turn the coffee machine off when the pot is still full?" I shout from the breakroom.

Now the damn coffee is cold, and I have to turn it on and rebrew more. Fucking idiots.

Mia comes storming in, likely having heard my outburst since her office is just down the hall.

"Hey, don't take it out on us that you make crappy decisions and push people out of your life!" she fires back before turning around and immediately leaving.

I slam my fist down on the countertop. I've about had it with their judgment.

I made this decision *for* Alexis. Can't they see how miserable I am?

"Everything all right in here?" Marcus peeks his head in.

I huff in frustration and turn to make the coffee, ignoring him.

"Still not ready to talk about what happened?" he says as he walks further into the space.

"I don't see why it's anybody's business. Besides, it's not gonna change anything. What's done is done."

Marcus leans against the counter next to me with his arms folded.

"Still wouldn't hurt to talk to someone about it. It might make you feel better. Or maybe it's not too late to change your mind."

A bitter laugh escapes me. "You heard what Mia said. I broke her heart...she'll never talk to me again."

"It's worth a try. Maybe explain to her why you did it."

"Just fucking let it go!" I shout.

"Maybe we would let it go if you would stop stomping around here taking it out on everyone else."

He pushes off the counter and disappears.

The coffee can't brew fast enough. It feels like forever, but I finally pour myself a cup and walk quickly back to my office.

Even the additional caffeine isn't making it easier to concentrate, though. I've been trying to read through this contract for hours, and the coffee has done nothing to help.

It's been two weeks since she moved out.

I can barely sleep at night. Half the time, I wake up in a cold sweat, but I can't seem to remember what my nightmares are about. I wasn't even this messed up when Angie left.

Then there's Sienna, who constantly asks me about Alexis, telling me how much she misses her and how badly she wants to see her soon.

Between that and my family, I'm struggling to keep it together. How can't they see that I needed to let her go? They know how young she is. They *must* know what I would be asking if I asked her to stay with me.

At five o'clock, I decide to call it a day. The contract isn't done, but I'm getting nowhere, and it's pissing me off.

When I walk through my parent's front door, the moment Sienna is in my arms, I feel a few seconds of relief. It's always fleeting, but I've come to look forward to it.

"Hey, sweetie!" I squeeze her tight. "How was your day?"

"Awesome! We baked pies today," she exclaims.

I walk farther into the house to see a huge line of pies scattered across the kitchen.

"Wow, you weren't kidding," I tell her as I see Ma boxing them up.

"These are for a church bake sale," she says before I can ask what the hell is going on.

"These two have been hard at work all day," Pa tells me as he joins us. "You're quite the helper." He pinches Sienna's cheek, who then giggles in my arms.

I put her down. "Go pack up your things," I say.

"She asked about her again today." Ma eyes me.

I groan. "Ma, I'm not in the mood to hear this from you, too."

"Well, that's just too bad. Mia called me today. Told me you were walking around the office, taking it out on them again. You gonna tell me what happened? Why you just pushed her out of your life when you're so clearly in love with her?"

"She was a keeper, son. I can tell these things." Pa joins in on the criticism.

"I'm not doing this. I was just trying to do what was right for her. I thought my family would support me and have my back," I growl out as I stomp out of the kitchen.

I find Sienna shoving her toys into her backpack. I help her finish packing up and then head straight to the door.

"I'll see you guys tomorrow," I shout to my parents.

It's not exactly the warmest goodbye, but they're lucky I'm not storming out and slamming the door behind me.

Dinners with Sienna are now full of painful memories. Memories of the laughter that used to fill our home when Alexis was here.

Now I struggle to keep it light for Sienna. I don't want her to feel the missing energy, and yet there is only so much happiness I can offer, especially when it's forced. She's been a good sport, though, always laughing and giggling at my jokes, as weak as they may be.

After I get her tucked into bed, I pour myself a glass of wine. It's my nightly routine now... Drink wine and do everything in my power not to text Alexis and beg for forgiveness.

It's when I'm alone at night when I'm the weakest. I'm only thinking about myself and my happiness instead of what's right for her. I hope she's out there finding her own path that will bring her joy, finding what life is meant to offer her.

After a couple glasses of wine, I end up right back where I knew I'd be: writing and deleting text messages to her.

Me: I miss you. I never should have let you go.

Delete.

Me: Sienna misses you. She talks about you every day.

Delete.

I'm not going to bring my daughter into this and guilt Alexis into possibly forgiving me, not that she ever would. How could she? I made her feel like she was nothing to me. Worse, like I used her.

I deserve to feel like this for the rest of my life. But that night, after we made love, I knew I could never say goodbye to her. If I stayed for one more second, everything I was feeling would come pouring out of me, and then I would never know if she stayed for the right reasons.

I knew that nagging feeling would haunt me forever. Little did I know, I would be haunted either way.

After deleting another message, anger boils up in me.

Why the fuck can't I shake this?

I chuck my phone across the room, watching as it bounces off the marble fireplace and shatters.

Fuck! What the hell am I doing?

Chapter Twenty-Nine

Alexis

"I think you should take it," Alicia says.

After I told her all the sordid details of what happened with Gabriel, she was my shoulder to cry on for as long as I needed it. Then, she gave me a necessary pep talk to pursue my interests and find a career that I'm going to enjoy.

She just poured us a glass of wine—another reminder of him—to celebrate my job offer. I'm still on the fence if I want to take it. Staying here in Cleveland wasn't the plan, especially knowing he is so close yet so far is like torture.

But I can't deny that it's an amazing opportunity. Mr. Albertini hooked me up with an interview at one of the largest event management companies in the country, specializing in sporting events. It's for a Financial Analyst role, and it seems perfect for me.

"I don't know." I sigh into my glass.

"What's holding you up?" she asks. "Does it have something to do with *him*?"

Doesn't everything have to do with him lately? It's only been a couple weeks since he broke my heart, but my brain has been able to think of nothing else. I have no appetite, no motivation. I cry all the time, especially at night when I'm alone.

To top it off, my parents have both managed to go the entire summer without checking in on me. I think my mom texted me once in the beginning to make sure I made it safely.

"Of course it does. I'm just not sure I want to settle down in the same city. I know the odds of running into him are slim, but just knowing he is so close..."

"It's only been two weeks. You'll forget about him eventually. You just need some time."

Will I, though? There's no way I will ever completely forget about the moments we shared. They were too transformative. All I can hope for is that maybe, over time, it will hurt less, and I won't think of him as often.

Plus, it would be nice to stay here and be near Alicia. She's been the biggest supporter in my life, and the thought of living apart from her fills me with dread.

"Alright," I exclaim as I hold up my glass.

"Alright, you'll take it?" she asks hopefully, sitting up straighter.

I chuckle at her excitement. "Yes, I'll take it. I don't wanna live apart from you."

"Yes!" she shouts as she clinks our glasses together. "To a fresh start and sexy office romances."

I laugh. "I don't think any of the men I saw at my interview are my type."

"Well, you'll just have to find one of the athletes at an event then."

One step at a time. First, I need to go to bed without crying myself to sleep.

"I think this means we need to go apartment shopping," she squeals. "Your starting salary is hefty enough that you can definitely afford your own place if you want."

"Yeah, I think I would really like that. I've never had a place to myself," I tell her.

"It's not too shabby. I've enjoyed my naked Tuesdays. I can walk around in whatever I want, be as messy as I want, and there's nobody here to judge me."

"Naked Tuesdays?" I lift an eyebrow at her.

She shrugs. "Don't knock it till you try it."

"Noted. I guess I should get started on apartment hunting this weekend. I'll call tomorrow morning and accept the position."

With my lack of sleep lately, my eyes are feeling heavy by the time I finish my glass of wine.

"Alright, girl. I'm gonna go get some more work done on my laptop in my room. You look like you could use a good night's rest. I'll see ya in the morning."

"Mmm k," I say through a yawn.

I lie down on the couch and wrap the covers around me, seeing his face just as my eyes close. An instant jolt of electricity courses through my body, and I know I'm not getting sleep anytime soon.

I miss him so damn much. I know I only had the warmth of his body at night for three weeks, but it was so comforting, and I didn't realize how much I had come to need it.

I felt so safe in his arms, so loved and adored for the first time in my life, and now it's all gone.

I keep trying to play it out over and over in my head. Where did I go wrong?

Could I have acted more confident on what I wanted in life? Was my confusion something that scared him off? Did it make me seem too young and naïve?

But that's the hardest part of all of this, when I thought about leaving him and Sienna, I felt confused. But when I was with them, I had never felt more secure and happy and confident in what I wanted.

I hope I'm making the right decision in staying here. Hopefully, Alicia is right, and it will get easier with time. I really do want to stay near her, and the job opportunity is fantastic. Plus, it's close enough to home that I can visit my siblings but still have enough distance from my parents.

What I could use right now to fall asleep is one of my Sienna snuggles. That girl burrowed her way into my heart so fast. I miss her laughter and her sweet affection.

One of these days, I'm going to find out where I belong. For now, I'll have to settle for where I am.

Chapter Thirty

Alexis

I'm desperately trying to get this stupid piece of hair to cooperate. I just got off work and Alicia wants to get some fancy dinner to celebrate her promotion at work.

I've been at my job for three months now and living in my own apartment for two. Work has been going well, the people are super nice, and I've even made some friends to do happy hour with occasionally.

I still think of Gabriel and Sienna all the time, but the pain has begun to subside. I'm no longer crying myself to sleep, which I'm counting as a win.

I miss them, though.

Fortunately, work has been keeping me busy. It's just the distraction that I need. Weekends are a bit tough, especially when Alicia is busy, mostly with all the dates she's been going on lately.

She's been begging me to go on double dates with her, but I'm not ready.

There's no way I could even fake being interested in another man when Gabe still has my heart.

My hair was still damp when I went to sleep last night, and now there's a piece of hair in the back that wants to stick up at the root an inch over my other hair. Finally, after going over it with a straightener eighty times, the crimp is gone.

"Girl, come on! We have reservations I don't want to miss," Alicia shouts from the kitchen.

"I'm coming," I reply.

She met me at my apartment downtown because she said the restaurant is close, but she won't tell me where we're going.

"Am I dressed alright? It would be easier if you just told me the name so I knew the vibe," I exclaim as I come out of the bathroom.

"Damn. Is that a new dress?"

"It is!" I look down at my new white dress that hugs my curves on top and flows out at the waist. Paired with my strappy black heels, I'm feeling good. "First time in my life I've been making some real money... I thought I'd treat myself."

"Well, you're dressed perfectly for where we're going," she exclaims, and I note that she's wearing a similar dress in black with her favorite gold heels.

"Where the heck are we going that we need to be this fancy anyway?" I continue with my interrogation.

"What does it matter if I tell you the name? It's not like you're going to know what it is, considering you're not going to fancy dinners all the time, and I know we've never been here."

She has a point there. I don't ask any more questions about our dinner the entire time we're in the car. We decided to take an Uber so we can drink as much wine as we want. Apparently, it's only a five-minute walk, but it's November in Cleveland, and walking the short distance in a short dress is a hard no in my book.

Alicia is in the middle of telling me all about what her boss had said to her during her promotion meeting when the car pulls up to our location. My stomach drops.

We get out of the car, and I stand frozen in place as I stare up at the sign.

"Come on, girl." She grabs my arm and she begins to drag me toward the door. "You're gonna love this place. It used to be this old bank. The food is out of this world. My dad takes me here all the time."

"I've been here before," I manage to get out.

She turns quickly. "You've *been* here before? When?"

"The one and only time he took me out on a date."

Her eyes open wide. "Shit, I'm so sorry. I had no idea." Her head looks around the surrounding streets as we stand out here in the freezing cold. "Do you want to go somewhere else?"

My brain instantly wants me to shout *yes*! But I don't want to let him ruin this place for me because it was amazing—the food, the vibe, the drinks, everything. And I should be able to go anywhere I want to eat.

Plus, it's frickin' freezing out here, and I just want to get inside.

"No, let's go. It was one meal, one time. I'm not going to let it ruin our night." I smile at her.

"Atta girl!" She turns around and walks through the doors.

The place instantly makes my stomach churn with its memories, but I ignore it. The hostess seats us at a table in the center of the room. We thank her and take our seats as both of our heads turn left to right to take in the room.

"No matter how many times I've come here, I'm still always sucked in by the old architecture," she leans across the table to tell me.

"I don't know how you could not be."

Alicia insists on splurging and orders us a bottle of wine to split. After our glasses are poured, I hold up my glass.

"To a much-deserved promotion. Keep doing your thing and kicking some ass, girl. Show those men it's a woman's world," I say, trying to keep a straight face.

Alicia's eyebrows raise in surprise as she clinks our glasses together. She can't control the fit of laughter that escapes her after she takes a drink.

"What the hell kind of toast was that? Do we hate all men now? Are we becoming big feminists?"

I laugh. "No, I just wanted to see what your reaction would be."

"Oh, god. Okay, good. I thought you were having some kind of quarter-life crisis."

I finally let myself settle into the evening after a glass of wine. We haven't even gotten around to looking at the menu yet, too busy laughing and reminiscing.

"I need to use the restroom. You need to?" I ask Alicia.

"Nah. I'm gonna look at the menu."

I nod and scan the room until I find the corner where the bathrooms are. I don't want to leave Alicia for very long, so I try to make it quick.

As soon as I leave the bathroom, I'm weaving through the room when my eyes catch a familiar figure a couple tables ahead. There's no way... Life can't be so cruel as to make me run into him in this place on the *one* night I'm here.

When he looks to the side, I realize it is, in fact, Gabe. What's worse, his new position allows me to see who he's with: a beautiful woman looking up at him adoringly.

I do my best to keep my head held high as I walk past him, hoping he doesn't notice me. My entire body feels like crumbling to the floor as I pass, but I somehow manage to make it back to my table.

I risk a quick glance in his direction, finding his dark, heated gaze holding onto mine.

What the hell is he so angry about? The nerve of this asshole.

His date must say something because his eyes leave mine for hers.

I feel like the room is closing in on me as it becomes harder to breathe.

"So, I was thinking that the lamb sounds really good," Alicia says as she keeps her head in the menu.

When I don't answer, she finally looks up. Noticing my chest is rising and falling in rapid succession, she sits up straight.

"Alex. Are you okay?" she asks. "What's going on? Are you going to faint? You look pale and sweaty."

"He's here," I say as a stupid tear escapes. "With another woman."

"Are you fucking serious?" she whispers.

"Get me out of here. Please," I beg.

She grabs her purse, throws bills on the table, and stands up. I start to walk forward on wobbly legs and almost stumble until I feel her arm on my back.

"I got you, girl. Just get outside," she whispers.

One foot in front of the other... That's all I need to do.

As soon as the cold winter breeze hits me, my tight muscles are able to loosen up, and I can take a deep breath again.

My body is still trembling as hot tears begin to roll down my cheeks. I shudder inwardly at the thought of him going home with her tonight.

Where's Sienna? Is she in bed at home or at her grandparents' house?

I feel so damn stupid. He really didn't care about me. He's already on a date again while I'm still trying to put back the pieces of my heart that he shattered. And to bring her *here* of all places.

Does he bring all of his dates here to seduce them?

"I'm trying to get a car right now. Here, put your coat on."

I take the coat from her, not evening realizing I left it behind. I slip my arms into it and wrap it around my body.

"Alexis." I hear a deep voice. "Alexis!" he repeats in the same cool tone.

I turn around, too exhausted to hide my tears. I have no words for him.

"What are you doing here?" he asks with a shaky voice.

A bitter, sarcastic laugh escapes me. "What am *I* doing here?"

He takes a step in my direction, but I take a step back. His eyes follow my move, and I see a look of despair flash across his shocked face. I don't care. He has no right to act like he's in pain.

"Why are you here...in Cleveland?" he asks.

"I live here."

"Car's here, Alexis. Let's get out of here," Alicia calls.

"I need to go. Have fun on your date, Gabriel," I bite out.

I head for the car, desperate to get away from him. To get away from these feelings of betrayal. Because they aren't my feelings to have, he was never mine to begin with.

As soon as I get in the car, I look up and see him pacing back and forth as he pulls at his hair. Part of me wants to feel bad for leaving him in this state of anxiety, but the other part just needs to remember how he left me that night.

Thank God Alicia is here. She manages to tell the driver my address and get me back to my apartment without me even realizing it. I've been stuck in a state of shock the entire time.

"Okay," she says as she places me on my couch. "Let's get you some water."

"Wine!" I correct her emphatically. "I need wine, not water."

"Got it. Wine it is."

She disappears into the kitchen, thankfully knowing exactly where I keep everything. I'm still trying to stock the place, so I only have two wine glasses. Luckily, I've only ever had her here, so it hasn't mattered.

What the hell made me think I was enough to hold the attention of a guy like Gabriel? The man has a damn wine cellar in his house. He lives in a mansion, drives fancy cars, and wears suits that probably cost more than my rent.

Shit, his wine collection alone is worth more than my life.

I'm just a college grad who still doesn't know where she fits in this world. Someone who feels like they are wandering around trying to figure out who she is, where she fits in. Maybe I never will have that sense of belonging that I desire. Maybe it's my childhood scar, always there to remind me of my inadequacy.

How could I be enough for him when I wasn't even enough for my own parents?

Alicia joins me on the couch and hands me a generously poured glass of wine.

"I think tonight calls for another toast." She smiles. "To us. To always knowing our worth and never letting any smug bastard make us feel any less than the incredible women that we are."

Her little speech makes me chuckle into my wine glass. I hold it up and cheers.

"Nice try," I say before taking a big gulp.

"It's true, though. Don't let this guy get you down. He's not worth the—" She gets cut off by a loud bang on my door.

We look at each other, confused and worried. She's the only one who knows where I live. Well, her and Mr. Albertini because he helped us look for a place. He said if I was living downtown and my parents weren't coming in to help me, he wouldn't feel right unless he approved the location.

The knock comes again, even more aggressive this time. I place my glass on the coffee table and slowly stand.

"Wait," she whispers. "You can't answer that. What if it's a serial killer?"

"I'm just gonna look through the peephole," I whisper back.

I take soft, careful footsteps to the door, trying my best not to make a noise. When I look through the hole, my heart stops.

What the hell is he doing here? And how did he find out where I live?

"Alexis," he shouts as the knocking continues. "Are you in there? Open up. Please?"

I turn to Alicia, who is now sitting wide-eyed on the couch.

"Alexis!" he repeats.

I'm worried he's going to wake up one of my neighbors, and then I'll forever be looked at as the disruptive one on the floor.

I swing the door open just when his hand is in the air, about to knock again.

He looks disheveled. His hair is a mess, his suit jacket is discarded, and his top buttons are undone.

"Can I come in?" he pleads. "Please?"

I open the door for him. He walks in and stops in the kitchen when he sees Alicia on the couch.

She looks nervously between the two of us.

"I'm... um... gonna go home. I'll call you later," she says to me.

"You don't have to," I say, but she insists.

As soon as the door closes, there's a silence that falls in the room. He puts his hands in his pockets, a gesture I've learned he does when he's not entirely comfortable.

I look down at the ground, finding it difficult to see this man standing here in my space.

"So..." he begins. "You live here now."

"I do." My hands go behind my back nervously.

"Why didn't you tell me?" he asks with a hint of anger in his voice.

The words coming out of his mouth make no sense. I can't help but feel my own mood veer sharply to anger.

"Why didn't I tell you? Why does it matter? You're already moving on and dating again."

"You never told me you wanted to stay here."

There it is again, an accusatory tone. One that implies things would have ended differently if I told him.

"I don't see what difference that would have made," I say, fury almost choking me.

His arms open up wide. "It would have changed *everything*, Alexis."

I advance on him as my finger points at his chest. "Don't you dare make this about me. You were the one who ended us before we even began You were the one who decided our future for us without even asking me what I wanted. Nobody ever asks me what I want."

His shoulders fall at my words. "That's what you think? You think I decided for you?"

I ignore his sad tone.

"That is what happened. You never once asked me what I wanted. You just *told* me what you *thought* was best. I deserve better than that. I deserve for my voice to be heard."

That part's a lie. He made me feel special in every way possible, until the very end where he ripped the rug out from under me.

His head falls in defeat. "I see. I'm sorry you feel that way." He walks forward, stopping in front of me. "I know I fucked it all up, but all I ever wanted was for you to find your own happiness. You deserve the world, Alexis. Goodbye."

He sidesteps me and walks out the door, leaving me in complete shock.

I fall to the ground as I release a choked, desperate cry, a raw and primitive grief taking over.

How could he do this to me? Why would he say all those things and then just leave? Because I don't believe them. He thinks I deserve everything, but he doesn't realize...*he* is everything,

Sienna is everything. They are my happiness. I've been miserable without them.

Now I'm here, left all alone, like everyone else has done my entire life. He treated me no better than my parents do. And he had the nerve to stand there and tell me he thinks I deserve to be happy.

A bitter despair takes over the holes of my lonely heart.

Chapter Thirty-One

Gabriel

My mind is so fucked up about the fact that she's living here in Cleveland. That she's been here the entire time.

Why the hell is she here? Why didn't she tell me? How could she choose to stay and not think to mention it to me?

And fuck my stupid brothers for setting me up on that damn date. I could kill them.

Her face, when she saw me and then noticed who I was with, was like a knife to the heart. I didn't even want to go. When they came into my office in the morning and told me I was meeting someone for a blind date that same night, I told them to fuck off.

They told me it was a done deal, and I would be a dick to stand her up. I didn't want to be that guy, one that let some poor innocent woman left to think the worst of herself because my brothers refused to call it off. They insisted that if I wasn't going to make it right with Alexis, then I had to move on.

But I didn't want to move on then, and I still don't want to move on.

Especially now that I know she's here.

As soon as she and her friend hopped in that car last night, I called Allen immediately. I told him it was an emergency and I needed to find her. I'm sure he's getting his ass reamed by his daughter by now if the look she gave me when she left us last night was any indication.

I hear my front door open, and my sister comes barging into the living room.

"What the hell is your problem?" Mia starts shouting at me. "Ma and Pa called me saying you called them last night and asked them to keep Sienna all weekend. They said you sounded awful. And...what the hell is that? Are you drinking wine right now? It's eleven in the morning. You need to snap out of this shit. It's been almost four months. Shit or get off the pot."

"Nice to see you too, Mia," I growl out. I'm really not in the mood for her storming into my home and insulting me.

"Don't give me that crap." She takes a seat on the chair diagonal from me. "Seriously, I'm starting to get worried here. You're not acting like yourself, and it's been long enough. What's going on?"

I take a generous sip of my wine.

"Give me that," she says, stealing the glass from me. "Talk. Now."

"Maybe I don't *feel* like talking, Mia."

"Tough shit. I'm not here for you, I'm here for my niece. She deserves more from her father. You know... the only parent she has left."

I lift my dark eyebrows in shock at her words. "That's a low blow, even for you, sis."

She looks a bit deflated. "I'm serious. Please talk to me."

"It's Alexis," I admit, assuming it's the exhaustion that makes me give in so quickly.

"Go on..." she drags out.

"I ran into her last night."

Her back straightens. "She's still here?"

"Yes, and she saw me on the stupid date Marcus and Lucas set me up on. Oh, and did I mention they happened to pick the same restaurant I took Alexis to for our first—and only—date?"

If Mia's cringe is anything to go on, I fucked up big time.

"Damn, that's some shitty luck you've got there, big bro."

"Yeah, thanks. I'm aware."

"So," she continues, "what happened? Did you talk to her?"

"Yeah. You should have seen her face... She basically sprinted for the front door, and I chased her out of the restaurant. When I got outside, she was crying, and then her and her friend jumped in a car before we could really talk. Long story short, I tracked down her apartment. Yeah, you heard that right... She has an apartment here. In the city."

Mia raises her hand. "I hate to interrupt, but I have to ask. Please tell me you didn't just ditch your date in the restaurant without saying something?"

"God, no. I ran back in there and gave the waiter my credit card and told her something came up. It was a dick move, and I still have to go back and get my credit card back, but at least I called a car for her."

"Oh, yeah. Huge dick move. That poor woman will have some issues after last night. Go... on."

"Anyway... I get to her place. I don't know what made me so mad at her, but I hated that she didn't tell me she lived here. It would have changed everything."

"*You* were mad at *her*?"

"The only reason I ended it was because I thought she deserved to make decisions about her future on her own, without me adding any pressure to stay here for me. She told me California was on the table, I didn't want to get in the way. You don't know her past."

"I'm gonna cut you off right there. First of all, you're a moron. Second, I actually *do* know some of her past. Her and I had a long talk that night we were all at TOLI. You think she wanted you to ditch her and make her feel even more unlovable than her upbringing made her feel? I can tell you right now... that's a big fat no."

"You don't understand. I did it *for* her. I don't want to be a decision she regrets. I've already been that for one woman, and I can't bear to do the same to Alexis. She deserves more than that."

Mia scoots to the edge of her seat like she's preparing to say something I won't like.

"It sounds to me like you were protecting yourself. Do you think there's a chance you did all this because you were actually afraid to put yourself out there again and get hurt down the road?"

"No!" I defend. "This was for her. I didn't want to be a thorn in her side. Something she looked back on in five years only to realize she'd compromised her own happiness for me."

"And why would you think she would come to that conclusion instead of maybe... you being everything she ever wanted? I saw the way she looked at you, the way you looked at her... You guys were in love. How does letting someone you love go without them being an equal part of the decision help that person? I think you did it because you were afraid of another woman regretting being with you. Especially knowing she was considering California, the one state that took your daughters momma away from her. You're bringing Angie's issues into this part of your life and projecting them onto Alexis. Alexis is nothing like Angie. She loves you, and she loves Sienna. Based on what I heard of her past, she was just looking for people who loved her enough to *fight* for her. Not push her away. You did what you thought would protect yourself in the long run."

"I..." I begin, but the next words don't come.

Is she right? Did I do all of this because I'm afraid of yet another woman making me feel like I was the one who messed up their chance at happiness?

Oh my god. She's right. All of this... was for me. I'm the selfish prick who was afraid to love again. I'm the one who didn't want her to look back and regret it because *I* would be the one who couldn't take the rejection. Not her.

Of course, she would want me to fight for her. She's never had anyone in her life do that. I threw her out and made her feel like another disposable person, just like she's felt her entire life.

"You're right…" My voice lowers as I realize the coward that I am. "It was for me. I'm scared."

Mia gets up and sits right next to me, grabbing my hand.

"It's okay. You didn't realize what you were doing. And Angie did a horrible thing to you, it's only natural that you would be afraid to get hurt again."

"But…" I take a deep breath. "I pushed away my one real chance at love because of it. Alexis could never forgive me."

"Hey," she says, nudging my side. "Don't sell yourself short. You can be a pretty darn romantic guy when you want to. You might be able to win her back."

I look over at her. "Might?"

She shrugs. "I can't promise anything, but I think you've got a chance."

"You think?" I ask.

"Absolutely. You just need the ultimate grand gesture," Mia suggests.

"What's that?" I probe, waiting for her to reveal the answer.

"That's up to you. You need to think about what it is that means the most to her, and then give it to her."

What means the most to her? I know she appreciates loyalty, and her friendship with Alicia. Thinking back to our long talks, I know she's always felt like her family didn't care about her.

They've always put others first and never really done anything to show her that she matters to them.

"I'll leave you to it." Mia pats my knee. "Let me know if you need any help."

After she leaves, I spend the time trying to think about what I could do to show Alexis that I love her, that she belongs with me. That her happiness—well, hers and Sienna's—is all that matters to me.

Chapter Thirty-Two

Alexis

"What kind of a prick says that shit without explaining?" I'm pacing back and forth in my apartment while Alicia sits quietly.

It's been a week since I ran into him, and he decided to play a mindfuck game with me.

You were everything to me.

His words have played over and over in my head. I'm surprised I haven't gotten fired at work for how little I've been able to focus since that night.

"What do you think he meant by it? Do you think he regrets what he did? Maybe there's more to it than we know," Alicia suggests.

"I don't know, but he's killing me here. It's like...what the hell do you want? You know? He waits until the day I'm supposed to move out to tell me it's over, but now he's sending me things, and mad at me because I didn't tell him I was living here. "

I'm pacing back and forth, not sure what I want to do next. The adrenaline running through me is making it impossible for me to sit down.

"You're right. He's being super confusing. I'm just saying we all have our demons. Maybe he's battling one of his right now. He's clearly messed up over you. I mean, he ditched his date and called my dad begging to find out where you would have gone."

There's no way that can be true. How can he be messed up over me? He's the one who did this to us. It just doesn't make sense.

A sudden knock on the door startles me. When I look through the peephole, there's no one there. I open it up and look left and right.

"Huh. Weird," I say.

"Anyone there?" Alicia sits up.

"No, but I swear someone knocked."

When I look down, there's a box sitting on my doormat with an envelope on top. I grab it, and as I walk over to my countertop, Alicia jumps off the couch and joins me.

"Who's it from?" she asks as she leans over my shoulder.

"I don't know." I pick up the envelope, which then reveals the bakery design on the box.

Corbo's

"Ooh, I love that place," Alicia squeals behind me. "Open the card."

This can't be from him. Can it?

I open the envelope with shaky hands to find a handwritten note.

Alexis,

I can't drive by this place without thinking of you and your obsession with their cannolis.

I hope you enjoy these treats and know that I'm thinking of you every second of every day.

I know I messed up, and I'm currently working through my own issues right now. I promise I will explain everything to you. For now, just know that none of this had anything to do with you.

You're perfect.

Love,

Gabriel

"Shit. I knew there was more to the story. He's totally in love with you." Alicia sighs behind me.

I gasp when I open the box, finding there must be at least fifty cannolis.

"How much does the man think you eat?"

I slam the lid shut.

"What am I supposed to do with this? He wants more time? I'm dying over here and he thinks a box of cannoli's will make it all okay?" I bite out and walk away.

Two days later, I'm on my way home from doing some holiday shopping, juggling my bags as I dig for my keys outside my door when I notice another box sitting on my front doorstep.

It's heavy and takes a bit of muscle to carry into my place.

I stare at it for several minutes, wondering if I have the heart to open it. I gave in the other day and ate a few cannoli's, bringing the rest to work the next day. They weren't freshly filled anymore, but everyone enjoyed them.

Curiosity gets the best of me, and I tear it open.

Alexis,

These bottles of wine are my favorite. I used to think about how I longed for a woman who was as bold, beautiful, and sexy as these wines.

You came into my life and blew me away. I've never felt the way I feel about you. To say it's scary for me is an understatement.

I've been burned and bruised before. It made me shut down and close my heart off to everyone, until you. But that doesn't mean I made all the right choices once you came along. I've screwed up and didn't treat you like the rare bottle that you are.

I opened a new brand the other day, and even the best bottle in the world doesn't hold a candle to your taste and beauty.

Enclosed are all the bottles I have left of the first wine we drank together. I can no longer appreciate them without you by my side.

Love,

Gabriel

Tears prick the edges of my eyes as I try to fight back the monsoon of emotions that threaten to release.

This is the Gabriel I thought I knew. The one who made me feel like I was something special, something he valued and adored, from the minute I woke up in his arms to the minute I fell asleep on his chest. I know his ex must have hurt him, but I'm not her. And even if you're damaged or scared, you don't just walk away from someone you love.

How can I forgive him? Is he even asking for forgiveness, or is he just trying to explain himself? I don't even know what he wants from all of this.

Does he still want me? More importantly, *do I still want him?*

I hate that my body ignites so quickly at the thought of being in his arms again. My brain and my heart are not so easily persuaded.

The wine he sent me is still sitting on my kitchen island. I can't get myself to open the bottles without him either.

I've picked up the phone so many times to call him, but in the end, I'm still scared.

What if he hurts me again?

It's a risk to take that leap again. How do I know that this man actually loves me? For starters, he hasn't actually used those words. And maybe he isn't even there yet. We were only together for three weeks, but we did spend the entire summer together. And I know I fell in love with him.

I open my door to head to work and am struck by another box on the ground. Is he the one leaving these for me? How does he have the time?

When I pick up this white box, it's warm. It couldn't have been sitting here long. Luckily, I'm an early bird at work, so I have some time to open it now. I know there's no way I'll get much done at work if I don't see what's inside.

When I open the box, there's a huge stack of sprinkled pancakes sitting in the middle, surrounded by bottles of sprinkles that I used with Sienna every morning.

There's an envelope tucked in the side of the box. When I open it, a picture falls out of the card.

It's a picture of Gabe and Sienna in the kitchen as they seem to be mixing together the pancake batter. They are both smiling so wide, it makes my heart ache with how much I wish I was there with them.

Alexis,

Every morning I wake up with Sienna and we make pancakes with sprinkles like you two used to make.

I went ahead and ordered your special magic sprinkles, as I call them, in bulk. I'm not quite sure why these are the only ones that don't completely dissolve away in the batter, but of course, only you know these things.

You came into my home and my daughter instantly fell in love with you. The way you were with her, it was like watching the life I wish I had for her. You were patient, caring, and generous with your love. It was one of the things that had me so drawn to you.

I know I'll never be able to take back what I did. I just hope that you will find it in your heart to forgive me.

P.S.: Sienna asks about you every day. We are both miserable without you.

Love,

Gabriel

Seeing the two of them together is about all I can take. God, I miss them. I *need* them.

The problem is that if life has taught me anything, it's that it's best to be guarded. To only need myself.

I somehow managed to make it through my entire workday today without crying.

After I pulled myself together this morning, I grabbed the pancakes and ate them on the way to work, the warm, yummy flavors taking me back to my time with Sienna. That's the trick with adding the sprinkles, they offer a little sweetness to it without having to add syrup.

As soon as I get back to my apartment, I kick off my heels and walk straight into my pantry for a bottle of wine.

Sometimes you just need a little something to take the edge off.

Before I even open the bottle, a knock sounds at the door. I practically run over with excitement, not even thinking to look through the peephole this time. When I swing it open, ready for my next surprise, Gabriel is standing there.

I let out a gasp. He was the last thing I was expecting.

He's wearing a dark blue suit and looking more handsome than ever. I try to take a breath, but it feels like it's stuck in my lungs.

"Hi," he says, offering me a small smile.

My jaw has fallen open as I take in his tall, dominating presence. I have to remind myself to speak.

"Hi," I breathe.

He looks my body up and down as his eyes grow a bit darker. I guess he's never seen me in work attire, but it seems like he likes my black slacks and white silk top.

"Wow," he says. "You look incredible."

"Thank you."

His hands go in his pockets, showing he's a bit nervous.

"Can I, uh, come in?" he asks.

"Um, yes. Sorry." I open the door.

He walks into my apartment as I close the door.

Okay, take a deep breath. You can do this. Just play it cool.

I turn around, and he's right there in front of me.

"Alexis," he starts. "God, I'm so fucking sorry."

I look down at my feet, trying to stop the tears, when I feel his hand on my chin, lifting until our eyes are on each other.

"Don't hide your tears from me, baby."

Hearing him call me baby again cracks the armor I'd constructed around my heart.

"I just don't understand. Why did you push me away like that?" I cry.

"I'm an idiot. I never should have let you leave like that, but I panicked. After being with you, after making love to you, I just knew that I wasn't going to be able to say goodbye. If I spent one more minute with you, I knew I would beg you to stay."

"Why didn't you want me to stay?" I whisper.

"I wanted you to stay with every ounce of my being. But I didn't realize that I was afraid. I was afraid of giving myself to someone again and getting hurt. I didn't want to give you all I have just for you to tell me down the road that I wasn't enough. The night at the restaurant, you said you might want to move to California. It was an instant trigger for me. That's where my ex moved. That was the place that was worth more to her than me and Sienna. I kept thinking...what if she stays and regrets it, and leaves me for California too? I covered my fears up and pretended I was just looking out for you. I didn't realize that at the time... so I told myself that I didn't want to hold you back from finding your own happiness. I thought if I asked you to stay, you would regret it down the line. Sienna is a big responsibility. What if you woke up one day and decided you weren't ready for that kind of commitment?"

I feel my body take a step closer to him, our bodies almost touching.

"You think I could ever regret choosing the two of you?" I ask him in shock.

He shrugs his shoulders. For the first time, I see a wounded boy, not sure if he's good enough for the world.

"Gabriel. You and Sienna mean everything to me. I've been so miserable without the two of you. I don't know what led your ex to decide she didn't want you guys... didn't want that life, but I couldn't dream of a better life than being with you two."

He takes in a deep breath as I see his eyes look off in another direction. I know that move. He's trying not to cry.

When his eyes meet mine again, they are slightly shinier.

"I love you, Alexis. I'm so damn in love with you, I didn't know it was possible to feel this way about another woman."

It's my turn for my eyes to go glossy.

"I'm so sorry for what I did to you. You didn't deserve that, no matter what kind of pain I was trying to prevent for myself or my daughter. Is there any way you can forgive me? Because, Alexis, you belong with me. We belong together. I've never been surer of anything in my life."

I can't believe the words I'm hearing.

I look up at him. "I've never belonged anywhere before."

He shakes his head. "That's not true. You've always belonged with me. It just took some time for us to find each other."

"And now that we've found each other?" I raise an eyebrow at him.

He leans down closer to me, our lips a breath apart.

"Now we live happily ever after," he whispers.

I smile as his lips come down on mine. We both wrap our arms around each other and sink into the kiss. When he pulls away, I can't contain the words I've thought but not said for so long.

"I love you, Gabriel."

He growls at my words and slams his lips back on mine. I let his hands roam my body and bask in the sweetness of the moment. Finally, I've found where I belong. It was never a city, a job, or anything I tried to conjure up in my mind. It was right here in this man's arms.

THE END

Epilogue

Gabriel

Two Years Later

I look over at Alexis as she spreads suntan lotion all over her body. She's in a white string bikini, lounging next to me by the pool.

"You better hurry up and apply that lotion before I drag you back into our villa."

She giggles while continuing to work it into her skin. "You're gonna kill me. I've already had two orgasms this morning."

"Well, we can't let that happen. How would I explain to everybody back home how you died on our honeymoon?" I smile at her.

We both settle into our seats with our coffee and look out at the view. The rolling hills look like they go on forever, and the medieval town is off in the distance. I booked a trip to Tuscany for our honeymoon after Alexis went on and on for the last year about how she wanted me to take her someday and show her my favorite vineyards.

We're staying at a luxury villa in Panzano, which is one of my favorite towns to visit. It's in the Chianti region of Tuscany, and it's only an hour drive from Florence.

"This is amazing, babe. I don't wanna go back tomorrow." She sighs. "I'm only going home because I miss Sienna."

Sienna wasn't too fond of us leaving her for two weeks, but my family has it covered. We've talked on the phone with her every day we've been here. I told Alexis she can go a day or two without talking to us, but she insisted.

I couldn't have dreamt up a more amazing mother for my daughter. Sienna was so excited when I told her I was going to propose. The first thing she asked was if she gets to call Alexis her mom from now on, which goes to show just how perfectly Alexis slid into the role.

There's another reason I wanted to take Alexis far away from everybody for two whole weeks. I want a baby. Sienna isn't getting any younger, and Alexis would look sexy as hell carrying my baby.

It's all I've been able to think about in the months leading up to the wedding.

It's been two years since, by some miracle, I won her back. I was ready for her to move in permanently right away, but she said she wanted to date and stay in her apartment for the remainder of her lease.

I didn't like it, but I agreed. It was better that way with Sienna. We eased her into the idea, not that it was necessary. She loved Alexis from day one.

"What's the plan for our last night here?" she asks after she takes another sip of coffee.

"I thought we could head into Panzano this afternoon. Their outdoor market is open. We could get a bottle of wine, get a little tipsy, stroll around town eating meats and cheeses. Then I thought we could come back here, and I could eat you before dinner."

She laughs her uninhibited laugh that I've come to adore.

"You think I'm joking." I raise an eyebrow at her. "But I'm dead serious."

"Honey, I know you're completely serious. That's what I love about you. You somehow can start off by saying the sweetest, most romantic thing and follow it up with something crass."

"I can't help it that your body was made to perfection. I just can't wait until I put a baby in there."

She rolls her head back. "Ugh. You're going to be disgusted with my body once that happens."

"Never. Every single perfect imperfection that comes from our babies is going to be sexy as hell."

"You sure know how to flatter a woman."

I'm not sure if she thinks I say this stuff to make her feel good, but I mean every damn word.

"Hey, did you notice Marcus acting funny at the wedding?" she asks.

I think about it. He did seem a bit on edge, maybe even a bit angry at times.

"I did. Do you know what's going on?"

She shrugs. "I don't know. Maybe he's stressed out with trying to balance work and teaching at the university."

"I don't understand why he wanted to take on that class anyway. It just sounds like a headache to me. It's not like he needs the money."

I told Marcus that, but he just shook his head at me and walked away. I guess I'm in a different headspace than he is. He sees the value in taking on a temporary professor role teaching a class three nights a week, and I see it as working from sunrise to sunset three days a week.

"Because it was an honor to even be asked," Alexis fires back.

"Whatever makes him happy. He just hasn't seemed all that happy lately."

"You should talk to him when we get back."

I nod my head. I'm not sure he'll want to talk to me about it, but I'll give it a shot.

Right now, I have other things to focus on, like spending the last moments of my honeymoon soaking up my time with my wife.

I stand up and reach my hand out.

"What?" she asks as she looks up at me.

"Let's go get ready for the afternoon."

She places her hand in mine and squeals when I pull her up abruptly. When she's standing, I hoist her up onto my shoulder and start walking toward our room.

"Gabriel. Put me down this instant!"

I swat her sexy ass. "I need you in the shower, my tongue on your pussy, before I have to behave for an entire afternoon in public with you."

Her laugh echoes as we enter our room.

Never would I have thought that the sexy, young nanny that walked into my life two years ago would be the one to heal my heart. But I'm glad she was lost and looking for a place to belong because with me was always where it was.

Lucas and Savannah

Are you ready for Lucas and Savannah's story next?

<u>Where We Met</u> is coming to you on <u>September 8th, 2023.</u>

A sexy student/professor romance that you won't want to miss.

Click on the link below to pre-order your copy today!

<u>Pre-Order here!</u>

Also By Nicole Baker

The Brady Series

Enough

Impossible

Irresistible

Persuade

Protected

The Giannelli Series

Where You Belong

Where We Met

Follow The Author

To have access to a Bonus Scene with Gabe and Alexis – visit my website and subscribe to my newsletter with *Bonus Scene* written in the message!

www.nicolebakerauthor.com

Facebook @nicolebakerauthor

Instagram @nicolebaker_author

TikTok @authornicolebaker

9 781088 158241